Uneasy Peace at Castle Rising

This fifth continuing chronicle of the de Lorme family is shadowed by the problems of post war recovery during the fledgling years of the roaring twenties. How the Family set about combating their difficulties forms the background to the revelries of the younger generation. The famous castle ballroom is transformed into a nightclub by the heir who hosts a dance for which a negro jazz band is brought over from America, and some of the most dangerous inhabitants of the castle's White Zoo are drawn into a celebration which evokes startling press headlines. The youngest son vanishes in an escapade which nearly ends in disaster; and a schoolboy cousin and his two friends earn the scorn and contempt of them all when they devise – with precocious skill – a confidence trick which nets the trio £45,000. Finally, a grievous death in the Family leads to a marriage which they had all thought could never come to fruition....

Other books by Fanny Cradock

Fiction
The Lormes of Castle Rising
Shadows over Castle Rising
War Comes to Castle Rising
Wind of Change at Castle Rising
Scorpion's Suicide
My Seed Thy Harvest
The Rags of Time
O Daughter of Babylon
The Echo in the Cup
Gateway to Remembrance
The Eternal Echo
The Land is in Good Heart
Women Must Wait
Dark Reflection
Shadow of Heaven

Children's Books
When Michael Was Three
When Michael Was Six
Always
The Dryad and The Toad
The Story of Joseph and Pharaoh
Naughty Red Lion
Naughty Red Lion Beware
Fish Knight-Sea Maiden
The Gooseyplums of Duckpond In
The Dip
Brigadier Gooseyplum Goes To
War
The Gooseyplums By The Sea

*Cookery and Travel. By Fanny and
Johnnie Cradock*
A Cook's Essential Alphabet
The Daily Telegraph Cook's Book
Fanny and Johnnie's Freezer Book
The Sherlock Holmes Cookbook
The Practical Cook
The Ambitious Cook
The Daily Express Cookery Book
Bon Voyage
Bon Viveur in London
Around Britain with Bon Viveur

Bon Viveur's London and The
British Isles
Bon Viveur in The Austrian Tyrol
Bon Viveur in Barcelona and The
Balearics
Bon Viveur in Belgium
Bon Viveur in Denmark
Bon Viveur in Holland
Holiday on The French Riviera
Bon Viveur in Sweden
Holiday in The Touraine
Bon Viveur's Guide to Holidays in
Europe
Cooking with Bon Viveur
Bon Viveur Request Cookery Book
Wining and Dining in France with
Bon Viveur
Beginning to Cook with Fanny and
Johnnie
Children's Outdoor Cookery with
Fanny and Johnnie
The Young Chef with Fanny and
Johnnie
Children's Party Cookery by Fanny
and Johnnie
Veg and Vim
Cabbages and Things
The Daily Mail Cookery Book
The Cook's Book
The Sociable Cook's Book
The Cook Hostess's Book
Common Market Cookery—France
Common Market Cookery—Italy
Three Hundred and Sixty Five
Puddings
Three Hundred and Sixty Five
Soups and Their Accompaniments
Home Cooking
Problem Cooking
Giving a Dinner Party
Colourful Cookery
Fanny Cradock Invites
Eight Special Menus
Modest but Delicious

Uneasy Peace at Castle Rising

Fanny Cradock

W. H. ALLEN · London
A Howard & Wyndham Company
1979

Printed in Great Britain by
Fletcher and Son Ltd, Norwich
and bound by
Richard Clay (The Chaucer Press) Ltd, Bungay, Suffolk
for the Publishers W. H. Allen & Co. Ltd,
44 Hill Street, London W1X 8LB

ISBN 0 491 02219 0

To Simon Buck who corrected
my historical references accurately
when he was only ten.
With love, Fanny

Contents

The Family from 1907, descendi

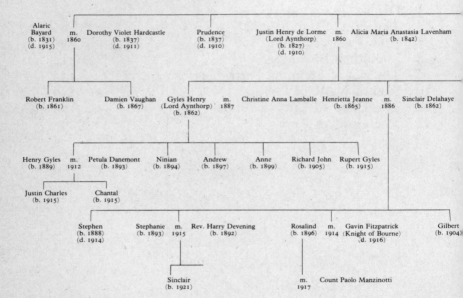

Alaric
Bayard   m.   Dorothy Violet Hardcastle   Prudence   Justin Henry de Lorme   m.   Alicia Maria Anastasia Lavenham
(b. 1831)   1860   (b. 1837)   (b. 1837)   (Lord Aynthorp)   1860   (b. 1842)
(d. 1915)   (d. 1911)   (d. 1910)   (b. 1827)
                                                         (d. 1910)

Robert Franklin   Damien Vaughan   Gyles Henry   m.   Christine Anna Lamballe   Henrietta Jeanne   m.   Sinclair Delahaye
(b. 1861)   (b. 1867)   (Lord Aynthorp)   1887   (b. 1865)   1886   (b. 1862)
                                    (b. 1862)

Henry Gyles   m.   Petula Danemont   Ninian   Andrew   Anne   Richard John   Rupert Gyles
(b. 1889)   1912   (b. 1893)   (b. 1894)   (b. 1897)   (b. 1899)   (b. 1905)   (b. 1915)

Justin Charles   Chantal
(b. 1915)   (b. 1915)

Stephen   Stephanie   m.   Rev. Harry Devening   Rosalind   m.   Gavin Fitzpatrick   Gilbert
(b. 1888)   (b. 1893)   1915   (b. 1892)   (b. 1896)   1914   (Knight of Bourne)   (b. 1904)
(d. 1914)   (d. 1916)

Sinclair   m.   Count Paolo Manzinotti
(b. 1921)   1917

m Lord Aynthorp

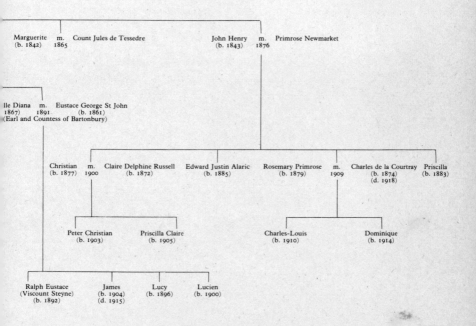

Marguerite   m.   Count Jules de Tessedre
(b. 1842)   1865

John Henry   m.   Primrose Newmarket
(b. 1843)   1876

lle Diana   m.   Eustace George St John
1867)   1891   (b. 1861)
(Earl and Countess of Bartonbury)

Christian   m.   Claire Delphine Russell
(b. 1877)   1900   (b. 1872)

Edward Justin Alaric
(b. 1885)

Rosemary Primrose   m.   Charles de la Courtray   Priscilla
(b. 1879)   1909   (b. 1874)   (b. 1883)
   (d. 1918)

Peter Christian
(b. 1903)

Priscilla Claire
(b. 1905)

Charles-Louis
(b. 1910)

Dominique
(b. 1914)

Ralph Eustace
(Viscount Steyne)
(b. 1892)

James
(b. 1904)
(d. 1915)

Lucy
(b. 1896)

Lucien
(b. 1900)

CHAPTER I

'The Old Order Changes ...'

Castle Rising was in summer dress. There were striped awnings over the French doors on the south terrace. Cygnets ventured hesitantly onto the waters of the lake. Larks soared under the sun into a cloudless sky. Roses were splashing colour over the little Countess Marguerite's cherished rose gardens. The long herbaceous borders strewed their bright ribbons against the protective arms of the topiary while the old, stone urns erupted with Sawbridge's cherished fuchsias and lobelias.

The crisp June sunlight filtered through the newly unfurled leaves of the trees in the home park where the deer cropped and drowsed. It sparked diamond splinters of light from the window panes of the great, grey sprawl of stone, shafted the flying buttresses above and the gargoyles which gazed out enigmatically.

On the south terrace Sawby had sent his footman George and footwoman Raikes to draw out the chaises longues, plump up the cushions and set small tables in readiness for the post-luncheon service of coffee and *digestifs*.

As they turned away the stable clock chimed twice. The family now took luncheon very early on those Saturdays when the Museum and Zoo were opened to the public. The first of these were already approaching. A charabanc load of them clambered out to stand and stare down over the wide valley bowl from the vantage point of Puck's Hill Lane from whence they could see the great sweep running down and soaring again on the farther side to the famous Saddle Back of King's Ride.

Deep in the valley the Castle sprawled in all its fairy-tale splendour, wearing the river like a glittering necklace which wound protectively between the Zoo spread and the Museum spread, forming a natural boundary to the Castle and its pleasure gardens.

To the hill-top spectators this made a Lilliputian scene. Home farms with their roofs of thatch and apricot slates were reduced by distance to toy dwellings as were the barns, byres and carts resting on their shafts, while, within the toy yard boundaries, distance-miniatured pigs, geese and hens picked and rootled. From them stretched the fields with their meticulous cut and laid with bordering elms under whose shade the farm hands had eaten their frugal luncheons before resuming work which would continue through the long afternoon until twilight came. Even the grazing cattle and sheep, the horses cropping in the paddock were made miniature, yet still seemed a little awesome to these watchers to whom trees, flowers, fields and animals were pathetically unfamiliar. They had been brought from London's East End; from their world of food barrows, sleazy public houses and mean streets for a day's outing which would almost certainly be the only holiday any of them had ever known. The women still clutched the shabby bags which had contained the food they ate in the charabanc on the way down; halting thereafter to drink ale or lemonade at a 'public' in Epping Forest.

Their guide now cleared his throat and began to speak.

'We stop here first,' he explained, 'to give you a bird's eye view of one of the oldest castles in England, built by the first Henri de Lorme who came to these shores with William the Conqueror. After the Battle of Hastings in 1066 and after the new king had been crowned in Westminster Abbey, that first French de Lorme came riding into Essex. That was when he fell in love with England. He never went back to his own country again. He built Castle Rising out of English oaks. It is said that a whole forest of them was cut down just to make the roof of his dining hall. Later he built the stone castle you are looking at now, and there it has stood for over eight hundred years. To the left of it is the white building you are going to visit – the Museum. If you've sharp eyes you can just see the two fountains playing on either side of the steps. Right over on the other side,' he waved an arm in indication, 'where you can see the river sparkling, that spread of buildings is the Zoo – the only white Zoo in England.

'Right through the centuries de Lormes have lived in

Castle Rising, handing down from father to eldest son up to the present day.' Again he paused and a wide-eyed girl asked shyly, 'and is there one to come after the present lord?'

'That there is Miss, and his name is Henry like his ancestor. This one fought too, in the Great War. He was taken prisoner; but came home alright and he now lives there with his wife and twins, a boy and a girl. The de Lormes live in the French way, drawing all sorts of members of the family into the pattern and they all live together under the one roof.'

'Looks like there's room enough,' grunted a wizened little man in a lurid cloth cap. The nervous titter which this evoked was eloquent of the impression the scene made upon them all.

A narrow-faced woman clutching her bag with work-worn hands murmured to the man at her side, 'Looks kind of safe Will, don't you feel? like nothing could ever be changed.' A small boy broke the spell by wailing, 'Mum when do we wee-wee? I want to wee-wee.'

The guide consoled him. 'Just as soon as we get down this hill sonny, so hop in. There's places for you all to use outside the Museum and the Zoo too, so the sooner you scramble in the sooner we'll be off and you can all relieve yourselves in the conveniences.'

This created the requisite impetus. The small boy clambered up the steps working his way forward until he clung, cross-legged, from the back of the driving seat. The charabanc filled up. The guide slid in beside the driver, the vehicle eased off the verge and down they went.

'Are we goin' ter Zoo or t'other plice naow?' the child demanded.

'Zoo first,' answered the patient man, 'then you can see all those white animals and birds. After we'll take you to the Museum where you can have tea.'

'How much sir?' the mother leaned forward anxiously.

'Ninepence for bread and butter and home-made jam, tea with cakes, one and threepence with strawberries as well, and you gets a rare big pot of tea either way.'

Gyles Aynthorp succeeded to the title on his rip-roaring father's departure to more lofty realms where his surviving family were confident he would promptly set about bullying the archangels. Gyles reverted almost immediately to his old wish to make a Museum on the estate. Justin Aynthorp had pooh-poohed the idea; but when Gyles raised it again after his death and canvassed opinion the consensus was unanimous. The Dowager, his widowed mother the redoubtable Alicia welcomed it, as did her sister-in-law the little Countess Marguerite, largely because the ransacking of the Castle for suitable objects for display would provide them with a most entertaining ploy. The rest considered it an investment which might well prove to be profitable in the future. All agreed that it must be situated in such a way as to ensure the complete safeguarding of their shared privacy.

The project was duly launched; but came to completion too near to the outbreak of the Great War. It was no sooner opened than closed again. It remained shuttered and barred in the keeping of a septuagenarian caretaker until the cessation of hostilities. Then Henry returned from his prison camp and while in London encountered disabled men singing in the gutter as he strolled down Bond Street. He brought the matter to his father's notice, inveighing against such a fate for men returning to the promised 'land fit for heroes to live in'. Between them father and son staffed the Museum with such men, and placed others in posts left vacant by those of their own employees who would never return. More disabled men were found employment in the staffing of the Zoo.

By this time Gyles was convinced that the future hope for the survival of Castle Rising in these changing times lay in the creation of a market for their produce from game to bacon, through eggs, poultry, butter and cream. Even when Gyles sent two blind men to St Dunstan's to learn a craft, he did so having explained to them that their future wages would stem from the baskets and game bags they would make and his new company 'Aynthorp Enterprises' would sell. Gyles believed in Aynthorp Enterprises as the prime, logical solution to the problem of rising prices. He was far ahead of his time. Thus he came in for a fair amount of criticism from 'the County'; but when these lifelong friends and neighbours felt the weight of increased wages, taxes and 'benefits' themselves; the rising prices of everything from farm implements to cattle fodder and discovered too that they would need more staff as working hours were curtailed, they switched from carping to copying; but not before one or two families had gone to the wall, finding themselves forced to sell up or at the best to sell some of their land – the most heinous offence in all their eyes.

The men who bought from them were chiefly what the Dowager described scornfully as 'rich cits', men for whom a prospectus had more significance than a pedigree and whose knowledge and understanding of the men who worked on the land was comparably minuscule. These new landowners put in managers, drove down occasionally, sitting back smoking big cigars in large and shiny motors and wearing the wrong clothes, but prospering none the less in everything but social contact with the de Lormes and their friends who closed ranks against them resolutely.

One of the initial ventures launched by the little Countess was that of flower arrangements. She had a genius for this ploy and until she became too frail poor Sawby never succeeded in getting one of his 'arrangements' into the Castle edgeways. It was all done either by, or under the microscopic surveillance of the little Countess. Today a team of 'nice gels' as she called the talent gleaned from her neighbours' daughters, kept half a dozen London florists supplied, also sending arrangements, cut flowers and shrubs to half a dozen of the leading hotels. Meanwhile Gyles, approached by no less a person than Monsieur Ritz himself, who had it must be admitted been dismissed with a metaphorical flea in his ear by his late lordship, now supplied the Ritz with both pheasants and partridges, and latterly with butter and cream as well. The irresistible, round butter pats, each one stamped with a fleur de lys, were exactly to the Ritz clientele's taste and generally the Enterprises widened steadily.

While the rest of the family made its leisurely way through the French doors onto the terrace, Gyles' third son Andrew fled from the dining room, grabbed his tennis racquets and blazer from the hall table, seized two black cash boxes and dashed, laden down the steps towards the Museum. He had forgotten to hand these over to the girls who manned the two stalls which, on 'open' days, were now drawn up outside the two respective entrances, piled with cut flowers, pot plants and little baskets of fruit and vegetables for sale.

Andrew arrived panting, apologetic. 'Almost forgot, I'm deuced sorry girls. Here's your petty cash, five pounds. It's mostly in small silver and pennies, all written down on a bit of paper inside. Just hand it over at the receipt of customs when you've finished and old whatsit will send it up to the Castle. He gives it to Plum and Plum hands over to Sawby y'see.'

The rest of the tennis party, which included the only two house guests for this particular Friday to Monday, were already skirting the lake on their way to the tennis courts in their white frocks and flannels. As soon as Andrew had chatted dutifully for a few moments he excused himself and pelted in pursuit.

As had so often happened in the past, amid the complexities and dramas of de Lorme life, the family was enjoying a brief period of comparative calm which gave respite to the older ones after the curtain had come down upon the chilling drama of the Lady Lucy St John's marriage to the young portrait painter Mr Piers Fournes.

Lucy had been advised not to travel with her bridegroom who was even now on his way to Switzerland on a stretcher and in the company of two fresh-faced nurses who thought their patient 'most romantic' and the marriage 'terribly sad'. So, while Piers sped towards the clinic for tuberculosis run by the famous Doctor Spahlinger, Lucy had been driven down by her devoted chauffeuse Elizabeth to pay a brief visit to her new in-laws. Her brother and partner in Lucy et Lucien Couture was off with a group of his new theatrical friends to a party at Henley. His parting shot to his sister, as he leaned over the opened window of her silver Royce, was a petulant, 'Have fun lovey. Hurry back. I am hoping I can have just a little more of your attention and just a little less talk of illness which frankly sickens me my dear Mrs Fournes.'

Accompanied as it was by a rather shrill laugh this made Lucy drive her nails into her clenched palms. It also provided considerable food for speculation for the impassive Elizabeth as she let out the clutch and eased the car into the Friday night traffic. Lucy just bent her head to Mr Silk, the

King Charles spaniel which Piers had given her. Her slow
tears dripped down onto the silky head. For once in her life
Lucy was uncertain of anything any more. This was an alien
experience which filled her with an impending sense of
horror. So, most unusually for her, she wept.

The terrace group settled themselves, sipped away and indulged in the easy desultory conversation which is only
possible among people of immense intimacy. Presently even
these idle exchanges dwindled. Gyles settled his straw hat
over his patrician nose and drowsed. His wife Christine
glanced at him, smiled tolerantly and began work on her
embroidery frame speculating on how best she might lead
Constance Danement into a discussion concerning the pre-
cipitous and unexpected marriage between Lucy and Piers.
    Constance was simultaneously reflecting on how closely
the de Lorme pattern resembled that of an average linen
draper. At the inaptness of the simile a slight chuckle
escaped her.
    'Tell?' invited Christine.
    Constance hesitated, then repeated her thought adding
hurriedly, 'Let me explain dear before you are too enraged.
For the linen draper there are recurring sales during which
there is a general state of uproar. When this subsides there
comes the comparative tranquillity of what is called stock-
taking. It is really very similar to what happens in this
household during any one of the frequent family dramas
which I have shared with you, whether a ball or a somewhat
more distasteful episode.'
    Christine nodded. 'And this you see as stocktaking time?'
She spotted her advantage and pressed on, 'When we all try
to arrive at some satisfactory conclusion as to why that
extremely difficult child Lucy, whom I might add has
resolutely refused some of the most eligible men in society,
should suddenly rush into a hole and corner marriage with
a young man who is likely to make her a widow at any
moment.'
    Constance stiffened inwardly, tranquillity vanished and
every nerve alerted. 'I really do not believe Piers will die
my dear.'
    'Surely that begs the question?'

'Not altogether.' Constance moved to an attacking position deeming it the best defence in the circumstances. 'Lucy may be ruthless, yet contradictory as it may seem, I believe she has a great deal of pity in her.'

'You think she married Piers out of pity?'

'Not necessarily. You know that he fell violently in love with her the first time they met?'

'So I understand.' Christine laid aside her embroidery. 'I also know he gave her a superb jade heart. When I was in that fantastic bedroom of hers at Halcombe Street it was on her bedside table,' she faltered, then honesty forced her to admit, 'with a photograph of Lucien of course. I also know that Piers painted that ceiling with all those cherubs and love birds and that he and Lucien furnished it all for Lucy; but what does that prove?'

'Not much.'

Constance glanced around her. Gyles slept, Charles, her husband also slept, the Dowager was reading and Tante Marguerite was clearly nodding off. 'I think you know the answer,' Christine said softly. 'Please will you tell me?'

Constance, who could not tell her anything, struggled to avoid a direct lie. Eventually she compromised. 'I know that if Piers recovers, as I believe he will, then he and Lucy will do very well together provided Lucien is not too jealous, too demanding or too neglectful either.'

Christine pounced on this trump hastily, 'Because you know Lucy loves Lucien more than anyone else and always will?'

'What else my dear? Be reasonable; but if things can be made to run on an even keel between Lucy and Lucien I still believe all will be very well indeed. Piers will of course need a great deal of care and attention even when he recovers. His is a difficult temperament at the best of times. Three creative artists under one roof are likewise creative of problems,' she added drily.

In this manner, exerting the greatest caution, Constance steered her friend and neighbour away from the danger zone; but having so done she drew no comfort from it. She was inextricably enmeshed in the situation both because of her past knowledge of Piers and from her involvement in what had occurred recently.

Such knowledge could not be shared, and as a result her involvements had become a twin secret. The times in which she lived required it and there could be no escape. As Lady Superintendent of the Castle Rising Convalescent Home for Officers to which Piers had been sent, Constance had sat by his bedside and listened to him when he was delirious, so she knew and could never share the knowledge that although Piers had fallen in love with Lucy on sight he had then met her brother and had been forced to ask himself thereafter 'what in God's name am I?' a question which he answered for himself in those same delirious revelations. Piers was hopelessly in love, but not with his wife, for he was obsessively, tearingly in love with her brother Lucien.

Constance had managed to convey two things to Piers thereafter; that she knew, and that she would keep the knowledge to herself whatever happened.

She had hoped when Lucy and later Lucien broke away from the family to fulfil Lucien's ambition to be a great couturier, that Piers would then break with both of them. Instead he had become even more deeply enmeshed. Then came a brief period of respite when he went to India. For those months of absence Constance had been less anxious until like a thunderclap Lucy had telephoned her in the middle of the night, begging her to come immediately, sounding completely distraught. She had gone, of course, driven through the night by Charles to whom she said no more than, 'Piers is with Lucy and Lucien. He had a very bad haemorrhage, Lucien has collapsed and Lucy is beside herself with distress. We must go at once.'

So they had gone. The rest lay hidden in the most secret corridors of her mind. How else could she live with the knowledge, and above all keep it from her husband that Piers had haemorrhaged *while in Lucien's bedroom*? Constance knew only too well that for her Charles there was only black and white. He was totally unable to countenance or accept any intervening shades of grey. It was alien to both his nature and his times. Yet the plain fact was that Lucy had forced her brother to carry Piers into her bed; had calmly announced that she had been sleeping with Piers which was quite alright as they were to be married as soon as Piers was well enough. To say that Constance was

appalled when the truth dawned on her was to understate
her reactions on many counts; that the delicately nurtured,
totally innocent little Lucy could not only undertake such
an awful commitment, but carry it through with a ruthless-
ness worthy of a Sabine woman, took her breath away. That
Lucy so loved her brother that no other course presented
itself to her and that such love and sacrifice was based upon
a totally false premise concerning Lucien's peril or safety
and finally that Lucien, brilliant though he undoubtedly
was, yet remained one of the most shallow, worthless, self-
centred human creatures she had ever had the misfortune to
encounter, merely piled the Pelion upon Ossa.

Nevertheless Lucy had her way. The announcements
were made. The press was immensely sympathetic. The
only thing Constance did not know was that when Piers
slipped the wedding ring onto Lucy's finger it was engraved
inside with the words *Toujours à Trois*.

Sometimes during the nights Constance would try to
decide if any one else knew anything at all or even suspected
anything. There was Miss Poole of course, Lucy's erstwhile
companion/chaperone, now practically controlling their
business for them, aided by the stuttering ex-tutor Mr
Sissingham; but sooner attempt to open an ormer with a pin
than extract any confidences from Miss Poole! There was
also Elizabeth, the mannish chauffeuse whose devotion to
Lucy was so obvious. Always at this point Constance forced
herself away from such speculations. There were such
perilous conjectures open to anyone who debated the
inmost preferences of those with whom the disastrous pair
had chosen to surround themselves. Somehow, with all her
medical experience, which in itself was far ahead of her time,
Constance was not ready to accept that the running of Lucy
et Lucien Couture was in the hands of 'abnormal' men and
women, controlled by only one deeply religious spinster
with enormous powers of observation and an extremely
acute intelligence.

There was another member of the family to whom the
Lucy and Piers marriage was a source of considerable dis-
comfort. After the wedding, when the family had left and
were sitting in the car preparatory to being driven home by
Grantham, Gyles had asked Henry if he had made a few

appropriate remarks of welcome to the family to his cousin's husband and when he stammered 'nnnno sir', he had been packed off so to do. Henry found Piers alone and resting. His famous temper flared with uncontrollable suddenness and he had made what was to him an unpardonable remark.[1] He too had his suspicions – though no knowledge – as to the *raison d' être* behind it all; and he too, like Constance with her Charles, could not even confide in his Petula. It was an impasse for the pair of them and abysmally distasteful to both.

Suddenly Christine said into the long silence following Constance's last reply, 'I am still convinced there is more in this marriage than meets the eye. However, if you do not know we shall just have to wait and see how things develop.'

Constance answered weakly, 'Well Lucy and Lucien are coming down next week for a Friday to Monday. Perhaps she will be able to throw a little more light on things. Now I really shall have to rouse my dormant Charles for it is well past three o'clock and we are menaced by a visit from the redoubtable Podge and his Duchess for five o'clock tea which in his case means a stiff brandy and soda and a lecture on the parlous state of Government.'

Christine chuckled, 'He delivered himself of a tremendous explosion last Thursday when he came to luncheon. Gyles saw him off so received the full force of his invective which one supposes he considered was not suitable for my drawing room.'

'What was his theme this time?'

'The iniquitous increase in gardeners' wages. He paid twenty-five shillings a week before the Great War and provided a cottage with a bit of land to each one for growing cabbages and potatoes. On that the men "did famously", his words, remember, not mine. They also managed to raise plenty of healthy children. Now thanks to the Government – it is always the Government with him – he has to pay five pounds a week. He said he will be ruined if things go on like this. He simply did not know what the country is coming to. Then his footman held open the Royce door for him and his chauffeur drove him home while he fulminated

[1] See Book 4, *Wind of Change at Castle Rising.*

in luxury in the back of a very costly car. Sometimes I wonder if there is not a touch of the Marie Antoinette about us all. Then I too begin to speculate on where it will all end!'

CHAPTER 2

Nesting

At precisely seven-thirty Dawson came tiredly through the
Museum doors to stand on the top step, easing his cap back
with his one hand and gulping in the air laden with the
scents of summer. From his vantage point he could see
Plum's youngest stable boy wheeling away the emptied stall,
and one of the 'Enterprises' vans drawn up, doors opened
for the collection of unsold fruit and flowers.

'Had a good day Miss?' Dawson called down.

'Ripping – all we have left is a pot of geraniums' – in which
she was in error for it was a pelargonium – 'one bunch of
flowers and a few new potatoes.' She hesitated, on the point
of closing the van doors. 'You'd better give the flowers to
your wife and the new potatoes to Plum, he'll be coming
round for the take as usual won't he?'

Dawson affirmed this, went down the steps to receive his
bonus as the girl Becky slammed the doors quickly and
jumped into the cab. 'We're going to a dance,' she told him,
'so I'm in rather a hurry. Say goodnight for me to Mrs D.
please.' Then she too disappeared in a cloud of dust.

The man went in again, closed the doors, shot the bolts
then made his way to the back.

In the stables the outrageous Plum, head coachman extra-
ordinary who enjoyed such enormous licence with what he
called 'my fambly', came out of his noisome old harness
room with a straw between his teeth and a deplorable cap
pushed back from his rosy pippin face. Bowling off on his
bandy, gaitered legs, he headed towards the Museum,
shouting back 'Pinkie, git that barrer inside, then cut orf
'ome I'm orf meself in a minnit.'

This was the hour Plum liked best in his seventy-two-hour
working week. He was about to collect the Museum 'take'
from the custodian and deliver it to Sawby in the servants'

hall. He confided in his wife after the first of such visits, 'It's as good as a play Mother so dont expec' me Saturdays wen that there Museum is open and don't cook too much supper, I usually gits a bite in the Castle kitchen.'

Having collected his *raison d'être* Plum rolled his way contentedly towards the entrance to the Castle's kitchen quarters. In the outer scullery two kitchenmaids were standing at the zinc sinks up to their elbows in soap suds while two more were washing potatoes for staff supper.

As Plum greeted them the last echoes of the second dressing gong thundered out on the evening air, confirming that it was seven forty-five and therefore the gentlemen of the household would be making their way up the great staircase en route for the ministrations of their valets.

This too Plum explained to his 'missus'. 'Ladies takes longer ter git inter their finery, so it's up aloft with them at seven-thirty wen the first gong goes and all of 'em downstairs again sharp on eight-fifteen. Very partickler abart time is 'is lordship like what his dear dead lordship was likewise, only this 'un doesn't 'oller so I'm tole wen one of them young limbs is late down.' By which Plum referred to Gyles Aynthorp's sons, Henry, Ninian, Andrew and Richard, the remaining youngest, Rupert, being far too young to dine.

Mrs Parsons welcomed Plum with astonishing affability. The clement weather was appeasing her corns. These constituted an unfailing barometer to the entire staff which was generally stuck at 'wet and windy', or when especially painful at 'gale force'; but tonight she was in high humour as she waited in her old chair by her stove for the completion of 'me brown dinner rolls' as she called her evening's baking – hands on vast knees, feet comfortably unhampered in a pair of over-large carpet slippers.

'Catch 'im as he comes down,' thought Plum seeing Sawby's back disappearing through the green baize door which separated those below stairs from those above. He then obeyed Mrs Parsons' affable invitation to 'come and set down alonger me', needing little persuasion so to do. To him there was a kind of magic abroad in these vast kitchens at the hour when the labours of the day were coming to their peak immediately prior to the lavish ritual of family dinner. It fascinated him. He likened it to a beehive where orderly chaos prevailed as everyone went about their appointed tasks with the ease of long practice; every few minutes glancing up at the old kitchen clock on the wall.

Chef André, high priest of these rituals, now stood at the long scrubbed table which ran between the spits and the great stoves. His starched high bonnet absorbed most of the sweat on his forehead, but little trickles escaped to run down into his neck cloth as he set tiny shapes cut in black truffles, in minute designs on the *chaudfroid* sauce which covered a dish of *Médaillons de Jambon aux Pointes d'Asperges*. As usual he worked with both hands at a speed which held Plum's mouth agape while, with waxed moustaches twitching, Chef continued hurling instructions and invective alternately at his attendants. Between the two rooms beside an open cupboard, footmen were shrugging into their livery waistcoats with the de Lorme silver buttons on them; the parlourmaids were hastily tying themselves up with the stiffly starched strings of their white aprons, while little wizened Boots scuttled between, dodging his way to the stoves to empty more and more hods of coke into their glowing maws. The clock hands moved forward relentlessly until suddenly Mrs Parsons heaved herself upright, lifted her oven door with a clang and withdrew the baking trays. As she bent to this task so she displayed her ample rump, the huge girth of her black stockinged thighs, green bloomers above and a glimpse of red flannel petticoat. Plum averted his eyes, coughed and bang went the first tray onto the table.

''Ave one,' Mrs Parsons invited, beginning to pile the hot rolls into a napkin-lined entrée dish, 'there's some butter on the corner.'

Edward the head footman came rushing down the stairs on the back of his heels crying, 'Are me breads ready the 'ot plates is on Mrs P?'

''Ow you 'avent broke your neck long ago,' Cook observed, eyeing him balefully, 'beats me it does. Peltin' down them steep stairs and gettin' away with it is more than you deserve and that's a fac'. 'Ere's yer rolls. I'll keep the rest 'ot till you send for 'em.'

Stodging at his liberally buttered roll Plum's attention was diverted by the sudden whisking off of everything from

Mrs Parsons' table to make way for the requirements of
Pansy and two kitchenmaids who instantly began covering
it with tazzas, trays of peaches from the stove houses,
baskets of forced cherries and a great rack of crystallised
fruits.

'Where are the leaves and flowers?' exclaimed Pansy
crossly, 'get a move on girl, time's flying.'

The kitchenmaid flew too. She came rushing back with a
tray of dark, polished leaves, pink and white camellias and
the young, pink leaves of *Acer brilliantissima*. Plum gawped
anew as Pansy's skilled fingers mounted the fruits into
pyramids and decorated them with the leaves and flowers.

George the second footman was beside her now, stacking
the completed tazzas onto his tray, which he then carried at
the double up those steep stairs, the tray balanced on the
palm of one hand.

'One day 'ee'll drop the lot,' sniffed Mrs Parsons, 'and
that's the Rockingham I would 'ave 'im know.'

Dead on cue Boots, clutching yet another hod, mis-timed
his scuttle towards the stoves, stepped back to avoid Rose,
cannoned into the kitchenmaid Daisy and down went the
hod with a horrendous clatter.

'Wot's that?' screamed Mrs Parsons.

'Coke,' she was told which appeared to frustrate her.

'Well clean it up Boots,' she snapped, 'sharp's the word
naow, I declare my pore nerves is torn in ribbons.'

They were all as accustomed to her nerves as to her corns.
Work continued at the same speed, Boots scraped up the
coke, ran for a broom to sweep up the mess and paused
broom in hand as Chef began to spin sugar, flicking a loop
whisk dipped into the dark syrup to and fro at flashing speed
over a long wooden rod, making the fine hairs fall like
summer rain as the deft hand threw the syrup unerringly.

'It *is* magic!' Plum exclaimed hoarsely.

'He's clever orlright,' Mrs Parsons agreed, 'even I'll say
that for 'im. You stayin' for a bite to eat? I've got a nice bit
of game pie 'otting up when this lot settles down, an' a
drop or two of porter ter wash it down. You're welcome
enough.'

Plum hesitated. 'It is a long time since tea, I don't deny,'
he agreed, 'but I carnt keep Mum waiting too long Mrs P.'

They turned automatically to the ruler of their lives, the clock which now stood at only ten minutes to eight-thirty.

Three of the four kitchenmaids then marched towards Chef carrying three gondolas sculptured in ice and set on silver salvers. Swiftly André ranged giant prawns down either side, thrust tufts of watercress in a dark green central line and flicked his hand in dismissal.

'Catch hold of that *tamis*,' he shouted as the third girl turned with her burden. Raikes then slipped between them crying 'I'll take them gon-dolas, leave 'em be and help chef dearie.'

Raikes and Vera grabbed the opposing ends of a large piece of flannel. Whipping a copper pan from the stove chef tipped in the steaming contents and began working the sauce through with the back of a wooden spoon.

'Tweest,' he shouted, 'tweest the ends, one one way and one the other, *mon dieu que vous êtes imbéciles*, not both the same way.'

The tempo was rising steadily. Plum's eyes gleamed. The footmen and women sped up and down those alarmingly steep stairs. Then Sawby appeared adjusting the lapels of his black coat.

'Evening Mr Plumstead,' said he with unwavering calm. 'Come with the take? Good man –' he broke off, shedding benevolence, 'get up stairs the lot of you, and where are my soups, why are they not ready?'

'Coming now Mr Sawby,' George and Edward erupted from the still room with two silver tureens handled and adorned on the lid with raised fleurs de lys.

Sawby meanwhile received the chamois leather bag from Plum as if it were the collection and he in church on Sunday.

'I'll put it into the safe as I go up,' he stated, 'a little over three minutes still so there is no great rush.'

'Pay no heed to me,' said Plum hastily, 'priv'lidge to be 'ere.' He stood aside as Sawby nodded and began his return journey up the perilous stairs as if he were an actor hearing the call by 'Mr Sawby please ... beginners on stage. *Mr Sawby* IF you please.'

Suddenly the rooms emptied. The housemaids fled up the back stairs to tidy the bedrooms and turn down the beds, something Christine would not permit until after everyone had dressed for dinner. The kitchenmaids reappeared lugging huge iron kettles into the scullery where the scullery maids were preparing the wide sinks for the onslaught of plates, cutlery and silver which would soon be coming down to them. Boots vanished into his broody hole under the back stairs and even Tabby the tortoiseshell kitchen cat, aware that there would be no pickings until the first plates and dishes came down, emerged from beneath Mrs Parsons' chair, stalked across the room, leaped onto the window sill and disappeared thence to, as Mrs Parsons would have put it, 'oblige herself outside. That's a nice clean cat that is.'

From above the sonorous gong declaimed its final summons to the family. Raikes held the doors of the White Drawing Room open and as George replaced the drum on its rack Sawby stalked across the great hall not unlike Tabby the tortoiseshell cat to announce in the opened doorway 'Dinner is served my lady.'

'This is nice,' Christine murmured contentedly as she shook out her napkin, 'did I hear that you children were going to a dance after dinner?'

'Not a dance,' Henry objected while debating the merits of *Crème St Germain* against *Consommé au Xerès*, 'just an informal hop at the Priory. Daphne has some new records, a cousin has brought them from America. The feller's volunteered to teach us all some new dance from New Orleans, where I understand it's all the rage.'

Dinner progressed without incident. For once no controversial subjects were mooted, Gyles was at his most bland and the small coinage of family conversation was passed from hand to hand. When the covers were drawn, Appelby's decorative tazzas set on the gilded surface of the bare, beautiful table, the overhanging chandeliers switched off and the table left floating in a pool of candlelight, Sawby surveyed the scene as usual and as usual made his soft 'pstt' sound of dismissal to his underlings. He watched them march soft-footed and decorous through the doorway then proceeded after them leaving the family at last able to talk freely on any topic considered tabu in front of the servants.

Presently, when John Newmarket had peeled Christine a

peach and the port had completed its first circuit, Christine collected eyes, rose, smiled at her eldest son as he sped to do what he called 'door duty' and the women left the dining room to their menfolk.

Not long afterwards the occupants of both the dining room and the small Blue Drawing Room heard the sound of engines revving up in the drive proclaiming that the younger de Lormes and their two guests were off to their 'hop', probably, as was their custom in fine weather, sitting all over two small open sports cars instead of taking four and being content to occupy the seating. In due course the men appeared in the drawing room, which settled down to a pattern of remarkable tranquillity.

Suddenly the Dowager put down her latest piece of *petit point* the better to deliver a massive *non sequitur* – since until she spoke the topic had been exclusively that of horse-flesh.

'It seems to me,' she observed to the room in general, 'that there is a plethora of nestin' goin' on around us at this moment.'

'Indeed Mama,' Gyles laid aside his *Times*, 'I must confess it had escaped m'y notice.'

The Dowager waited a moment or two to assure herself of everyone's attention then commenced, holding up one finger, 'Permit me to enumerate. Firstly, my dear son, your third male and Podge's niece are rushin' about practically carryin' wisps of straw in their mouths.'

It always amused her relatives to hear the almost forgotten nickname for the duke of Barton and Sale as they tended to forget it and also that little Alicia had spent many holidays with little Podge's parents before any of them had been born – with the sole exception of little Marguerite.

'Andrew and Victoria,' said Gyles looking up from his *Times* rather vaguely.

'Certainly my dear. It's as plain as Podge's nose. Moonin' over her. Takin' her on jaunts to those depressive London night clubs' – her own single visit had jaundiced her opinion of these playgrounds – 'in my opinion it would be a sound match, in fact I favour it and so I believe does Christine.'

Gyles raised an eyebrow at his wife who nodded. 'I like her,' she confirmed, 'very much and I agree with Mama.'

Characteristically Primrose remarked, 'Gel's got an excellent seat, tends to rush her fences occasionally but she's a fine horsewoman.'

Her John merely grunted.

'Then,' pursued the Dowager holding up another finger, 'there's poor young Charles who is head over ears in love with our Sue-Ellen who has no eyes at all for anyone but your number two, Gyles.'

'Ninian!' Gyles exclaimed now, genuinely astonished. 'Oh come Mama, that's doin' it a bit too brown. I admit Charles is slightly *épris*.'

'Oh no indeed, Alicia is perfectly right,' exclaimed Marguerite warmly. 'You have only to examine the facts. Ninian takes four years to venture here after James' death and when he does come he is at pains to point out that it is only a flyin' visit and that he's wedded to his regiment. What happens? He sees Sue-Ellen and goes dashin' off to London only to return with astonishin' celerity to announce he's chuckin' the army and lookin' for a place of his own to base on, anyrate for the huntin' season. He and Sue-Ellen take long walks together, ride together, not just occasionally mark you, but every single day. We don't claim either of 'em know it yet but anyone with half an eye can see they're powerfully attracted, If you doubt it just ask Petula.'

The Dowager chuckled. 'Petula,' she observed, picking up her needle once more, 'is showin' every sign of growin' into another me. She misses nothing and in Plum's words is in a fair way to gettin' her finger into every pie.'

'I beg of you Gyles, do nothing in that quarter,' Christine spoke with some urgency, 'discuss the matter like this if you wish but pray do nothing to show your hand. Remember we are dealing with two young people who have been sorely hurt already and although there is every sign thank God that their wounds are healing now, I believe the slightest probe would start them throbbin' once again. I think it would be perfect for them if ever it came to pass; but just bear in mind that however deeply Ninian may come to care for Sue-Ellen her fortune would almost certainly make it impossible. The dear girl is so immensely and, as it turns out, so unfortunately rich. Ninian, alas, only has his allotted income and the thirty thousand my father left him. I believe Papa left him some other things besides, but nothing of any great importance. I must remember to ask him at a suitable moment.'

Gyles listened to this in silence. When the discussion deteriorated into a speculation between Primrose and John as to just what Ninian's 'effects' left by his maternal grandpapa might be, he spoke.

'The Trust ensures Ninian's income doubles should he marry,' he reminded them adding thoughtfully, 'I wonder if he even knows that.' Seeing their expressions he appended, 'Now please, none of you say anything either one way or the other. I will contrive to bring the matter up in due course. Come to that I'd prefer to deal with father's bequests Christine if you will consent to leave it to me.'

Christine smiled at him without bothering to answer. There the matter was left except that the Dowager reminded them a trifle crossly, 'I have not finished, for,' she held up a third finger, 'there is another bit of frustrated romance afoot, your Anne my dear Christine is moonin' over young Charles who is Sue-Ellen besotted.'

Christine nodded. 'I know Mama, but I think there again we are wiser to let the matter work itself out. Sooner or later Sue-Ellen will give young Charles his *congé*. Being the gel she is she will do it gently enough when the time comes and then we shall see what we shall see. Any fingers in pies there at this juncture would only cause trouble, of that I am assured.'

'There is no need to look at me like that,' retorted the Dowager. 'I shall not be here. Marguerite and I are goin' off quite soon. Aren't we Meg?'

At this moment the door opened disclosing Henrietta and Sinclair so the matter of where the two old naughties were going was left in abeyance.

Even so what had been said formed a sound preface for a little scene which was enacted the following morning at the breakfast table. Sue-Ellen and Ninian had been riding beforehand so, as was his custom, Sawby had placed their letters beside their covers.

Sue-Ellen set hers aside having glanced through the envelopes but Ninian, after obtaining the necessary consent, ripped open his small pile grunting, 'Bill ... invitation ... bill ... those damned tailors are never satisfied! ... Ah, this might be interesting.' He withdrew a number of folded, type-written sheets from a long envelope, glanced at them, turned over several pages, then extracted one saying, 'I rather like the sound of this, may I read it to you? It really might suit. It's from the estate agents, they've sent me the particulars of several houses. I must say this one looks promisin'.'

He read: '"Situate a few miles from the Suffolk/Essex borders on the outskirts of the village of Much Heneage"... I must say these estate agent wallahs use the most extra-ordinary language; now where was I, oh yes, "delightful old world gentleman's residence, tiled and half timbered with fine oak panelling and massive beams, carved staircase, large hall with open fireplace, 3 good reception rooms, 2 small additional rooms on ground floor plus usual offices, 9 bed-rooms and dressing rooms, set in picturesque surround-ings, half a mile from Much Heneage station, standing in old-world walled garden running down to the River Flush; good fishing, excellent stabling, 5 loose boxes, ample accommodation for two motors, easy access to fine huntin' country, price £3,000 freehold with vacant possession." What do you think of that?'

'Daylight robbery,' said Gyles shortly, 'I know the place well. The Grimthorpes sold it to a feller called Stukeley in '05 for, wait a bit, let me think, yes for one thousand six hundred pounds.'

'Steady a bit Pater,' objected Henry, 'prices have rocketed since then. I suggest Nin you give the place a thorough goin' over. It don't cost anythin' and it sounds toppin', bang on, just the job.'

'Henry,' snapped Gyles, 'pray speak English and not this appalling slang.'

'Sorry sir.'

Sue-Ellen spoke. 'Ninian how many bathrooms? You didn't mention them?'

Ninian sought the answer. 'I'm afraid,' he admitted, 'it only says "bath and 3 toilets". Ugh! toilets is such a lethal word ain't it?'

Petula joined the fray. 'Nin you don't need nine bedrooms and dressing rooms so you could add bathrooms surely?'

'Any mention of central heating?' Sue-Ellen asked suspiciously.

' 'Fraid not.'

'Oh you English!' she exclaimed.

'Oh you Americans,' he retorted without rancour. 'Care to come with me and have a look?'

'I'd love to.'

This last caused a good many surreptitious glances to be exchanged.

When Sue-Ellen and Ninian returned Lucy and Lucien had arrived for luncheon and the over-riding topic had become Lucy's hair.

Gyles strolled into the drawing room for his pre-luncheon madeira, stopped short at the sight of Lucy, hatless and bobbed, and came forward slowly thereafter. 'My dear child,' he exclaimed, 'surely not scarlet fever?'

Lucy failed to connect, the Dowager choked and Sinclair stammered in her defence, 'I l-like it Gyles. D-don't be unkind.'

The light dawned, but not before Christine had swept to Lucy's defence, saying, 'Now Gyles, I think it is most becomin'.' In moments, as usual, the entire family had taken sides. In a lull Sue-Ellen, newly come in was heard declaring, 'I think it's just adorable. What did you say the man's name was Lucy dear?'

'Antoine, Paris,' Lucy replied as Ninian interjected, 'Oh no Sue-Ellen. You mustn't. Your hair is so lovely,' which for some reason seemed to have a quelling effect on everyone except this girl. She replied airily, 'Don't be silly Ninian. I can always have my hair made into a transformation and then that will mean I can still wear it up for grand occasions. I think it's such a practical style. When we add up the countless hours our maids spend just brushing our hair it may be a, whaddyou call it, "crowning glory" but I should be glad if I could just pop mine on when needed.' She caught a gleam of sympathy in Petula's eyes. 'Pet,' she urged, 'come with me and we'll both have it done.'

Petula looked doubtful. 'I'd love to,' she admitted, 'Henry what do you think?'

Henry nodded. 'Why not indeed? You can also buy one of

those very long jade cigarette holders and get a hat like a candlesnuffer, Lady Mendel had one on last Thursday. She couldn't see a thing. You won't either so I'll have to come along to lead you across the streets.'

'Stuffy old pig,' Petula said angrily. 'It's terrible to find my husband is nothing but a stick-in-the-mud who refuses to move with the times.'

Into the silence which followed Gyles was heard to say blandly, 'Thank you my dear for describing me so accurately.'

She had the grace to colour, but before she could frame a suitable disclaimer, little Marguerite contributed her mite. 'Well I really think I shall have it done. Palliser is already shortenin' all my skirts. Admittedly she sniffs all the time but then if that woman was ever offered the choice of two evils she would be bound to take them both.'

Gyles then enquired icily, 'Mama I take it you will not subscribe to this inelegant lunacy?'

'No my dear,' the Dowager agreed, 'but then I do not propose to wear the extremes of current fashion either. I simply do not see myself smothered in bangles, hung with beads and bandaged across the forehead.'

Lucien looked over his sherry. '*Tante* Marguerite could wear it,' he pronounced, 'but then so could you Aunt Christine, you have such a lovely neck and with your figure you can wear my latest clothes perfectly.'

This caused another uproar, over which the unlikely voice of Primrose could be heard demanding, 'But isn't that what every woman wants? After all, isn't this man Voronoff with his monkey gland which restores youth, absolutely *thronged out* with women hoping to regain their lost youth? I should have thought that having a short hair-do was a lot easier than trotting off to Switzerland for *injections*.' This set them all off once more.

Then Lucy recalled her duty as a young bride. Once the noise had abated sufficiently she interjected, 'I must tell you, Piers sent messages to you all just before I left him in Switzerland, but,' here she pulled her mouth down suitably, 'when I saw Dr Spahlinger he asked me particularly not to come over to see Piers again until he gave permission.'

'Poor love,' murmured Christine sympathetically. 'How was he when you left?'

'Not very well,' replied Lucy, looking sad, 'we thought he had stood the journey splendidly; but then he had another haemorrhage after I had left him at the Clinic. It is a lovely place though, and the Doctor is a most delightful little man. He exuded confidence. He was insistent even then that Piers would get well. He said the three prerequisites – plus his treatment, of course – were complete rest, almost total immobility for at least four months and Swiss air.'

'Through wide windows one supposes?' Gyles mused.

'No Uncle, Piers is wheeled out onto a long terrace during the day. All the patients' beds are on wheels so that they get the air without even being transferred from beds to long invalid chairs.'

'I see,' Gyles seemed rather at a loss to know what else to say and the awkward pause was filled by Henry, who asked, 'what happens to that little dog of his, Lucy?'

'He is with Piers' mother. I went down last week to stay with them. They were so very kind and welcoming.'

'Poor love,' said Claire, radiant at having her Christian back home safely, 'what a rotten way to start your marriage.'

Lucy smiled at her, 'We'll make up for it later on,' she said reassuringly, 'Piers wants us to have a small house near mine. At the rate business is increasing we shall need all my house quite soon, so I am looking round for something suitable already.'

'Good girl,' approved the Dowager. 'It must be a dreadful thing for that poor boy not being able to paint.'

'He's willing to wait *Belle-mère*. He plans to write a fairy tale when the Doctor gives him permission. He will illustrate it himself. Though I am sure that as soon as he is given a sketch book he will begin on some of the new faces. There is an old gardener who caught his eye the very first morning he was wheeled onto the terrace.'

'How fortunate you are in having your work,' exclaimed Priscilla, 'and in having Lucien with you.'

Lucy nodded. 'Yes,' she agreed, 'Lucien and I can talk about him as much as we want without the fear of being boring.'

On that note Christine deliberately changed the conversation, uncomfortably aware that as usual Lucy was proving more than a match for her and if there were anything to conceal her niece would be the last person to reveal it.

Subsequently two things happened which drove Piers from the forefront of their minds. Eustace gave Gabrielle the requisite grounds and their divorce went through with comparatively little publicity for which he was immeasurably thankful. No sooner was the *decree nisi* granted than the Dowager took the centre of the stage to announce that she and the little Countess Marguerite had decided to pay a round of visits to relatives and friends in France. This proposed canter was promptly christened by Henry 'the Old Naughties' Progress'. It led, inevitably to a complicated discussion concerning the running of the floristry department of Aynthorp Enterprises in their absence. At length Petula provided the solution by undertaking to co-opt Sawby's wife, Appelby, whom she assured the family would be in transports at such a suggestion and who besides was possessed of considerable talent in this direction. She then committed the cardinal error of describing Pansy Appelby's abilities to the little Countess as 'nearly as good as you my darling' which so piqued the old gentlewoman that it nearly put the solution out of court.

As soon as this matter had been resolved and the old pair waved to from the front steps as they set off with Palliser and sufficient baggage for an army, Anne's long delayed 'come out' became a new bone of contention. Gyles had already made plans for a business trip to Australia and made it abundantly clear that he expected Christine to accompany him. He was only persuaded to hold off departure until after Anne's debut as the summons had already arrived for Christine to present her daughter at one of the earliest courts. Wearing an expression of extreme martyrdom Gyles agreed, albeit with a fine show of reluctance, that none of his recently acquired Australian interests would suffer unduly by a few weeks' delay. This did not deter him from moaning at the prospect of 'all that London season fandangle', nor to looking distinctly put out when he was denied full participation by the stout and forthright Duchess of Barton and Sale.

'All stuff and fiddlesticks Gyles', she declared at his luncheon table a few days later. 'I'm givin' Vikki a ball. There's nothin' simpler than to include Anne. After all it is only what Christine did for Rosalind and Lucy.'

'That would indeed be wonderful,' exclaimed Christine.

'Think nothin' of it. What's more . . .' she broke off to peer into the entrée dish George proffered at her elbow, 'what's this? Ah, *Soufflés Froids aux Pointes d'Asperges*, never could resist 'em! What a mercy it is that the commissariat is gettin' back to normal at last.' She promptly took two, enquired, 'now where was I?', picked up the thread without assistance and concluded, shouting as if she were on a barrack square, 'what's more my dears there's absolutely no need to open up your place in Arlington Street. You can bivouac in our great barracks of a place until both gels are out and then cut off to Australia while I sit like a broody hen with the fishin' fleet. If I don't succeed in marryin' Vikki off by the season's end you can do a stint next year and see if you can get the gel off our hands.'

Christine's mouth twitched. The Dowager dabbed busily with her table napkin and Gyles slid one long hand across his mouth. The Duchess concluded, 'These soufflés are superb' and loosed a comfortable belch which served to supply cover for a significant exchange of glances between Victoria and Andrew.

Gyles responded, 'Deuced good of you Kitty – George the soufflés to her Grace,' then he turned to Henry and demanded 'feel you could run things here with yer brothers durin' our absence?'

Henry grinned, 'Of course sir,' at which Christine intervened saying with unaccustomed force, 'I have a proviso to that undertaking.'

Gyles raised an eyebrow, met his wife's eyes and smiled a trifle wryly. Without being told he knew what the stipulation implied. However he confined himself to a dry 'How much, may I enquire?' and she retorted 'Quite a considerable sum I suspect. I am of course referring to that old saw, that all work and no play, etc, with which I know you will concur.' She abstained from explaining that what she was about to propose stemmed directly from her own experience.

Under the late, extrovert, autocratic Justin, neither she nor Gyles had ever been given any opportunity to as she thought of it 'flex our wings'. They had both longed for a chance to entertain untrammelled by the controlling hands of the Dowager and her rumbustious spouse, so now Christine saw the perfect opportunity to give to Henry and Petula that she had been denied. Gyles waited.

'Well,' she began, still somewhat uncertainly, 'you will also agree that we have done precious little real entertainin' since the war?'

'Of course.'

'Here we are then, surrounded by our own young who are growin' up, makin' their own friends, as is only right and proper, bein' entertained by them in their parents' homes and it seems to me only fair to suggest that if we are layin' the burden of our responsibilities on Henry and Pet, we should also give them a chance to try their wings in an entirely different way.'

'Meanin'?' Gyles' caution commanded the table's silent attention.

'Why not let them tackle some entertainin' without any help from us?'

'Such as?'

'I thought perhaps a dance for all their friends. In any quandary they would have our nonpareil neighbours Constance and Charles to turn to for advice or counsel. How say you, love? Would it not be good trainin' for when they do have to take over the reins entirely?'

'Admirable,' Gyles agreed. 'I make only one proviso of my own.'

Henry and Petula had sat very still during this exchange, but at the word 'admirable' which they had suspected might have been 'preposterous' Petula clapped her hands excitedly and Henry's hand went up to his copper head.

'Pray leave your hair alone at the luncheon table,' Gyles commanded. 'I think this is a most excellent suggestion. My rider is purely commercial. You two can do what you like, choose what date you wish and have the entire staff and any additional labour you require, without let or hindrance. I merely ask that you keep a strict and detailed record of expenditure as part of the exercise. Whatever you do I do

not believe you will bring us to bankruptcy and the staff
will be in transports, particularly André. It would also
constitute practical trainin' for when you take over. No
matter what is involved just *rendre compte* to me when I
return. I must also remember to check our champagne
stocks and remind you that Berry Brothers will supply you
with anythin' vinous or indeed alcoholic you may need
additionally.'

Henry erupted into speech. 'It's perfectly rippin' of you
sir and Mama's a corker for suggestin' it but, well, you see all
our chums are drinkin' champagne cocktails now, it's, er,
the thing; but to do 'em with your Perignon would be a
mortal sin. Have I your permission to lay in some ordinary
non-vintage stuff for all the mixin'?'

'No,' said Gyles shortly. 'M'gratitude. These pernicious
"cocktails" as you call them – such an inelegant word – are
nothin' more than a number of good ingredients totally
ruined by bein' mixed together, but,' he raised one elegant
hand, 'that is only *my* opinion, and you will serve what you
wish. However,' his pleasure was manifest, 'it is gratifyin' to
know you would not commit mayhem with our good stuff
and anyway prices have soared since the war in a way which
is positively criminal.'

In the ensuing excited babble which broke out the two
Aynthorps exchanged glances of extreme content down the
table and nodded to one another.

Almost immediately Petula began making lists. Henry
had filched one from her after she had been shopping in
the villages. He cherished it for it contained the entry 'hair
nets for melons and me'. Sawbridge, having been persuaded
to try his swelling canteloupes suspended in 'Lady Fayre'
baby blue hair nets, was heard afterwards saying with
reluctant admiration, 'That Mrs Pet is a blooming marvel
with substitoots even if baby blue ain't a head gardener's
favrit colour for 'ot 'ouse fruits.'

While she and Henry were engrossed in their party plans
Ninian bought his 'gentleman's country residence' in Much
Heneage. Sue-Ellen instantly defected from her Zoo. She
drove with him to London to bully the firms who were
engaged to put in central heating – the little Countess's gift
which Sue-Ellen had managed to persuade him to accept.

When it came to a matter of bathrooms the pair were highly diverted by the language mystique which the purveyors of these things employed. They hooted over 'toilet basins with running H and C', and similar linguistic eccentricities. These reached their zenith when Sawby entered to announce that Messrs Plug, Pullit and Crapper were on the telephone with an urgent query.

'What?' grunted Ninian who was learning to play mahjongg at the time. Sawby hesitated, glanced down at the scrap of paper in his hand and managed, 'They are enquiring sir if you wish to have a P Bend or an S bend on your low level suite.'

'Good Gad,' Ninian looked up nonplussed, 'can you interpret?'

'I think so sir,' he replied calmly and did so.

'Tell the clot I'm not a bloody pigmy.' Ninian snapped. Sawby remained impassive. Sue-Ellen intervened, 'Tell him nothing of the sort please, but say it is of no consequence provided either will be concealed when the enclosing panels have been affixed.' She added for Sawby's benefit, 'We wish to retain the, er, box affairs and merely install more modern plumbing.'

Out of this incident grew what they called 'toiletry lingo', until Christine put her small foot down on being asked at the luncheon table by her eldest son 'Might I trouble you to pass the condiments, Ma.' She fought a losing battle. Having ruled, Ninian said, 'Granted soon as asked,' while Henry was heard remarking, 'I don't mind if I do,' when offered a dish of *rognons sautés au Madère* by George, which caused the dish to wobble alarmingly in the footman's hands.

The pair were finally threatened with a box on the ears by their incensed Mama who declared, 'Even if I have to stand on a chair to administer it.'

When the estimates arrived Ninian was appalled.

'I'm going to be ruddy well ruined,' he groaned passing them to Sue-Ellen, 'I haven't got a stick of furniture yet.'

'Oh yes you have,' responded Gyles, 'yer Mother and I have been talkin'. You may have all that rather splendid oak in yer Uncle Alaric's suite which includes a first Elizabeth four poster, if you are not too toffee-nosed to accept it. You

may also take Sue-Ellen with you to our attics. There's
enough good stuff up there to furnish half a dozen homes.
Take yer pick. That rabbit warren aloft is long overdue for
a turnout, and besides it's only right and proper. You may
be an adult but you are also my son. Furthermore,' his
expression was almost baleful, 'we intend launchin' you
with a couple of thou' so pray be quiet while I read my paper
in peace.'

Henry chuckled and was glared at. Ninian flushed,
then muttered, 'Most grateful sir, ... indeed quite overcome.'

After this, 'We'll go to country sales,' Sue-Ellen decided
which led to some unprecedented Lorme behaviour as she
and Ninian haunted dusty salesrooms, prowled through
other people's houses on view days, repaired to country
pubs to eat bread, cheese, pickled eggs and onions, sitting
tucked into old settles or perching on bar-stools where
Ninian rediscovered the alchemy of laughter and Sue-Ellen
silenced bar-parlours as she walked in.

When they came back with an extremely early Bible Box
the family went into transports. Finally Sir Charles asked
mildly, 'Might one commit the solecism of askin' what you
paid for this?' To which Sue-Ellen replied, 'Two pounds,'
which drew a murmured 'To them that hath ... there is no
justice!'

Eventually the day came when all their 'loot' was taken to
Much Heneage and carried in to 'Farthings', a name which
Ninian observed drily was 'fittin' in the circumstances'. Sue-
Ellen said nothing but found him a very gloomy companion
for a time thereafter. Soon afterwards a new consignment of
birds arrived for the Zoo and Ninian was left to 'go it alone'
which drove him right back into his old silences.

Sue-Ellen was sitting at her desk working out the cost of
feeding twenty-four penguins, when she looked up to see
Ninian's large frame in the doorway.

'Hullo,' she exclaimed, 'I thought you were at Farthings.'

'No good,' Ninian grumbled, 'needs a woman's touch. I've
shelved it until you've got sorted out here. Can you give me a
job?' which again achieved his main objective of being with
her. After that Farthings remained filled with cases, furniture, rolled rugs and carpets for several weeks, while the

Dowager and the Countess set out upon their Progress and the time drew near for both Anne's presentation and Gyles' and Christine's departure thereafter.

CHAPTER 3

Rupert

Christine had been shocked to learn that their Majesties were insisting upon the retention of simplicities which had so startled Society the year before. 'No feathers!' she wailed. 'No trains! Oh what a disappointment.'

Despite these strictures mother and daughter looked very well, and Anne's willowy beauty evoked much praise. Her parents stayed with the Duchess until after the joint ball for which all the Castle young drove to London. They remained until they had given the Aynthorps a rousing send-off, after which Henry drove his Petula back to the Castle and called a conference.

The immediate problem was one of dates. With three or four balls a night in London during the season it could not be expected that anyone would turn up for a country dance until it was over. Then the great exodus would begin. Hugely dampened, they were forced to put the date forward until the end of September. Once this was decided, they would begin preparations from the first of August when all the nursery brood would be safely installed in Bognor with Nanny Rose, they settled to a mixture of work and play, in which they took turns to attend the London balls; using their leisure in between to play tennis, ride before breakfast, swim in the newly-installed swimming pool and dance to a gramophone at their own or other people's homes.

Everything was running smoothly when suddenly a white-faced Nanny Rose brought the information to the breakfast table that the youngest de Lorme, Rupert, had disappeared.

'I put him to bed as usual,' Nanny blurted out, 'he'd been such a good boy all day I didn't think to lock his door as I do when he's been terrible ... I looked in again at ten o'clock

and he seemed to be sleeping peacefully ... then when I
went to wake him this morning ... his bed was empty. He
had dressed himself in plimsolls, white shorts and a blue
blouse, they was all gorn and his little red corduroy coat. At
first I thought he must have waked early and got out for a
stroll. Nanny used to lock the door to the nursery wing but I
was always up afore any of them ever stirred so I didn't think
it was necessary. I dressed as quick as I could and then ran
down to the Servants' Hall, but they had seen nothing of him
so I went to Mr Plumstead. He hadn't seen him neither. I
asked him to tell all the other men while I went over to the
Zoo, but no one had seen him there so though I'm ever so
sorry to trouble you Mrs Henry, madam, I thought you
ought to know. I'm that worried with her ladyship away I
just don't know what to do next.'

Henry put down his table napkin. 'Give Rose a nice strong
cup of tea Pet,' he advised. 'Come along Nin and you
Andrew, we'll ride down to the villages. Nin you take Lower
Aynthorp, I'll take Upper and Andrew can get over to
Pletched. Be sure to tell everyone you see. What was it again
Nanny? White shorts, blue blouse, what colour was the
coat?'

'Red sir, oh just suppose something has happened to him!'

'We won't suppose anything of the sort,' said Henry
reassuringly. 'Come on you chaps, and Pet, you and Sue-
Ellen start ringing round. The blighter may have gone
calling for all we know.'

The three brothers pelted from the room. Primrose and
her husband were not yet down, nor Henrietta and Sinclair,
so Sue-Ellen hurried off to tell them while Petula began
telephoning.

By eleven o'clock everyone had drawn a blank. The only
clue they had gleaned came from their old postman who
claimed he saw a small boy in a red coat sitting on a tractor
which had lumbered up Lower Aynthorp main street just as
he was setting out on his rounds.

'I never noticed,' said old Groby shamefacedly, 'I could
kick myself, that I could.'

By the time the country people had settled at their kitchen
tables or under hedges for their mid-day dinner every
farmer with a tractor for miles around had been contacted

to find out if they had one out which had gone through Lower Aynthorp high street. None had, but two admitted that their tractors were out and that their drivers just might have taken a long way round. Both promised a rare trouncing for such dereliction when the offenders put in an appearance again.

By three o'clock Constance and Charles, together with young Charles, had joined them. 'Better telephone the police,' Sir Charles advised sombrely. 'Not our local bobby; but Chelmsford for a start, and then ring round the surrounding towns. Give a full description each time. And may I say I consider that age entitles me to the privilege of giving that young devil a sound walloping when he is found!'

By nightfall Nanny Rose was in hysterics and a very grim household faced the fact that they had as Ninian put it 'drawn every ruddy cover without success'.

Dinner was a farce. Every time the telephone rang – and it rang almost incessantly – they started, Henry rushed to answer it and came back each time to shake his head. 'Nothin', just wantin' to know if we had any news,' he told them again and again.

'How much money had he?' asked Andrew suddenly. 'Let's ask Nanny Rose.' They waited. The girl came in, her face swollen with weeping, her eyes red.

'He's took his money box,' she told them bursting into a fresh storm of weeping, and then through her sobs, 'an' I left my handbag on the nursery table with two pound in it and some pennies. It's all gone.'

'He meant to go!' exclaimed Petula. 'He planned this. But where in the world would he make for?'

Sue-Ellen said quietly, 'The wireless. Can we not get someone to ask about him on the wireless like we do in the States?'

Henry started up. 'I'll ring, but it'll put a cat among the pigeons. We'll have the press here in hordes!'

'I'll deal with them,' promised Sir Charles. Then they all sat silently waiting for Henry to return.

'I got passed from hand to hand,' he apologised, 'in the end I got a feller whom I knew. I told him all over again. I also told him that father and mother were on their way to

Australia. He asked me to hang on, but when he came back on the line he said it will be done after the nine o'clock news.' He glanced at his wrist watch, 'about half an hour, and then we shall have to man the telephone right through the night in case someone rings with news.'

They streamed into the library and sat around with earphones clamped securely in position.

Sawby came in with the liqueurs, George with the coffee, so Henry removed his earphones to say, 'If you want to hear the appeal to anyone who has seen Master Rupert you had better get downstairs to your wireless.' Then he replaced his earphones.

The news seemed much longer than usual. The announcer waded through his report, ... on unemployment ... about a small outbreak in the West Country of foot and mouth disease ... the continuing wheat surplus ... crops ... weather report, until they all began to twitch. Then it came. The measured voice said clearly, 'Now here is an appeal. Missing from his home in Essex since last night, six-year-old Rupert Michael de Lorme. It is believed that the boy is wearing white shorts, a blue blouse and plimsolls. He is also either wearing or carrying a red corduroy coat. He is tall for his age with dark red curly hair, hazel eyes. He has a small scar over his left eyebrow. Will anyone who has seen this boy please telephone Scotland Yard, number 1212 or Chelmsford Police telephone number 731904.'

Their hands went up like those of Duchesses at a Coronation. Off came the headphones and Henry got up with a sigh. 'Would anyone like some brandy?' he asked wearily.

Primrose took Marguerite's place to dispense coffee.

Charles Danement was the first to speak. 'If we could try to think ourselves into Rupert's devious young mind we might come up with a likely source of enquiry. Henry, where would you go? What would you want to do? What could cause you at Rupert's age to run away? He must have had some objective.'

Henry's hand flew to his copper head and he ruffled it desperately. 'I dunno, sir, though wait a bit, *I* was potty about circuses, has there been one anywhere round here recently?'

Charles nodded. 'Suggestion number one. Andrew, what's your thought?'

Andrew scowled at the brandy in his ballon. 'It was trains with me,' he remembered, 'I was crazy about trains. I used to go AWOL to watch them come into Lower Aynthorp station. I had a little book in which I recorded numbers, but then it palled because there were so few really. Then I got a passion for ducks, but those kept me within our own boundaries.'

'Right,' Charles looked round, 'we've got trains, and circuses, anything else?'

Priscilla nodded reminiscently. 'With me it was gypsies. I met some once when I was quite small, about seven as I remember. They were camped in that field near what used to be that old hut in the woods where that poacher lived before Henry got him up to Clangowrie.[1] I met a funny old woman who asked me to cross her palm with silver. I told her I hadn't any but she took my hands and stared at them. She told me. . . .' She broke off, flushed, stammered and managed, 'Well she talked a lot of rot about the future men in my life. Then a young man with flashing eyes and dark curls came up, I think it was one of her grandsons. He had a hedgehog, which he proceeded to cover with wet clay. He raked over their fire while I sat beside the old woman and watched. He pushed the clay ball into the ashes, covered it completely with more; why, now I come to think of it I can even remember what he said; "tastes better than all your fancy foods at the Castle missy. Baked hedgehog's wunnerful." I stayed until it was roasted. All the while the women sat by the fires making clothes pegs. At last the gypsy broke the clay putting a tin plate under to catch the juices which simply flowed out. All the hedgehog's prickles had stuck to the clay and there was this white flesh exposed, and a most wonderful smell. It tasted good too, just as he said. As a result I was late for luncheon and old Nanny spanked me.'[2]

'Gypsies, circuses, trains,' mused Charles, 'anyone got any other suggestions?'

Ninian looked at Sue-Ellen. 'When we took the little blighter with us to Farthings the other day didn't he say

[1] Book 2, *Shadows over Castle Rising.*
[2] Book 1, *The Lormes of Castle Rising.*

something about wanting to be a sailor when he was old enough. Now what *did* he say?' he frowned, trying to remember.

Sue-Ellen answered, ' "When I can escape from all these women I'm going to be a sailor". That's what he said. I wonder...? Charles, where is the nearest port? He might just have got the idea into that wicked little head that he was going to run away to sea.'

'Tilbury. It's no distance really, he wouldn't even have to cross the river.'

'How would he get there?'

'Well now that's the problem. It would be a cross-country journey by train. Would anyone give lifts to a boy of that age?'

'Yes,' said Petula firmly, 'if he had a story which would hold. That young devil's combined charm and inventiveness would probably work the oracle. He's got the Lorme charm to excess remember. But what I do not see, and I cannot accept any of these theories until someone convinces me, is what set him off?'

Henry rose, crossed to the chimney piece and pulled the bell.

'Goin' to ask the servants,' he said simply.

When George appeared, it was clearly his turn for late duty. 'Ah George,' said Henry, 'is Nanny Rose below stairs or has she gone to bed?'

'Oh no sir,' George looked shocked, 'she's with Mrs Parsons who's trying to comfort her.'

'Right, thank you George. Is she in the Servants' Hall or the Steward's Room?'

George looked puzzled. 'The Steward's Room, sir, with Mr Sawby and Pearson is in there too. The rest has gone to bed.'

'Then I'll come down.' Henry rose. 'It's better than havin' her up here, I'll see if there is any clue she can give me.'

When he had gone Petula said despondently, 'Nanny Rose said he was a very good boy yesterday, gave her no trouble for once.'

'Exactly,' Charles' eyes gleamed, 'is not that in itself unusual?'

'Um, yes ... I suppose so.'

'Well then let us wait and see. Constance my love, more coffee?'

'Yes please if it is still hot.'

'It is,' Primrose assured her, holding out her hand for the cup. 'What's in your mind Charles?'

'Only the most nebulous fancies at present. But let us suppose Rupert had planned it all sometime ago and was only waiting for Christine and Gyles to go. He knew exactly when they sailed. He even asked how long the sea journey would take, because I remember hearing him when they came down from the nursery to say their goodnights. He would know that they were still on their way – in baulk as it were – for even the Lormes cannot have a ship turned around, even supposing we contacted them by radio telephone. Might he not have decided to bide his time? If so it would explain his behaving like a Christian for a whole day, just to lull Nanny Rose into tranquillity. I don't suggest he settled well ahead for any particular date, but he was playing it very cool. When he saw, just before he went to bed that Nanny had left her handbag in the nursery, he checked the contents, found that two pounds and tuppence and decided this *was* the moment at last. So, he went to bed and foxed sleep when Nanny went in to check on him at ten o'clock, then he waited a bit longer, got up and dressed himself, crept downstairs and let himself out by one of the garden doors. I wonder what he did then though? He would know he was perfectly safe until the household awoke. He would also know there was no chance of a train, or a lift until daylight, so he would look around for somewhere to lie up. Yes that's it. Now where would that be?' he looked around expectantly.

'Zoo!' exclaimed Sue-Ellen. 'He knows exactly what time my men start work in the morning. If he crawled in with one of the smaller animals, the man who brought their feed would be sure to wake him so that wouldn't do, because by that time there'd be too many people moving about, someone would be bound to see him. Now where would he be sure to be wakened really early...?' she demanded.

'Cock crow in fact, that's what we want,' said Andrew. 'Gosh! I've got it!' His face lit up. '*He slept with the white bantams*. There are five cocks among them. No one could sleep through that din, not even a little boy. I say, why don't we go down and have a look? He might just have left some sort of clue.'

When Henry returned to the library he found to his astonishment that it was empty save for Andrew who had agreed to take the first watch by the telephone and was now stretched out beside it, sound asleep and snoring steadily. He promptly woke him up.

'Wassermarrer,' murmured his brother, sundered at mid-snore by a hand on his shoulder.

'Wake up you clot,' shouted Henry, 'where's everyone gone?'

Andrew sat up crossly, 'I was just having a wonderful dream about ... well never you mind, but what the hell do you want?'

'Where has everyone gone? that's what I want to know,' Henry demanded wrathfully.

'To see the bantams, ... lookin' for clues ... go 'way Hen you bastard,' after which brotherly endearment he closed his eyes again.

'Bantams! At midnight!'

Without bothering to open his eyes again Andrew mumbled 'Charles had an idea. Now push off there's a good feller. I'll sound the alarm if the telephone rings.'

Henry gave an exasperated grunt, hesitated, then flung himself in a chair saying, 'Might as well wait here. What lunacy! chargin' round a Zoo in the middle of the night.'

The search party arrived at the bantam house armed with torches. There was no moon; but the night was warm and filled with the drifting scents from borders and shrubberies. An occasional, drowsy bird cheeped as they went by. Slight rustles denoted the presence of small nocturnal animals on the prowl. As they came to the first of the cages there was the rustling of bodies in straw and as they went by some of the many owls, one screeched in the darkness, a startling, mocking sound. Now too there wafted towards them a warm conglomeration of animal, furry, feathered smells.

'I feel an intruder,' whispered Sue-Ellen to Claire, as they went arm in arm. Then someone stumbled against one of the

new grass verges and 'God dammit', came from Ninian,
followed swiftly by, 'I beg your pardon girls.' They heard
Constance giggle. At length they reached the bantams, 'I'll
go,' Ninian volunteered, contrite at his bad language. He
switched on his powerful torch, relic of his service days.
There was a soft cluck-clucking of protest as he pushed open
the door to their sleeping quarters and a whoosh of stirring
wings, followed by a fluttering as some awoke and dropped
down from their perches. The beam, focussed on the straw-
deep flooring, showed a deep hollow in one place, as if a
larger body than any bantam's had indented it. The beam
worked round steadily. The rest crowded round the
entrance.

Suddenly Ninian dived down and began scrabbling in the
straw. 'Found!' he shouted in triumph, 'we are right, the
little fiend has been here.'

He turned, on his knees, much to the detriment of his
dress trousers, and held out one hand disclosing several
gleaming scraps of silver paper, 'Butterscotch,' they chorused, 'silver wrapping and sticky papers from butterscotch.
Christine gave them all some before she left.'

Ninian only grunted and went on scrabbling. This time he
came up with a stick of liquorice.

'Must have fallen from the pocket of his coat when he
curled up and slung it over him,' he commented passing it
back behind him. 'Oh yes, and here's his compass!' His voice
rose on a note of triumph, 'Rupert slept here and when the
cock birds began their dawn crowing he woke up and nipped
off not bothering to see if he'd left anything behind.'

They trudged back to the Library, stood blinking in the
bright light while Ninian fastidiously plucked chicken droppings off one black trouser knee, saying crossly, 'Turds,
dammit!' and flung them into the chimney piece among
Petula's carefully arranged wine-cooler of lupins and
delphiniums.

'Why a compass?' she asked.

'Because,' Charles told her, 'he had lessons in compass
readin' when he had that hare and hounds paper chase.
Don't you remember? for the village kids. Harry Devening
arranged it for the Women's Institute children and Rupert
asked if he could join in. He produced that compass and

asked Harry how it worked. All unsuspectin' the poor chap explained it to him. The little blighter must have used it to work out the shortest distance between the starting point and the finish for he tore ahead at the "off" for hounds, ducked through some woods, took the shortest point from start to finish and came in first. It only came out when someone asked how he had managed to run three miles in less than the current record.'

They had to laugh; but soon sobered.

'Point taken,' said Henry. 'I found out while you were caperin' about the estate ruinin' dress clothes and dirtyin' long skirts,' he ignored the howls of protest, 'that Rupert cajoled the Dowager when she went into the nursery to say goodbye, to show him where Tilbury is on the map book we used when we were kids. So, it's plain enough with hindsight that he was plannin' this some time ago. Nanny Rose remembers him askin' "*Belle-mère*, is that where big ships leave from?" and of course the old darling told him. *Quod erat demonstradum.*' He glanced at his wrist watch. 'We'd better get going. I suggest Nin and I go, we work well together in double harness, while you sir,' to Charles, 'let the police know how far we've got and alert their pals and River Police to search any ships which are on the point of weighin' anchor. Come on Nin let's get out of these togs.'

CHAPTER 4

The *Jolly Polly*

Henry's Bugatti snarled to a standstill at the entrance to Tilbury Docks as the first streaks of daylight began working their way through the smoke-hazed sky. An unenthusiastic character emerged from the door of a small wooden hut, reminding Henry of a badger emerging from its sett. He grunted at them, checked names, then jerked them forward with a battered thumb. 'Inspector's waitin' for yer,' he told them, grudgingly.

Their exchange of courtesies with the Inspector was more encouraging. He was a burly man with shrewd eyes and a pleasant smile but he had little to tell which might hearten them, just that a protracted search of ships due out on the morning tide had drawn a blank; but that there was one British coaster which had slipped through unchecked, going downstream a little before midnight with a cargo of pig iron. She was bound for Gothenburg where she might, the Inspector guessed, 'Be expected to dock in approximately fifty hours, certainly not sooner. He explained, 'She lies pretty low in the water so cannot chalk up many knots per hour.'

He also told them that the search was still in progress and was likely to continue for a further couple of hours. Their faces fell at this, but brightened at the suggestion that a bit of breakfast in the police canteen might help to while away the time. In a matter of moments Henry had backed the Bugatti alongside a warehouse wall and the three were walking towards the source of a tantalising smell of frying bacon which wafted to them on the sharp morning air.

By the time three very thick plates – loaded like the elusive coaster – had been handed to them and they had embarked upon their first mouthfuls of eggs, bacon, sausages, fried bread and chips, the atmosphere became less strained. Then a mound of buttered toast appeared held in a beefy hand and a gruff voice said, 'Gents, you've forgot yer blottin' paper.' They looked up to see a very red-faced, burly constable towering above them.

'Hold hard,' said this character, 'an' I'll get yer tea,' by which time the brothers were grinning. The constable returned with three steaming mugs, easily contained in one hand.

The Inspector, clearly in benevolent mood, said, 'This is Constable Stiggings, gentlemen. You can rest your ass if you like Tom, these are the brothers of that scallywag that's run away.'

By the time Henry, as to the manner born, had wiped the last streaks of egg and bacon fat from his plate with a toast crust, the Inspector and 'Tom' had taken their measure and decided they liked what they saw. Then Henry's cigarette case went round. Tom said, 'I don't mind if I do.' After accepting a light, he lumbered to his enormous boots to get replenishments of tea.

'That coaster,' the Inspector explained, blowing ecto-plasmic clouds of smoke from his pipe, 'is called the *Jolly Polly*. This dirty lot around here calls her the *Jolly Pereneum*.'

Ninian laughed. 'Y'know,' he said, elbows on table, 'I had a number of dockers under my command during the last shindig. I thought they were splendid fellers and bloody tough,' which further enhanced the Lorme image.

'Inspector, what *will* happen to the little sod if he is found as a stowaway?' Henry asked abruptly.

The man, his eyes glinting, countered with a question of his own.

'Might I ask sir, does he resemble you gentlemen?'

Copper heads turned to one another questioningly. 'Well yes, I suppose so,' Ninian admitted. 'He's better lookin' though.'

'Well then,' another cloud of smoke enveloped him, 'I should say he'd be fed, watered and then firmly locked up in one of the crew's 'orrible pongy sleepin' quarters. There isn't much else on a coaster.'

'He'll love it,' Henry decided crossly.

The Inspector glanced up at the large wooden-framed

clock on the canteen wall. 'Well,' he said, 'it doesn't look as
if we're getting any joy.' His voice sounded apologetic.
'Would you, I wonder, care to come aboard with my men
and take part in a search? It's nearly as funny as doing one in
a men's railway station toilet. A real panic, for you know
every damned crew member of every ship is up to something
and their consciences show like a Can-Can girl's knickers,
leastways to us.'

Such company was very much to the Lormes' taste. They
quit the canteen and flanked by the two policemen strolled
towards their objective. Henry asked 'What will you do if
you don't find him here?'

'Contact Gothenburg,' said the Inspector promptly.
'Which we shall do in sufficient time to be sure they board
the *Jolly*, er, *Polly* the moment she heaves to. Then if the
lad's there they'll turn him round on the next ship and
we'll have a reception committee waiting for him here.'

The subsequent search had them choking with laughter
despite their anxiety. Scared faces, scuffles below deck and a
knowing what-did-I-tell-you glance from the Inspector
creased them and they were hard put to control themselves.
At length, strolling back they said their thanks to their hosts
and rather wearily backed the car out, turned her round and
began the return journey. Half-way home Henry nodded off
at the wheel so they pulled onto the verge and slept for a
couple of hours, eventually sliding into their places at the
luncheon table while a storm raged below stairs.

Intent on hearing the news as relayed by Sawby, who had
purposely replaced his footmen for pre-luncheon sherry
duty in the library, Chef André allowed his *Soufflé* Monte
Carlo to blacken. In a more powerful than usual Gallic
eruption he castigated Appelby and ended by hurling a
small copper chafer at one of the kitchen maids. Simultaneously Mrs Parsons took what she called 'h'umbrage'. Precisely on cue Sawby came down, very stately, enquiring in
full voice, 'Is my dining room soufflé ready chef?' He
stepped straight into the line of the flying chafing dish and
was compelled to duck with undignified haste. Into the
ensuing silence he then expressed himself with such fluency
that a scullerymaid burst into tears, her companions
promptly followed suit and over all sounded the ringing of

the dining room bell. Sawby did a neat about turn saying balefully as he mounted the stairs, 'You will hear more of this when I return.'

This was the last straw to the infuriated André who screamed after him, 'Tell 'em we'll 'ave omelette Somerset Maugh-ham *aussi vite que possible*,' all of which stemmed, if somewhat indirectly, from the delinquent Rupert.

By twilight the entire remaining family were out on the terrace beyond the White Drawing Room windows. They were steeped in forebodings, twitching with unease and anticipating at any moment a cable from Gyles demanding information. Their only comfort seemed to be in remaining close to each other. Charles and Constance joined them, their faces grave and anxious. Henrietta, as was natural, no longer possessed a face. According to Andrew it was just a swollen mess due to incessant weeping. In the end it was he, the least likely among them, who said what all of them were thinking.

'Can anyone tell me just what we do if that young blighter isn't aboard the *Jolly Whatsit*? We've done the police, the radio and there isn't a hospital in the country which hasn't been alerted. The papers have splashed it and there can't be a soul on this island who isn't on the alert for a flaming-haired boy of six in a red corduroy coat, white shorts, a blue blouse and plimsolls. How can he have vanished into thin air like this?'

Even now there was no one who would say what really oppressed them. Possibly they felt that to voice it would be to make it happen; but they were all weighed down with the dread that something *had* happened to Rupert.

Sue-Ellen was the first to crack. She had been sitting in the deepening dusk making cat's cradles with her fingers and staring out at the strange shapes the garden assumed in the fading light. Abruptly her control snapped. 'Oh, why don't we bring it out into the open!' she exclaimed, 'it can't be worse than bottling it up like this! He may be the naughtiest little boy in the whole world but even so he *is* only little. Just supposing we are all wrong and something awful has happened to him? It doesn't bear thinking about but *we must think* and we must do something.' She was crying now quite

unashamedly. 'I am just sitting here imagining what I
should feel like if it were my S-S-Stephen,' she groped for a
handkerchief and Ninian leaned forward to put one in her
hand. 'T-Thank you N-Ninian ... I am s-sorry everyone
b-but I j-just can't bear your s-stiff upper lip any l-longer.'

Ninian's hands were at his sides now, hanging down over
the arms of the rattan chair in which he sprawled. As Sue-
Ellen began to cry those arms moved to grip the sides of the
chair until the knuckles were white. He was obviously
fighting for control and quite unaware that both Sir Charles
and Constance were watching him intently. Petula jumped
up and put her arms around the weeping Sue-Ellen.
'Darling of course we understand. There's no reason to be
ashamed. I've been in torment since this thing started ...
wondering ... well wondering exactly as you have done.'

'Excuse me madam.' Petula whipped round at the sound
of his very familiar voice to see Sawby standing impassively,
framed in the open French doors.

'More trouble Sawby?' she queried, her arms cradling
Sue-Ellen still.

'Well, not exactly, madam. The Dowager has just telephoned to say that she and the Countess have a train to
catch so would not wait to speak to you. The line was very
bad but I understand we are to collect them from Lower
Aynthorp.'

'The eagles gather,' murmured Henry in funereal voice,
'next thing we'll have his ruddy lordship on the line and then
Godhelpus all!'

Petula cut across this very firmly. 'Mr Henry will take the
Royce Sawby if you will be good enough to have it brought
round, and see that one of the footmen is ready to accompany him and handle the luggage. Do you happen to know
the time of the last train, I can never remember?'

'It arrives at five minutes to twelve madam.'

Henrietta loosed a fresh storm of weeping over them. 'Oh
why couldn't they have waited! Traipsing all over France at
their ages. Oh the poor old loves!'

Never had two hours dragged by with more nerve-racking
slowness. They sat on until darkness was complete and the
night sky decked out in her jewellery of stars. The new moon
then launched herself, a silver crescent which, as it rose,

invested the silent gardens with an almost mystical beauty, while from the banks below a Davidia shook out her eerie handkerchief blossoms as if they were wraiths, wringing their small white hands.

'Such a very little boy, really.' Claire dropped the words into the pool of silence. Christian reached out to grip her hands. Young Anne was crying quietly.

'Come now, my love,' Christian soothed his wife. 'Rupert is very probably havin' a rip-roarin' time with the *Jolly Thingummy*'s crew. There is no cause to rend youself to shreds.' Then his voice dropped so that the rest of them could only hear its murmur.

They were silent again. Startlingly their old familiar barn owl hooted. 'Even Willie Wumperty sounds menacing,' Henry complained. Yet again Priscilla asked, 'What is the time somebody please? Henry mustn't be late for the poor old naughties.'

Back came Henry's, 'It's only just after ten m'dear.' Then silence again, into which Sir Charles quoted softly, 'In such a time as this it is not meet that every nice offence should bear his comment. . . .'

'But does!' cried Claire.

Petula stood up again. 'I'm going to sit with Nanny Rose for a while. She's being splendid poor dear but she is in a dreadful state.'

'Nanny Rose has nothing with which to reproach herself,' Constance protested.

'But she does,' Petula was now framed in the light from those French doors as she paused for a moment to reply. 'The stick she is using on herself is that she did not follow old Nanny's practice of locking the outer door to the nursery wing.'

As she vanished the rest of them heard the soft crunch of the Royce's wheels on the drive.

'Car's there,' Henry commented superfluously. He was caught up in a private nightmare of his own in which his twins had vanished as Rupert had done. A pulse in his head thrummed viciously. Sweat broke out on the palms of his hands. He could stand it no longer. He murmured some unintelligible excuse, ran along the terrace, down the steps and turned towards the stables.

'Gone to Plum,' said Ninian. 'I expect he's thinking about Chantal and Justin poor feller. It's bad enough with a brother, but when a chap has kids . . .' he broke off and returned to his own particular nightmare that something like this had happened to James, his 'Inseparable' and when he reached him it was too late, as it was in reality; but for a very different cause.

Upstairs Petula hurried to her sleeping children, bent over their warm flushed faces, angelic in sleep, murmured a prayer for *their* safety, added another, that they should have it within them by God's grace to be reasonable in all things, and tiptoed out again to Nanny Rose.

Henry, hands shoved deep in his pockets, walked to the dim light which fell from inside the harness room onto the cobbles, blaming himself as he went for his inadequate stewardship during his father's absence.

'Ar,' said a voice in the dark. 'That you Mr Enery, I thort you'd might be along. Come in. I went back fer me tea but Ma was in such a state I come back 'ere. I lef' 'er with Mrs Parsons who's a Job's comfort and no mistake, still some'ow them two gits along. Beats me. Now don't stand there ditherin' in me doorway!'

Henry came round the lintel, pulled out a stool, lowered himself, and began rumpling his hair desperately.

'You tell me,' he exploded, 'how a little chap with our hair, which can be spotted a mile off, can just vanish with the whole ruddy nation searching for him, and now it seems that France has got in on the act.'

'Ar,' said Plum, 'tell me then.'

When Henry had obliged Plum said, 'Well I may as well tell yer I never took to Master Rupert, 'air or no 'air. E'm a proper sod. Ee'll turn up orlright, mark my words though there's trouble ahead wiv' 'im, you see if there ain't. I mean, you was a warmint. Come to that all liddle Lormes is warmints; but there's warmints and warmints 'ef yer git my meanin' and that one's summat else. Ee's on 'is own fer my money. Wot time are yer meetin' the old 'uns?'

Henry was scandalised. 'Plum! do you mean the Dowager and the Countess?'

'That's right,' he agreed, quite unruffled. ' 'Er's got ter be 'ere. 'Er carn't miss 'avin' a finger in this pie like wot she's done wiv' all the other pies, and you're a fine brood of pie-makers you are speakin' from experience. Wen does the perlice find 'ef Sodsie's aboard that ship?'

'They have and he's not,' said Henry flatly. 'It's goin' to be a long night Plum and the women are run ragged already.'

'Not worf it,' Plum said sympathetically, 'ee ort ter 'ave been 'ung up by the thumbs and wallopsed twice every day! Ow's my lady-love takin' it? 'anging over them twins' cots I'll be bound.'

This drew a small chuckle. 'Don't you ever say cots to them,' Henry warned, 'they've long been promoted to beds. Did I tell you what Justin said to me yesterday?'

Plum had attained his immediate objective and his old eyes gleamed with satisfaction. 'Ain't seen yer with all this schermozzle, go on let's 'ave it.'

He listened, he interjected and led Henry on from one anecdote to another. Presently Henry drew two bottles of beer from his dinner jacket pockets and they drank together. Plum proposed a toast to his future master ''Eere's to a n'appy issue art of all that bleeder's afflickshuns, oi! do you know its long gorn eleven and we never even 'eard the stable clock. You'd best cut along. Go on push orf, I carn't 'elp yer no more so I may as well git along to fetch my ole missus.' Saying which he rose to extinguish the old carriage lamp which dangled from its even older iron hook while Henry disappeared into the moon-gilded garden.

CHAPTER 5

Diana

It was one in the morning before the two Old Naughties had been told the full story.

They had welcomed the suggestion to eat and drink, Sawby had set places for them at the library table then dismissed his footmen and waited upon them himself. It flashed across Henry's mind as his grandmother and great-aunt sat sipping cups of André's special chicken consommé that it was on this same table, on the night of Justin Aynthorp's funeral, that his father had set their Talisman and opened it after it had lain in its niche undisturbed for over eight hundred years. He thought now, 'And that set a cat among the ruddy pigeons for nothing has ever gone smoothly since. I wonder if we should have left it undisturbed.' Then he began to speculate upon his father's known superstition that they had in fact loosed a Pandora's box when the rusted lid was raised to disclose the treasure left by his ancestor the Lady Mathilde who had, so the story ran, died laughing, all those centuries ago.[1] He ruminated on the possible power of inanimate objects until his wife's voice brought him back to the present. 'Henry, *Belle-mère* asked you a question.'

He apologised hastily, the Dowager nodded as if she had read his thoughts and understood them. She repeated, 'I suggest Henry that you now send the staff to their beds. Pray do so without further delay.'

'As to you,' she said huskily to the rest, 'Charles you take Constance home immediately. None of us knows what tomorrow may bring. Hetty you look a wreck, upstairs with you now and bathe your face with witch hazel and for goodness sake save the rest of your tears until we

[1] Book 1, *The Lormes of Castle Rising.*

know something. Whatever does eventualise I beg leave to point out that each one of you will be of far greater use if you get some rest now. We have all lived through divers crises together. Pray be advised by me, and go along, *all* of you. Henry, be firm below stairs and make the staff do likewise. I intend to follow suit and so does *Tante* Marguerite.'

With only a slight pause for breath she ended, 'When this *débâcle* is over we both intend returning to France so have no doubts on that score either. Go along home Constance do and take your step-son with you. He's sound asleep as it is.'

A snore from young Charles, sprawled on the rug, confirmed her words. The old indomitable had provided the necessary catalyst. One by one they drifted from the room, leaving only Sue-Ellen and Ninian. He then went outside, returning almost immediately with an armful of rugs.

'I'll just cat-nap in here, if you don't mind. I'm too restless for bed. There's somethin' bayin' me, but for the life of me I dunno what. I don't snore by the way, and perhaps if I stay down here I may get a line on the answer.'

Sue-Ellen glanced up gratefully. 'That is exactly how I feel,' she confessed, 'though there's no reason that I can see.'

He persuaded her to put her feet up on one of the deep leather sofas. He wrapped rugs round her, then backed hastily to one of the old red armchairs. They talked on in a desultory fashion until he unwrapped himself again to extinguish all the lights except one small table lamp by the door. Presently he fell asleep too. He awoke soon afterwards, saw Sue-Ellen's rugs had slipped down so tip-toed across to tuck them in again. Then he stood looking down at her as she slept, sighed, and returned to his chair.

He woke again about four, went to the windows and stood staring out. All the while Diana, Gyles' beloved Borzoi, cat-napped, nose atop paws nearby. Gyles had left her in Ninian's care seeing how eagerly the bitch attached herself to him. The Family saw, but abstained from mentioning that man and dog were in a fair way towards becoming yet another pair of inseparables. In lieu of her master, Diana followed his son wherever he went even, as Henry observed vulgarly, to 'sleepin' outside the loo door while the rotter sits inside readin' the Pink 'Un.'

So it was now. As Ninian crossed to the windows on

stockinged feet Diana lifted her head. Thump, thump went
her tail in greeting. As this gained no response she rose, all
stately, padding across to nuzzle one hand. Ninian absently
gentled her but he continued to stare out as if some message
lay cached in the darkness which, try as he would, he could
not decipher.

As the first faint lightening in the sky declared the coming
of dawn, Sue-Ellen stirred under her rugs, sat up, put her
hands to her hair and then saw Ninian standing with the big
dog at his side.

'However long have you two been there?' she asked
sleepily, 'you look like statues.'

Ninian turned slowly. 'I couldn't sleep,' he confessed,
'Sue-Ellen I am baffled.'

'Aren't we all,' she echoed. 'Nin, I'm going to have a quick
bath, then I'll get into a pair of breeches and have a ride.
Would you care to come with me? It might clear our heads.'

'Of course. We'll take Diana, she hasn't had a proper run
for two days.'

He took the rugs, folded them with his own and followed
her into the hall.

'I'll shove these away then I'll bath and change. I'll wait
for you down here so that we can go to the stables together.'

She came running down half an hour later, a velvet cap
pulled over her curls, crop in hand. Together they drew
back the bolts and unlatched the great door letting in a wave
of fresh, morning air. Diana galloped down the steps, did a
swirling circle of pleasure and looked up at them. They went
directly to the stables, saddled their mounts while Diana
watched, feathering her tail. As they swung into the saddles,
'Let's go round by the Zoo,' Sue-Ellen suggested, 'then we
can cut across over your waste land that Uncle Gyles says I
may have for expansion when the time comes.'

'It's not exactly beautiful,' Ninian warned her, 'nothin'
ever did well there. We tried every known crop. Besides
which it made lousy grazing when we tried putting it down
to grass; there are rabbit holes galore so we shall have to go
very carefully.'

He spurred Night Star so as to pass her out. 'Let me go
ahead, you be a good girl and follow. I haven't been over
the ground in years myself.'

They trotted on. Ninian inevitably recalled the last time he had been this way – with James – and how they had scrambled through the furze which encircled those unfruitful acres and walked up what the pair in their salad days had called the Dung Hill, a fairly steep rise not unlike a small version of the Welsh Sugar Loaf.

They cantered on. A little later he called back, 'Damme we shall have to do somethin' about this furze and stop talkin' about it. It's like the Sleepin' Beauty's barrier forest, Lord how it's grown!'

They put another mile behind them, ringing the dense furze barrier, searching for a gap in the thicket it had become. Suddenly he turned in the saddle as, 'Ninian,' Sue-Ellen called, 'where's Diana? *She's* vanished now.'

He reined in until Sue-Ellen levelled with him. 'That's rum,' he frowned, 'she's as good as gold . . . never leaves me.' He rose in his stirrups, put two fingers to his mouth and blew a piercing whistle.

They waited. He blew again and this time they both thought they heard a faint, very muffled-sounding bark.

'Diana,' he shouted. 'Hello girl, Diana, to me!'

'Hush,' cried Sue-Ellen, 'I heard her then, barking, yes I'm sure.'

They both listened intently. In the clear air, with the sun now rising, the sound came again, a strangled, muffled bark.

'Surely,' Ninian exclaimed angrily, 'some ruddy poacher hasn't been setting traps on our land. I'll horsewhip him if he has.'

He shouted again and again the same sound answered them, very stifled. He flung himself down. Sue-Ellen followed suit. They tethered the mares to a nearby hazel tree and following the direction from which the sound came turned rightwards and went plunging into the furze. Ninian kept up a steady cry of 'Diana', with alternate whistles, 'Diana, come along girl . . . heel girl . . . Diana where are you?' He felt a small gloved hand on his sleeve. 'Listen,' she urged, 'it's more to the right, this way, come on.' She thrust her way forward, only pulling back in the nick of time. At her booted feet the ground fell away suddenly into a sharp descent on whose lip she teetered for a moment before regaining her balance. 'It's a kind of pit, I nearly fell!' she shouted. Ninian forced his way after her, pulled up short and exclaimed, 'God above, what's this? It was never here before; that I'll swear!'

They stood on the brink looking down at a litter of rubble and stones and tangled torn-up roots below, only now dimly seen. 'The ground must have caved in, rotten with rabbit burrows I suppose.' He stared disbelievingly. Then up from that steep drop rose the sound of Diana. She was whimpering again, barking . . . whimpering. 'She *is* in a trap!' Ninian cried, 'I'm going down. Hold on now, *don't follow*. She must have shot over and fallen in.'

'Hold on lass,' he called down, 'I'm coming.' He began lowering himself over the edge. Something large dislodged and went tumbling down. 'Watch it,' he shouted back, 'it curves away . . . to the left, where those bushes overhang.'

Now Diana began to bay, while slowly, gropingly, seeking each foothold, testing it, as tumbling rubble preceded him, he vanished. Sue-Ellen could only hear him calling, 'All right my pretty . . . Ninian's comin' . . . keep barkin'. . .'

The dog's howls became louder.

Sue-Ellen was on her tummy over the rim. She worked herself flat, leaned over and was peering down, but Ninian had vanished.

She called frantically, *'Ninian are you all right?'*

Instead of replying, a stream of blasphemy came rising to her astonished ears, followed by such a cry of horror that she started down over the rim, then paused, waving one foot in search of a hold. As she did so she turned her head, knocked off her cap and saw Diana's silken tail waving like a banner. She began working herself along. Suddenly she saw Ninian bending down over something and in that perilous position heard his cry, 'Sue-Ellen, it's Rupert: *I . . . think . . . he's . . . dead.* Darling, Sue-Ellen please do not try to come down here – go for help. Ride like the wind but be careful. Get strong tarpaulins . . . can you hear me?'

'Yes.'

Sue-Ellen was easing herself back inch by inch, his words stripping her of vertigo, making the return too urgent for her to feel giddy.

'Get Constance, and Jamieson, hot water bottles, rugs and

some milk and brandy, hurry for the love of Mike,' she heard him shout as she hauled herself over the edge.

Ninian fell to his knees. Dimly the sound of thudding hooves told him that Sue-Ellen was up and away, crouched over the mare's neck, stretching across that treacherous ground. He sent up a small prayer, then turned back. His youngest brother lay there in his once scarlet coat, dreadfully still, as Diana began licking the tear-stained, mud-streaked blue-white little face, all crusted with blood from a jagged tear down one cheek.

Ninian scrabbled his hands frantically below the small shoulders in an effort to get one arm underneath. One small hand moved . . . just. 'Hi chum,' said Ninian softly, 'it's Ninian. I've come to take you home.' He felt his eyes smarting as he looked down at the matted curls. His arm was through now and cradling the small shoulders. With the other hand he tore at his cravat, flung it aside, unfastened his coat and worked himself out of it murmuring, 'You're safe now Rupert, hang on old chap . . . hang on. . . .' He ripped off his shirt leaving it dangling by the one sleeve, drew the little body slowly, carefully against his own bared chest and as he did so the long lashes quivered and for a split second parted. Rupert opened his eyes, croaked a hoarse, 'Thirsty Nin,' . . . then the lashes closed again.

'I know you are,' Ninian drew the small body closer to him, feeling the icy coldness of him, the soggy wetness of the torn and filthy little blue shirt as he fumbled with the buttons and slid one huge hand in to feel for Rupert's heart. Then he drew in a sharp breath of thankfulness. It was beating steadily. Suddenly Diana crowded him, pushing in, licking frenziedly at any part of Rupert she could reach.

'Good girl, good Di, steady now,' Ninian praised her, but still she worried at them until at last it dawned on him what she wanted. He eased up and instantly Diana edged between them stretching her warm silken body across the boy . . . still licking, licking with her soft tongue. Ninian's eye moved to Rupert's hands. The nails were terribly torn, crusted with blood . . . telling him that for as long as the child could fight he had fought, scrabbling that rough ground with frantic little fingers . . . until his strength gave out.

Ninian's mind was racing. Three days without food or

water! Three days in the cold and in pain. The horror of it cramped him as the minutes dragged by. Then he saw something partially white, recognised it as one of Rupert's plimsolls, looked at his feet, one shod the other shoeless, swollen, misshapen. *He had only had his hands and one foot with which to fight, the other must have been damaged as he fell*, thus imprisoning him.

Sue-Ellen lay across the mare's neck, coaxing her. 'Come on my girl,' she urged, 'stretch it my beauty, ... show Sue-Ellen what you can do ...,' while her lips quivered and her blood chilled with the recollection of Ninian's shouted words.

Old Groby was lumbering across the line the mare took, atop his cart, heading for the kitchen, delivering the morning mail and papers. Sue-Ellen turned her head to yell. 'Get help Groby! It's Master Rupert, he's in a pit, either dead or dying ...' her words faded as she flew on in a flurry of hooves and flying turves leaving old Groby to shake his bemused head, gather his wits, flip the reins and urge his old cob to a trot.

By the time she reached the Castle steps the breath was whistling in her throat ... somehow she slid down, half ran, half clambered up, reached for the bell and tugged with all her remaining strength.

First into the hall was George.

'Master Rupert found dead or dying,' gasped Sue-Ellen, 'muster every able-bodied man, send someone for the Castle's Ambulance. No, telephone ...' she put her hands to make a funnel at her lips and shrieked with all her strength, 'wake up everyone ... help ... help ... help....' Her brain had told her it was quicker than fetching, quicker than telephoning so she just stood and yelled. In moments they were all around her. She gasped out her message, instructions, saw Henry thudding down, yelled again, 'Rupert dead or dying, in a pit, tarpaulin, hurdles, doctor, Constance.' Henry took her by the shoulders and thrust her down into the great hall's carven chair. 'Brandy, Sawby!' he snapped. She shook her head. 'I'm all right,' she gasped, 'I just wanted to rally you all. You must follow me or you'll never find it.' She forced him away, slipped under his arm, ran for the door, the steps, her sweating horse and was in the saddle by the time George, Sawbridge, Groby, Henry, Andrew and Edward jostled their way into and on top of the Bugatti as it came snarling up. She led them back, the Bugatti bouncing at her horse's heels. 'Down there,' she pointed, 'tell Ninian I'm coming.'

Crouching below, frenzied with fear and impatience, Ninian heard them and for a second his eyes were warm, then a voice yelled to him, 'Are you there Mr Ninian? It's George, I'm coming down,' and then another much more familiar voice, 'Like hell you are, stand back man I'm goin' down.'

Henry had come.

'Then get on with it you clot!' Ninian yelled back. 'Bring the tarpaulin and have the others send down ropes. We'll have to tie the corners and haul Rupert up, but we'll need four lengths for the four corners...'

'No need to shout,' said Henry just above him, slithering the last bit. '*Is he alive?*'

'Yes, but three days Hen without food or water... and the exposure.... Take him, will you. Di found him, she's warming him, the clever, clever bitch.'

With infinite slowness the transfer was made. 'Christ,' exclaimed Henry softly, 'look at the poor little blighter's hands.' He thought that Ninian had not heard. He looked up to see the ropes spiralling down, saw his brother catch the first dangling end and began knotting it. Ninian said thickly, 'He tried to escape but he couldn't use his left leg so he did what he could with his hands ... till his strength gave out.'

The second rope was in place. Andrew was down now and knotting a third. With the tarpaulin spread out they lifted the boy and the adamant, blanketing Diana into the centre. Henry stood up. 'Listen aloft!' he shouted.

'Listening sir,' came back from George.

'You've got Master Rupert and Diana to tow, so keep those bloody ropes level if you value your lives, you lot.'

'We're ready sir, we'll use every care...'

'Then begin to take the strain at my count of three, *one* ... *two* ... *three* ...'

Ninian was hand over hand, foot by foot, driving himself

to the top to receive the perilous burden which was now in mid-air. As his head showed over the rim he saw Dr Jamieson rushing from his car. 'Thank the lord, sir,' he gasped thankfully. 'He's comin' up. Will you take over?'

Dr Jamieson nodded, grabbed his bag, came forward. The tarpaulin rose above the uneven ground, the men lowered it. Sue-Ellen and Petula scrambled to their feet. Dr Jamieson knelt down while the *mêlée* of men unknotted the ropes. George bent over. 'Mr Henry sir,' he shouted, 'knot this around your waist, then hang on and we'll do the rest.'

Silently Henry obeyed. As his head cleared the rim he could see Dr Jamieson holding a cup of warmed milk to Rupert's lips; but the child was too exhausted to drink. The doctor drew a clean handkerchief from his pocket, dipped one end into the cup, forced it between Rupert's lips and said, 'Suck boy suck. Come on now, do as I ask. You can if you try.'

Rupert tried. He sucked. A few moments later with the silent group around him he croaked, 'More.'

Ninian had hold of the cup. 'It's all right,' said the Doctor gently. 'I think he will drink now.' This time Rupert drank. Then, 'Hungry,' he croaked.

Petula bent to him. 'Would you like a sponge finger Rupert?' raising a questioning eyebrow to Dr Jamieson who nodded, so she dipped a sponge finger into the remaining milk and Rupert took that too.

'More,' he demanded.

'Not for a while old man, we're taking you home now.' Dr Jamieson leaned to beckon to the two holding the hurdle.

'More,' croaked Rupert imperiously.

'Hells bells!' grunted Jamieson, tucking the blanket around him, slipping hot water bottles inside, taking the small grazed wrist to feel the pulse, 'you'll live to fight another day all right you young rascal.'

'Ninian,' came weakly from inside the blankets.

'I'm here,' said Ninian steadily, 'I'm ridin' with you in the car, I promise. Just let them slide you in and I'll join you as soon as you're settled.'

Sue-Ellen was standing apart, watching them with brimming eyes; but as they slid the hurdle in there was a sudden flurry as Diana shot in too, settling herself once more across the boy. For the first time in three days a slight ripple of grateful laughter stirred between them, then the Aynthorp van – for the ambulance had not appeared – began to grind slowly over the bumpy terrain while the rest hurried into the waiting cars.

On the way back Sue-Ellen said, suddenly mystified, 'Constance never came!'

Petula nodded. 'You'll see why in a few minutes,' she promised.

They tumbled out, they followed the cortège into the hall and down the long corridor to the Convalescent Home. Rupert was carried into the lift, but still Diana refused to budge. As it rose and the doors slid open they saw that Constance and Claire, both in their nursing uniforms, were waiting.

'Good girls,' grunted Dr Jamieson.

The lift went down again – fast – the rest were carried up. Constance and Claire were by this time walking on either side of the trestle.

Ninian and Henry dashed towards them. Constance's grey eyes met Ninian's blue ones. 'Alive,' she confirmed. 'But do you think you could dispose of this animal for me? I imagine she is not in need of surgery.'

When Rupert was wheeled out of the little theatre and tucked up in his own bed, Dr Jamieson emerged into the corridor where they were all gathered.

'That young man will sleep on and off for the next twenty-four hours, so there's no need to hang about here,' he told them. 'Cut along now and get some breakfast, do. Rupert may wake in a couple of hours for nourishment but he'll drop off again almost immediately. As for you Ninian I suggest when you have eaten you go to bed. You look as if you have been dragged through a bramble bush backwards.'

'What about his foot?' Henry asked, 'any permanent damage?'

'None, a very bad sprain, two torn ligaments but nothing that rest cannot sort out. He's got a nasty cut on his cheek, but we've cobbled that up and I doubt it will even mar his fatal beauty. Go along and I'll join you in a few minutes then you can have the full report.' He turned, paused, said over his shoulder, 'I'll tell you one more thing now. He's got the constitution of an ox, the stubbornness of about ten mules, and before you've done with him you'll probably have hell.'

When they streamed into the breakfast room the Dowager was in full cry. They heard her in mid-sentence proclaiming, 'Well *something* will have to be done or there will be tragedy ahead for him with that temper.' Then she broke off, 'Ah there you are children, the police telephoned, and I spoke to them.'

Henry eyed her with something akin to awe. She looked fresh, groomed and poised; the hustling across France left no trace on her appearance.

'Good morning *Belle-mère*,' Henry bent to kiss the proffered delicately-scented cheek, 'you are a bloomin' marvel. What did you tell the constabulary?'

'The truth of course,' she dabbed with her napkin at the corners of her mouth, 'where is Doctor Jamieson?'

'Comin' shortly to render unto Caesar.'

'Meanin', one supposes, to give his opinion on Rupert to me?'

'Precisely,' Ninian bent to salute her, 'he has already said in so many words that the little, er, that Rupert will be all right. Now one supposes we must gird our loins for another press invasion.'

'I think not,' said Petula sharply, 'I have prepared a statement. Sawby is to hand it to whomever calls, or if they telephone then to read it to them. Then I have warned him he will say to any further queries "no comment" and either replace the mouthpiece or close the door. I consider we have had enough.'

Little Marguerite slipped in during this speech. 'Good gel,' she said approvingly, 'and good morning everyone. How is that small person?'

They reported to her after which she nodded and said, 'That should then be that, Alicia. We, unless there is anything untoward in Dr Jamieson's report, shall rest today, and in the mornin' we shall return to France. In the meantime what has been done about your parents Henry?'

'Nothin' yet *Belle-mère*.'

'Then you must cable them immediately. Say something

ambiguous like "Pay no heed to garbled tales, Rupert safe and with us. Please continue trip, all's well".'

'Can we?' Henry eyed her dubiously.

'Certainly, on *my* responsibility.'

'And in the meantime? I mean when he gets on his feet again what do we do with him?'

'Clap him in irons?' Ninian suggested.

'Fiddlesticks,' the Dowager eyed him crossly, 'if you can manage a battalion of soldiery it should not be beyond you to manage one six-year-old boy until his parents return.'

'Lucky old Nin,' said Henry irrepressibly.

'Now cease this tomfoolery Henry and let me hear from Ninian how that child was discovered.'

Sue-Ellen and he immediately began speaking together. Petula, watching intently, felt a tiny warning tingle. The brightness of the Dowager's eyes seemed to her suddenly to denote a little more than natural interest in the tale. Somehow she knew that the Old Naughty was about to dip her fingers into yet another family pie. Swiftly she and Henry exchanged glances which confirmed for her that he too was suddenly alerted; but by what, neither could have explained.

Ninian and Sue-Ellen came to the point where Sue-Ellen had cried a warning to Ninian as he went over the edge and Petula saw to her astonishment that she broke off and the colour flooded to her cheeks. She sat there staring at Ninian as if she were seeing him for the first time.

The Dowager missed none of this, nor did Marguerite. Their faces were eloquent. It was as if they had declared their curiosity aloud: '*what happened at that moment between these two?*'

Sue-Ellen pushed her napkin deliberately from her lap, then bent to retrieve it, thus giving herself time to recover. She straightened up; but her eyes were over-bright still and she remained silent, just staring at Ninian. He broke off, said, 'Hi.'

She started, waved a vague hand, murmured, 'Go on, you finish,' and began staring at the lawn tablecloth, tracing with one finger the intricate embroidery done by the Beauvais nuns. She, of course, saw none of it, for superimposed was Ninian's face, the high-bridged Norman nose, the strong

line of the jaw and those other lines which sadness had
etched in after James's death . . . the steady eyes which were
sometimes, as now, grey-flecked. Her mind gave her the
picture and then her mind replaced his face with the image
of her childhood 'Mammy' and seeing that dear fat, black
face the head swathed in a knotted bandana handkerchief
imagination gave her 'Mammy' speaking, saying, 'Lawks
Mis Sue-Ellen baby, Mammy done think you gone fallin'
in love again.'

With the words ringing in her head she came back to
reality, she saw them all looking at her curiously, heard
Ninian saying, with sudden anxiety, 'Are you all right Sue-
Ellen?'

Up went one hand to her head as she stammered, 'I'm
sorry, I think I must have felt dizzy suddenly, I expect it's
only reaction, where were we? Really I must apologise.'

She made a tremendous effort to regain her composure
and eventually managed to take up the tale. 'Oh yes, well
Ninian called up to me, so I fled. I saw Groby in his cart
coming up with the post and paper, I shouted to him to
hurry, warn the servants, send the footmen and Sawby to
the front door, then I galloped on. As you must all
remember I yelled up the stairs, I must have shouted enough
to rouse the dead,' here she managed a deprecating little
smile. 'It was Diana who saved him. She picked up his
scent. She went down first and she barked and howled until
we found her. She knew well enough we would never go on
without her. All the credit goes to Diana, she even tried
to jostle Ninian out of the way to use her body to warm
Rupert. . . .'

Ninian smiled across at Sue-Ellen. 'Are you feelin' all
right now?' he asked anxiously.

'I,' said Sue-Ellen clearly, 'have never felt better in my
life.'

At that moment Constance and Dr Jamieson came in.
Chairs were drawn for them, coffee proffered and accepted.
Then their old friend spoke.

'It will be all right, Lady Alicia,' he said reassuringly, 'but
I never cease to marvel at the resilience of children. One
moment they are dying and the next moment they are trying
to see how far round the bedroom they can climb without

touching the floor. There must be a very special providence watching over small boys in particular otherwise very few would ever reach manhood.'

Constance took up the report saying, 'Rupert has a nasty cut on his face, but we've cleaned it up, put in a few stitches and done what we could with his hands. He'll have to keep them bandaged for a while but they will mend. He must have twisted his ankle as he went over, then I suspect he broke his fall part of the way down and fell on his knees. Both have some ugly lacerations, only superficial, but we must safeguard against septicaemia of course. As for the ankle, it's only, as I expect you know already, a very bad strain and a couple of torn ligaments. We gave him a whiff of chloroform while we stitched and generally cleaned him up and there is not the slightest indication that we shall have anything more serious to contend with than a slight chill from exposure. We can thank God it happened at this time of year and not in mid-winter. Even so it is remarkable.'

Dr Jamieson pulled at his beard as if it held some clue to the stamina of little boys. 'When I left him he was screaming for food, which of course would only make him sick after the chloroform. Just water to sip for the next few hours and then we'll begin feeding him slops.'

All the while Dr Jamieson talked Petula scribbled frantically. When he had done, he asked mildly, 'Mrs Henry, pray what are you doing?'

'Amended statement for the press.' She glanced up, smiled, then returned to her chore. 'A brief summary of what you said. If you will excuse me everyone I will just have copies made and then I think we might ring for some more coffee, don't you?'

'No,' said Henry loudly, 'champagne. This calls for a celebration if ever anything did.'

'What a very good idea,' the Dowager nodded her approval, so Henry rose and pulled the bell for Sawby.

They drank their champagne. They coped with the enquiries, the flowers, the gifts which automatically flowed in as soon as the luncheon-time editions of the evening papers had appeared with their banners, 'Peer's son found injured. No cause for undue alarm says family doctor.' Then, the following morning, the two old persons went off again to continue their 'Progress' through France. Within a fort-night Rupert was again causing chaos in the nursery, with only a slight limp to remind them all of those three grim days and nights.

CHAPTER 6

The End of Candlelight

Down through Castle Rising's rumbustious history ran a great tally of balls, all eloquent of Lorme extravagance and all much spoken of long after the last wick had guttered in the last candle.

The founder of the English line, Henri de Lorme, fourth son of Edouarde Count of Normandy, had quit his native soil in the service of Duke William – whom none dared call Bastard in Henri's presence lest he was run through by his sword.

Henri leaped after his Duke onto the Pevensey shingles. He was by his side when King Harold's arrow-pierced body was borne into the Duke's tent. He had been dubbed knight by him and was soon to be further elevated. He was also beside William again when the Archbishop of Canterbury held the golden crown of England above his black head.

Only then did Henri, himself nicknamed now '*tosjors feal*' or in more modern parlance '*toujours fidèle*', exert his privilege by riding into Essex to find himself lands which pleased him and there raise his first Castle Rising for which a great forest of oaks was decimated.

Under those oaks, which formed the beams of the scarce-completed Great Hall, the first measure was trod by King William and Henri's wife Thyra, daughter of Knut the Dane. There, when Henri's firstborn '*petit Henri*' was christened, the King led Thyra out and when the first measure ended the whole great company celebrated the Naming Day with dance and song.

Thus it continued. Another King Henry came, when new-returned from Agincourt, to lead Arabella, bride of Richard de Lorme, onto the rush-strewn flooring. A third King Henry, hot foot in pursuit of one Nan Bullen descended upon the Lormes with only a fanfare for warning, subsequently chased the lady round the new-grown maze and danced a stately pavane with her in the Great Hall. Half Whitehall came by coach to Essex for the ball given by the Long Lad's wicked favourite Rupert. His lady, the beautiful Marguerite, danced with King Charles in celebration of the restoration of the monarchy wearing, albeit unknowingly, the jewels her husband had pilfered from the King's already sadly depleted coffers; but the ball was a triumph even so.

The tally grew until it culminated in what was generally held to be the most dazzling of all Lorme balls.[1]

This was the one given by the late Justin Aynthorp for the coming of age of his grandson Henry. As it transpired, it was also the unexpected celebration of Henry's engagement to Petula Danement. Once again six hundred guests danced by candlelight. The old peer had insisted upon this, banishing the new-fangled electricity at what cost only he and his eldest son Gyles knew and merely restoring it thereafter.

Now for the first time in all those centuries the young heir and his wife were to play host and hostess to their friends in the absence of the ruling Aynthorp. It was in keeping with the times, as was the dropping of the word ball, in favour of 'dance': an entertainment given by the young for the young without benefit of advice or guidance by their seniors.

Tradition became a brooding wraith in rags, banished to the shades as the wind of change raced through the long corridors, the great rooms and, not surprisingly, blew strongest where it whistled about the Servants' Hall and Steward's Room in which comment and conjecture were rife and the passing of the old ways invoked dolorous predictions.

'Wot a terrible pity I should ever live ter see it,' bemoaned Mrs Parsons. 'Bringin' new-fangled ways into our stately 'ome. I'm 'orrified.'

'Who could ever have pre-dicted,' demanded Sawby, 'that I should be asked to serve "cocktails" within these walls to the offspring of the aristocracy? It pains me deeply.'

''Ow am I expected to create a buffet which will make marriage with such mix-mucks?' Chef André almost screamed, while Richard, leaning against the opened door-

---

[1] Book 1, *The Lormes of Castle Rising.*

way in his striped waistcoat enquired rhetorically, 'Putting things into champagne is sinful, if you arst me.'

'Well no-one did,' snapped Mrs Parsons, 'so just mind yer ps and qs young man. Wot they say *upstairs* is wot we 'as ter do *downstairs* and no ammounter grumblin' 'ull make a mort er difference. Where's me 'ot tea, this cup's cold!'

Pearson rose from her chair beside the fire. 'Two bands,' she said sepulchrally, 'and from wot I've 'eard one of 'em's coal black with trumpets.'

'OmiGod,' exclaimed Mrs Parsons, 'mark my words, we'll all be murdered in our beds. Niggers 'ere! It's more 'n flesh and blood can bear.'

André tugged frantically at his waxed moustache ends, ''Ow about keep-airs *à quatre heure du matin*?'

'Talk civilised,' snapped the cook.

'At four o'clock in the morning then,' André snapped back.

'But what is keep-airs?' Mason whispered, nudging Pearson.

'Kippers 'ee means,' explained George with a grin, 'wiv beers and shandy gaffs like we was in the old spit and sawdust at the Aynthorp Arms.'

While this resentment by the domestic staff only just stopped short of wailing – as at a wake – Petula, Sue-Ellen and Henry attempted to work out the details in Gyles' old office.

Petula had appropriated her father-in-law's refectory table at which she sat with Sue-Ellen at her side.

'It's no use,' the latter exclaimed, 'Parisian jazzbands are a completely unknown quantity. We shall just have to bring one over from the States.'

Henry and Petula stared at her in horror. 'But darling we simply cannot. Imagine the cost!' Petula exclaimed.

'Unthinkable,' Henry grunted, 'we're hock deep already.'

'But it's my score,' Sue-Ellen reminded them, 'you said I could contribute. So, I contribute the coloured band. I shall cable this afternoon. Why, every-one back home has two bands, it's crazy to think we could scrape by with just Ambrose. Besides, I know exactly which one to import.'

'Who?' came from two throats simultaneously.

'They call themselves The Original Dixieland Jazz Band.

They're all the rage in the States and oh my how those piccaninnies can blow!'

Petula twinkled, 'Darling you went very American on us just then. Did you know?'

Sue-Ellen shook her head ruefully. 'Damn. No, I did not. I want to sound absolutely English. I just must be more careful! I am the ultimate Anglophile and I mustn't talk borrowed English – ever.'

Henry frowned. 'What's borrowed English?'

'Why American. They borrowed it, then they made it over to suit them which they have every right to do except that it absolutely does not suit the English language as I have heard it spoken over here. One is through the larynx as it should be, the other is *vers le nez*,' at which she wrinkled her own delicious nose disapprovingly.

'Well thank the Lord you said it,' Henry grinned, 'if either of us had dared you would have turned and rent us. I suppose you know we shall have to sleep your southern darkies,' he added dubiously.

'Why not?' she retorted. 'Put 'em in the convalescents' rooms in the old Home, after all Uncle Gyles gave us leave to do as we please. Well, didn't he?'

A slight cough in the doorway put paid to Henry's reply. It was Sawby looking very stately and rather cross which Petula claimed always made him look pompous. His opening was strictly conventional however. 'You rang, sir?' he said, staring woodenly at Henry.

'I did, Sawby, I would be obliged to know from you just how many bottles of non-vintage champagne we shall need for making champagne cocktails for around three hundred.'

The way in which Sawby repeated, '*Non-vintage* did you say sir?' nearly undid them; but, struggling for composure, Henry managed, 'We would scarcely insult his Lordship's vintage champagnes by using them for cocktails would we now?'

Sawby refused to be appeased. 'I must suppose so, sir,' he agreed.

'In any case,' Henry continued, 'the amount is roughly the same as if we were drinking the stuff straight, so how many would you anticipate we should get through?'

The butler still hesitated. 'Well now, sir, it would depend

upon how long you intend serving these ... er ... champagne cocktails.' His mouth might have been rinsed with alum.

Petula intervened. 'The invitations are for ten o'clock, some will drift in from then and on up to eleven-thirty and then as we settle at the tables in the ballroom another round will be served before the champagne at supper. Bear in mind too that there will be four alternative drinks offered during that time.'

'More cocktails sir?' He now sounded like a man awaiting his own death sentence.

'Yes, of course, I'll take you through them later. They are very simple and remember we have engaged two professional cocktail-shakers, barmen from Mayfair who will be shakin' 'em. Then with supper we shall serve the good stuff.'

'Dom Perignon sir?'

'No, The Widow.'

Sawby repeated this.

Henry began to lose patience. 'We shall serve Veuve Clicquot. It is much more popular with *our* generation,' he mischievously stressed the 'our', leaned back and waited for the result. He had made up his mind to be amused.

'Might I then enquire if three hundred is to be your limit, sir?'

'Well now,' Henry tipped his chair back and deliberately sprawled. 'Give or take a few, yes. Of course, these days one is bound to have a few gate-crashers, even out here in the wilds.'

Sawby swallowed. 'Pardon my ignorance sir, but do you mean persons who endeavour to obtain admission without having received invitations?'

'Precisely.'

At this point Petula decided that her husband had gone far enough. 'I do not for a moment suppose there will be any gate-crashers,' she said reassuringly. 'Meanwhile there is another important matter which we would like to propose to you. Like the Countess you have developed a very special talent for arranging flowers, so I, indeed we all three, wondered if you and your wife would agree to taking charge of all the floral arrangements for our dance.'

Sawby stiffened, hesitated, but as they had suspected the bait was too alluring for him to hold out.

'I should be greatly honoured, madam,' the words came out almost despite himself, 'and so I am confident would my wife. Might I enquire if you have determined upon your colour scheme yet, and if I have your permission to discuss the matter with Appelby.'

Sue-Ellen riffled through her papers. 'I can tell you that now: Tango Orange and Jade Green. We also want the food to be in the same colours, in varying shades, of course, and here is the exact shade of Tango Orange for the flowers,' she held out a scrap of orange silk to the now visibly thawing butler.

When he had gone Henry hooted. 'What did I predict?' he crowed, 'they're off at Bogside! Now there'll be no stoppin' 'em! We're out of the wood and into the home stretch all right. Now let's settle to some details.'

An hour later these culminated in an approved draft for the invitations. It read:

The Forty-Four Nite Spot at Castle Rising requests the pleasure of .... company on
Friday
the thirtieth of September for a White Zoo Drinking Party followed by dancing to Ambrose Band and An Other. Tango-Orange Buffet, Cocktails shaken by Buck and Bud. Cabaret. Kippers and Beer at Dawn.

In the bottom corner:

R.S.V.P. The Honble Mrs Henry de Lorme.
Castle Rising   Aynthorp.   Essex.   Please bring this invitation with you.

This was received with great enthusiasm. It was left to Henry to supply the last poignant comment which he did with relish. 'Verry classy – just the thing in fact. Of course, it's enough to make the old "Octogeranium" turtle in his coffin ain't it?' by which he indicated his awareness of the fact that the late Lord Aynthorp would not have been amused.

An hour later Petula pushed aside the pile of papers she had been studying.

'I don't mind admitting,' she said ruefully, 'there is more to giving a party like ours than just sending out the invitations and buying new frocks. *Belle-mère* coped in her day with twice our number without any apparent difficulty; but even with such a marvellously trained staff it still leaves an awful lot for me to arrange.'

'You're telling me,' Henry grunted. He laid aside his pen, scowled at the ledger into which he had been making careful entries and glowered at his calculations.

'His ruddy lordship made it a condition I kept an accurate record of all our expenditure; but every time I get out a total someone pops up with something we've overlooked, then I have to start all over again.'

Sue-Ellen chuckled. 'You have to admit your mother knew what she was doing when she gave us a free hand. She knew perfectly well we hadn't the foggiest idea just how much work was involved.'

Henry nodded, 'Years ago,' he confessed, 'Pet stopped me short in my tracks when she turned me down for the third time.'

'What on earth has that to do with this party?' his wife expostulated.

'I'll tell you if you let me get a word in edgeways. You gave me my first sleepless night, I can remember as if it were yesterday. You made me realise what a useless feller I was; comin' of age, due one day to inherit this lot and without even the vaguest idea of what to do if, which thank God didn't happen, I suddenly found m'yself with the reins between me fingers. In the end I went to father and asked him to start trainin' me. In fact I'm still learning and I think my quiet Mama deliberately set us this task as a test. Anyway I'm damned if I'm goin' to admit, any more than she and *Belle-mère* have ever done, that there's more than money and good servants involved in mass entertainin'.' He looked at their two pretty faces severely.

'I'll tell you somethin' else. A good party is like plannin' a military exercise. Nothin' can be left to chance otherwise we're goin' to be in a helluva seethe on the night.' He thumped the table with such violence that both girls started.

'We've got to run it like a battle, that's what it all boils down to. Then when it's all happening we too can have some fun and enjoy our little orgy. Above all we have to work out our timings. It's not by accident that everything happens when it is meant to happen when Mama entertains. One slip up and the whole caboodle gets out of kilter, then it can easily turn into a flop.'

Petula eyed him gravely. 'You mean that absolutely nothing can ever be left to chance? It has to seem, well, just perfectly natural but it all has to be thought out now and by organisation and planning be made to happen just exactly as we want it to?'

'Including contingencies,' contributed Sue-Ellen thoughtfully. 'Things like what preparations are needed for people eating more or drinking more than we have estimated.'

'Oh surely,' Henry protested, 'we can leave the grub stakes to André, and the drinks to Sawby?'

Sue-Ellen shook her head vehemently. 'Yes, on the night, but the pre-vision and the pre-arranging must be checked by us. Just supposing for instance someone really important like the young Royals send a message saying they would like to bring someone else. There must be a margin for such eventualities in terms of tables, chairs and the amount of parking space. Just supposing we calculate for so many cars and find we've twice the number. If lots of our friends pile into cars that's one total; but if they pair up and come two to a car, that could make a terrific difference to the amount of parking space we have allowed.'

'Out that one,' Henry said more cheerfully, 'there's room for five hundred cars in the Museum parking area. We just lay on some skilled drivers to grab the cars and do the parking.'

Sue-Ellen shook her head. 'Are they supposed to guess which car is which? You'll need clear identification – except in the case of those who bring chauffeurs and the majority of your friends won't get their parents to supply them because they'll probably be needing them themselves.'

'Supposing it rains?' Petula stared from one to the other suddenly scared. 'We'll have to plan for that too won't we?'

At this precise juncture the door opened disclosing Sawby in the doorway.

'Oh come in Sawby,' said Henry thankfully, 'you're just the man I wanted.' He went on with a disarming grin. 'Among all the books and records we know you have kept during all the years you have worked for us, do you by any happy chance keep lists of the things which have to be done whenever we give a big party?'

For an instant Henry suspected his query sparked a gleam in the butler's eye, but it was so swiftly repressed that he might well have imagined it. Sawby merely said with his usual deferential calm, 'Most certainly sir. I asked her ladyship if I should bring them to you. She instructed me to hand them over to you if you or madam asked for them.'

'You do that then,' Henry nodded, 'in the meantime Mrs Henry and I will rough out a list of the specific queries we have in mind to raise with you.'

As the door closed behind Sawby three pairs of eyes met. 'I ... thought ... so,' Sue-Ellen nodded. 'She anticipated we would get stuck, she told Sawby what he was to do in the event and in the meantime she thought it might be salutary for us to find out as many of the complications as we could for ourselves.'

'How did you guess?' Henry mocked, 'though I never realised my Mama could be such a devilish wily schemer.'

Petula turned on him. 'Never underestimate your mother,' she said severely, 'for my money, anyone who could have lived most of her married life in the Dowager's shadow without being ruffled, steered a tranquil course through the luxurious Bedlam created by Grumpy, and all the while succeed in damping down your father with such loving subtlety has to possess a very considerable array of talents.'

'What do you mean "damping down the old man"?' Henry frowned.

'Well didn't she do just that? There was never a trace of the famous Lorme temper while Grumpy[1] lived; but within hours of his death your father erupted *if* you remember. He assumed the mantle of Elijah, became *his* father all over

---

[1] Book 1, *The Lormes of Castle Rising.*

again with the possible proviso that Uncle Gyles' temper was by comparison like a violin being played with a mute on.'

Henry thought this over in silence for a few moments. Then he sighed, 'My dearest love you've got a pretty tangle of mixed metaphors in that statement, nevertheless I take your point. And I suppose that when Mama hands over to you you'll set about manipulating me just as she has manipulated the old man.'

'What else,' Petula smiled sweetly, picking up her pen again, 'after all dear boy I was trained by experts.'

While all this was going on Gilbert Delahaye, son of Henrietta and Sinclair, and his two Wykehamist friends Joe and Lionel Brinkman arrived for the holidays. The Brinkmans were not particularly liked by the rest of the family. Their father, Lord Brinkman, was immensely rich but his wealth came from what Gyles was inclined to think of as shady sources. However, his sons were quiet and well-behaved and were soon accepted as a necessary evil which kept Gilbert from under their feet. The three boys gravitated as they had done on a previous visit to 'In Transit', the indeterminate room which had once been the sanctum of Ninian and James when the pair were in their early teens and therefore ineligible for dining formally with the family. Instead a footman waited upon them among their form books and old copies of the Pink 'Un. In point of fact Joe did qualify as he was over eighteen now; but no-one thought to advance his claim which pleased him greatly. Thereafter the three boys pursued the pattern much as Ninian and James had done save that their reading matter concerned ledger studies and frequent references to current copies of the *Financial Times*.

The trio breakfasted with the family, made suitable conversation, withdrew with decorum afterwards, locked away their reading matter and were seen no more. As soon as one of the footmen or footwomen brought them their pic-nic hamper and wicker-enclosed Asprey Thermos flasks they were off in Joe's car, ostensibly to pursue their declared passion for bird-watching which seemed innocuous enough if a trifle dreary.

After the first few days they were forgotten. In the light of what this unlovely trio ultimately achieved this was, to say the least, unfortunate. It also made, in retrospect, a piece of Lorme history in that these three succeeded in achieving the seemingly impossible by successfully drawing the wool over the Dowager's eyes, as she herself was to acknowledge later.

As the fateful day of the dance drew nearer an atmosphere of wild activity pervaded the Castle. This reached a first peak with the appearance of a lengthy procession of vans which forged their way up the main drive and were duly directed to the ballroom entrance. There the contents of the first dozen were offloaded, a small marquee erected as ordered for the use of the two bands during their rest periods. They also debouched all the tables and chairs for the dance supper while the rest were re-directed to the servants' entrance where they offloaded innumerable crates containing china, glass and wines. The two former were taken through to the room which had been used as a common room by the war-time replacement female staff where serried rows of trestle tables had been set up. Then all the china and glass was unpacked. When this was done Sawby reappeared and directed his staff to convey the wines to his lordship's cellars.

No sooner had the last van-tail disappeared through the main drive gates than a procession of vehicles drawing huge trailers began crawling towards the front entrance. On each trailer a cage was lashed. Boots was immediately sent scurrying in the direction of the Zoo to 'fetch Mrs Delahaye's men as soon as possible'.

They came. By this time work ceased entirely inside the Castle. Everyone from scullery maids to Mrs Peace rushed to the windows to watch the proceedings avidly. The temporary Zoo was about to be erected, with a *lèse majesté* which the older members of the staff found quite shattering, or as Mrs Parsons put it, 'In the front drive where his late lordship held the Invitation Meet on Boxing Day; whatever would 'ee 'ave said to this I wonder!'

'Let's be thankful he never lived to see it,' said Sawby sourly.

After the cages had been manhandled into position with the largest and heaviest placed by a small crane there was a hiatus, during which work was resumed by the household staff; but they were all back again at the windows to watch the animals being coerced into their temporary quarters.

Throughout this exercise Sue-Ellen directed operations with a chart in her hand standing atop an upturned crate.

Henry and Petula, with a twin hanging from each hand, were danced about by their offpsring who were in a state of delirious enchantment at the whole performance.

By nightfall two small huts had been erected, one mid-drive and one just below the steps. Then two braziers were brought, lit and set in readiness for the night-watchmen to 'brew-up' during the night. Nothing had been left to chance as Henry had insisted; in fact, just to be sure, he came out after dinner and went round the cages himself, testing every lock, bolt and bar. As he remarked to Petula afterwards, 'Fun's fun and the old man wouldn't mind any of it, but God have mercy on us all if one of those brutes escapes. Every ruddy male in the family will be talkin' in high-pitched voices after he's done with us.'

Below stairs was no better. Sawby had indigestion so was busy dosing himself with bicarbonate of soda.

'I tole you so,' snapped Mrs Parsons, 'you never should 'ave ate them gherkins. They always repeat on you something crool, you've only yerself to blame.'

Wisely, Sawby abstained from comment, vanishing instead into the Steward's Room.

Mrs Parsons then declared in full voice that she had, 'Come down with an 'eadache,' settled herself in her chair beside her stove and left Appelby, who had been working with her husband on the flowers since five o'clock, to do the breakfast rolls while she sat watching and nagging until she had the kitchenmaids on the edge of tears.

André and his cousin from Paris, who had, of course, been summoned immediately the project was launched, were quarrelling in mid-distance and in chef's bay over their spun sugar palm trees, while Boots, ducking and weaving like a snipe, scuttled as best he might between the screaming pair, shovelling hods of coke into the stoves and endeavouring to dodge the protagonists.

Into this chaos the head gardener inserted himself. He was clearly in sour humour. 'Me pines will be along in a minnit cook,' he shouted, 'I'm a boy short wot 'as set me back. You'll find them peaches on the truck, if so be someone could trouble themselves ter bring 'em in for I ain't the time and 'ef that truck ain't emptied quick I carn't turn round with the nex' lot.'

Two more extra footmen rushed to please, one of them saying, 'Well I'm shore it ain't our place but it's all 'ands and no mistake this morning although me corns is killing me.' As he said this he took one pace back and trod on Mrs Parsons' prime offender.

Her eldrich shriek rang out. 'Your corns is it, young feller me lad! Wot abart mine wot you've just trod on? And anyway you shouldn't be wearin' tight shoes.'

'I've got me slippers on,' the young man retorted.

Sawby, who had burped and vanished, was now followed by his wife who had just slid her last tray of rolls into their rack. They were hot-footing it back to the ballroom to join their two 'lady' helpers Victoria and Arabella from the Flower Shop and the hired help from the village, Jane, who had brought her stalwart but simple brother along for the heavy lifting.

As the Sawbys walked in over the thick drugget which had been laid down over the polished floor they could see that the ballroom looked entirely different already. Petula and Sue-Ellen's design was beginning to take shape. The estate's electricians, precariously balanced on a scaffold, were working at an intricate arrangement which was intended to be winking lights which would, or at least should, flash a sign reading 'The Forty-Four Nite Spot', for the guests to see as they approached down the long corridor.

Already, too, the platform was completed. Peak and his cousin were clinging like men on a cliff face atop tall pairs of steps, fixing the supports from which the Sawbys' cascades and hanging baskets would be slung. The remaining four extra footmen, in their shirt-sleeves, hauled tables and chairs into position, folding back drugget as they worked until the Aynthorps' gold and white ballroom with its priceless chandeliers looked like one of the new London night clubs, which was exactly what was intended. By the time Agnes, dishevelled as usual, stuck her smutty face around the half-opened doors, the baize under coverings were in place on the tables; all the chairs were in position around the gleaming, now uncovered rectangle in the centre where one hundred and fifty couples would shimmy, tango, two-step, glide and lock together in slightly tipsy and amorous embrace to the strains of the final 'At Three O'clock In The Morning...' which would be *vale* to the dancing and *reveille* to the below stairs, deeply resented 'keep-airs' and ale breakfast.

Agnes having done a thorough, adenoidal survey with mouth open and eyes wide, raised her voice to cry shrilly, 'It's elevenses Mister Sawby and Mrs Parsons says will you please ter come quick because Chef wants the Servants' 'all table fer finishing 'is palm trees and he wants ter know if he may borrer Poppy, that is Appelby.'

'Tell cook we're coming,' Sawby called back, 'then go and wash your face, straighten your cap and tidy your hair before so much as a drop of cocoa passes your lips.' After which he reverted to his ploys.

He and his wife were contemplating their prime invention. They had unearthed a quantity of silver trumpets from four enormous épergnes, housed in green flannel and stood long ago in a dim corner of the silver vaults. These they had swathed in green moss and secured by fine wire. Having nodded in unison, approving the basic structures, they proceeded to drop them, like branches into the holes bored in a dozen sapling ash trees which had been peeled free of bark first, then brushed with colourless varnish. They had likewise found in the vast top-floor china rooms to which all redundant china was banished, a dozen green indoor flower pots made by Josiah Wedgwood. They now acted as the ash supports.

Sawby dropped the last outward pointing trumpet into its socket, stood back once again and said with pardonable pride, 'I think that's it my dear. When our ferns and lilies spray out and hang down from them they will resemble trees from a tropical forest.' Such flights of fancy from the butler caused Pine to flash him one astonished glance before wisdom prompted him to bend his head again to his own task. He would wait until husband and wife had left the

ballroom before climbing down the steps to have a better
look.

Oddly enough, once she had recovered from her morning
miseries, there was nothing which Mrs Parsons liked better
than a milling crowd about her. The more there were to
bully the happier she became, so now, bustling about, corns
forgotten as she proffered ham sandwiches, urged one and
all to partake of her 'pang-der-piece' and exhorted George,
'Fill up the pot boy we're all parched.' She was in her
element. She even went so far as to beam at the hired
footman who said, with his mouth full, 'Tastes more like
gingerbead ter me,' nodding and agreeing, 'so it is my lad
but French, see, "pang-der-piece".'

At twelve-thirty the whole grinning bunch of negro
bandsmen would debouch onto Lower Aynthorp platform
with their instruments and suitcases. Two of the Castle vans
would bring them thence, after which they would be served
luncheon in the breakfast room while Petula entertained a
number of young things to luncheon in the dining room.

Lucy and Lucien were also expected. During the previous
week Sue-Ellen had telephoned to enquire about her frock
which, of course, Lucien had designed specially for her. He
came to the telephone himself sounding rather put-out and
using the new curiously emphasised form of speech which
was his latest mannerism, due Sue-Ellen suspected to the
rather strange young man who had recently become his
friend and ally. 'I just *hope*,' he told her fretfully, 'that your
party *is* a success of *course* darling Sue-Ellen, but I have to
tell you that I *never* want to see another Tango orange dress
as *long* as I live. We are *smothered* in tango-orange frocks;
simply *drenched* in tango orange shawls, stoles, capes and
huge feather fans; and I am sick, sick, *sick* of tango orange . . .
what? . . . oh yes of *course* your frock is ready, it's being put
on the two-thirty train to Lower A. You'll just have to send
someone for it pet. It's in the guard's van and the guard is
being given a *huge* tip,' . . . here a giggle came over the wire,
'which I shall *firmly* put on your bill my love. Now I must
rush, Lucy-Lou's *fantastic* outfit is not quite finished and
I'm on a treadmill. What's that. . . ?'

Sue-Ellen managed to get a word in edgeways. She asked

after Piers and was told in a rather offhand manner that Lucien supposed he was all right. 'Oh yes, he is no *worse* if that's what you mean; but no he couldn't have visitors yet and Lucy has a *long* letter from him and is bringing it down for you *all* to read.' Then ping and the line went dead. Sue-Ellen replaced the mouthpiece feeling somewhat shattered. Lucien had given her the very strong impression that he didn't give two hoots about Piers' condition. He was full of this new young man. Apparently he was a designer who did such very clever sketches that Lucien was thinking of taking him into the firm. He told her, 'He *understands* me, which is so *very* important as you will be the *first* to see angel.'

She walked away from the telephone trying not to be un-Christian. She managed in the end to persuade herself that the crux was that Lucien had become just a little bit jealous of the marriage and was pretending he didn't care. It was a comforting explanation which made her feel much better. After the luncheon at which excitement rose to fever pitch and the chatter was akin to several flights of starlings, she suddenly decided to collect her own dress as everyone had such masses to do. On her way back she dropped in on Stephanie, Henrietta and Sinclair's daughter, for a brief chat.

The girl was not far off her time now, very cumbersome and finding it difficult to get about, so of course she had excused herself from the dance. As her husband Harry refused to leave her, even for an hour, neither would be present. She looked well enough. She reported that Dr Jamieson was well-pleased and that she would have her baby at the Castle in the old convalescents' wing which would be freed of coloured musicians by that time.

She received Sue-Ellen warmly, thanked her very sweetly for her gift and then went into raptures over every single item, from the cot to the last nappy in the sumptuous layette which Sue-Ellen had provided. Harry came in just before she left, greeted the giver, then fussed over his wife insisting she sit down and put her feet up while he made them a cup of tea: but this Sue-Ellen refused, pleading that she had to return to the Castle.

The sight of this busy, contented pair, who had so little and considered they had so much, touched her deeply, even making driving a little difficult as her eyes blurred; for a shadow lay across her days now, a very large shadow which was Ninian. She had given up all attempts at deceiving herself over him. She knew and acknowledged to herself that she had fallen deeply in love with this second son of Gyles Aynthorp. Only too well she realised that there was absolutely nothing in Ninian's character which would ever make a very rich wife an acceptable one to him. She was almost certain that he cared too; but no way could she see any hope that he would ever tell her so.

She had also come to accept that she was someone whose tastes went from one extreme to the other. First there had been Stephen. She had always known that he was what the older generation were prone to dismiss as 'a wrong 'un'; she had fancied even so that she would be strong enough to change him . . . but that she could never know now for he had died instead. Now there was Ninian who was in every respect diametrically opposite to Stephen. He was steadfast and reliable, he was immensely kind and thoughtful and so completely inarticulate that he could never put any of his feelings into words. The most she could hope for, if matters ever came to a head between them, would be a muttered, 'You see old girl it's simply not done for a chap to live on his wife's money.' Then he would withdraw into his own pain and regret, as he had withdrawn over the loss of his cousin James.

One way and another Sue-Ellen was not looking forward with any great eagerness to the evening's celebrations. Andrew on the other hand was in transports over everything. He was head over ears in love with Victoria and already sufficient had passed between the pair of them to make him reasonably confident that she would have him if and when he found the appropriate moment to 'pop the question'. Above all he knew his parents thought well of her and that he even found favour in the old Duke's sight, 'foul mouthed old bastard that he is'. All this Andrew confided in his own reflection as he brushed his copper hair. Then he told that reflection, 'I intend to have a shot at it tonight.' So he came thudding down the great staircase, rather in the manner of the 'Inseparables', looking resplendent in white tie and tails with the added touch of elegance – a crisply starched white marcella waistcoat. He thudded across the hall, now transformed by Sawby into a bower of flowers, charged into the billiards room, only to pull up short as he saw that Ninian had forestalled him and was already twirling a magnum in its cooler.

'You look very spry I must say,' Ninian greeted him. 'Care for a drop of the "widow", Tertius?'

The Party had begun.

Sawby stood below the winking lights at the entrance to the ballroom checking the completed decorations. In the canopy-diminished daylight it looked like a garden; but when he pulled the master switch, flooding the scene with brilliance, it became one which he had never set eyes upon before. It was a giant version of a London night club. He permitted himself a low whistle of approval. They had done it again!

The buffets were completed save for André's *grands pièces* which would remain on their green and tangerine socles of ice until only moments before the first guest came into view down the wide corridor. It seemed to the experienced butler, who had seen so many completed buffets over the years, as if this one floated on a frothy sea of green tulle, punctuated by atolls from which rose the *leit motifs*, glistening, edible, palm trees. André and his cousin from Paris – where the young man had already made a name for himself as a brilliant *patissier* and *confiseur* – had elected these as their *pièces de résistance*. They had drawn out the curving, palm leaves in green spun sugar. They had clustered them over brown trunks made in gum paste and on the gum paste circular bases they had massed crystallised fruits, cape gooseberries dipped into tangerine glacé icing, *marrons glacés* enclosed in green, spun sugar, and exquisitely modelled, minute fruits and vegetables in almond paste which they had shaded in the chosen colourings. These included Lilliputian bunches of carrots and leeks, single pods bursting open to disclose *petits pois*, equally minute tangerines with tiny leaves on, bunches of white grapes and doll-sized pineapples and nectarines.

Each long buffet table was centred by a giant palm tree and flanked to left and right by the famous Lorme silver-gilt candelabras, whilst from the front down each length cascaded matching orange lilies interspersed with green *molucella laevis* and miraculously forced green *hellebores*.

Even the tables, covered in foaming green organza, seemed to echo the 'floating' as the light sparkled on the pale polished flooring below them, while forming that canopy above were miles and miles of green and tangerine satin ribbons which 'tented' the ballroom, being fastened to the branches of the chandeliers and then drawn out to the walls in lavish crescents. From all four corners, groups of the tropical 'trees' cascaded with the Sawbys' arrangements of lilies and ferns.

'I think it will do quite well,' Sawby decided. He switched off the lights, did a quick about turn and began moving down the corridor on his way to the White Drawing Room.

As he crossed the great hall, Petula came down the staircase looking like a naiad in floating green chiffons with naughty Marguerite's pilfered emeralds in her hair[1] and holding an enormous tangerine orange feather fan.

'Ah, Sawby,' she said gaily, 'just the person I was looking for. Are you ready for me?'

'I came to inform you madam, the ballroom is ready for your inspection if you can spare a moment.'

'*If* I can,' Petula laughed, 'I have been looking forward to this moment all day; but Sawby, Mr Henry must come too, I think he is on his way now.'

A thud sounded above them, then an expletive and then the future Lord Aynthorp came running down with his copper head gleaming. They waited.

'Looks like it was yesterday they were having their ball,' thought Sawby, 'they aren't a day older for all they've had to endure. She looks no more than the girl she did then, even though it's past eleven years ago.' Try as he would and despite his rigid training he could not keep the admiration from his eyes.

'Evenin' Sawby,' Henry galloped himself level with them, 'don't my wife look ravishin', eh?'

Sawby permitted himself a smile, 'Indeed sir, if I may say so without presuming, it was what I was thinking. Madam

---

[1] See Book 1, *The Lormes of Castle Rising*.

doesn't look a day older than the night you were betrothed.'

'Ah,' Henry tucked one hand under Petula's arm, 'that was a night wasn't it?'

Sawby just nodded, caught in a sudden uprush of emotional recollection.

'Thank you Sawby,' said Petula warmly, 'now come along, take us to see your ballroom.'

'It's not so much mine madam as mine and Appelby's and Chef André's and, well, all of us,' he told them.

They came to the entrance, Sawby pulled the switch again and stood back letting their cries of admiration and approval flow over him until a slow contented smile spread over his face. He forgot that his back was aching and that his feet throbbed. He forgot that he had been up since dawn with little prospect of seeing his bed before another one had broken. He became, instead of a very weary one, an extremely happy man.

'I think it's quite enchanting,' Petula turned to him enthusiastically. 'It is divine in fact, thoroughly original, new, different, oh, absolutely and completely what we wanted.'

'What's so dam' clever,' Henry added, 'is that it's bang on up to the minute and at the same time quite enchantin'ly pretty like Mrs Petula. Sawby you're a genius.'

Petula turned a shining face to him. 'I'll tell you one other thing,' she said with a mock note of warning, 'we shall all have to be very, very careful how we describe it to our favourite Great Aunt. I suppose you realise, lest the Countess might feel you had put her pretty little nose quite out of joint; and that we must never allow to happen.'

Until the day he died, Sawby remembered what they said. He cherished every word. In due course he repeated it often, sometimes to himself when he felt low or when Lorme fortunes were falling. Sometimes he told it all over again to his wife, then in turn to her son and daughter, his stepchildren. With the passing of the years he then told their grandchildren when he became a step-grandfather.

He controlled himself with a great effort now, long enough to follow what he thought of secretly as 'my lovely pair', pacing decorously in their wake as they chattered their way excitedly towards the drawing room again. He nearly burst a blood-vessel when at the White Drawing Room door Petula turned, held out her small hand and said sweetly, 'Thank you so very much Sawby, now please go and rest for a few moments, you must be so very tired.' He bowed low over the small hand, murmuring a trifle incoherently. He was then hand-shaken and thanked by Henry, after which he almost floated on his 'pore feet' below stairs again and recited all the golden words which had been said to him to his plump and appealing little spouse.

Upstairs in the small linen room where she 'did' the laundry for the nursery wing, the nurserymaid was regarding Nanny Rose with a woebegone expression. 'I jest know Nanny I put twenty-two sheets into that laundry bundle. Then I writ them down along of all the rest. Now comes a message from the laundry telling me as there were only fifteen sheets in my bundle which ain't, isn't possible Nanny. I never 'ave been wrong 'ave I?'

Nanny Rose was feeling lenient. She said, 'Well now that is true, I have never known you make a mistake with the laundry but I shouldn't let it bother you tonight. We will go into it in the morning when we're fresh. Let's forget about it now. Oh, there is one other thing though. I am going to lock up early tonight. Mrs Henry says I may watch from her bedroom window as all the guests arrive.' She paused, hesitated, then seeing the miserable little countenance before her she said, 'Why don't you hurry now and get everything done as fast as possible. Then you can come and watch with me, I'm sure Mrs Henry wouldn't mind. When they go into the ballroom we'll come back here and make a nice hot cup of cocoa to have before we go to bed. Would you believe it? Chef André sent up a plate of them petty fores specially for us to have too. Now cheer up chicken. I'll go round the children jest before ten, then I'll give you a call and we'll go down together.' So ending, Nanny dismissed the matter of the missing sheets and trotted off humming a little tune as she began her routine tidying up of the day nursery before supper came up from below.

Down in the stables, newly returned with 'Mother', his comforting and comfortable wife, Plum was preparing to be a spectator too. He had filched a couple of chairs from Pine and a couple of horse blankets from the harness room and was busily occupied in settling the chairs and swaddling them both in the blankets. They settled down, tucked into an angle of the terrace from which they could spectate to their old hearts' delight without being observed.

To while away the time Mrs Plumstead asked, 'How's that young limb Master Rupert gettin' along these days? I only know he's proper on 'is feet again and spry as a linnet.'

'He'm spry orlright,' Plum confirmed grudgingly, 'Mr Ninian's took 'im in 'and while 'is pa's away. I must say ee's bin better be'aved. Come to me 'ee did, as nice as nice tother day. "Mister Plum" 'ee says, "wot is the very strongest knot in the world?" so I tole 'im o' course. Then 'ee says, wheedlin' like, "could a boy of my age learn to make those knots?" So I tole 'im of corse 'ee could, then I sez you come in alonger me and I'll learn yer, wot I did and 'ee done 'em first time right and proper. You know Mother that danged young warmint thanked me ever so nice afore 'ee run orf. Ooo look Ma! there's a car comin' now!'

A posse of drivers had been engaged to take over the non-chauffeur-driven vehicles of which, as Henry had predicted, there were many, as was soon obvious. Young things with streaming scarves tied round their heads debouched from low slung sports cars and the knees of the young men who accompanied them as Bentleys, Bugattis, Napiers and Lancias snarled their way round the last drive bend. They were stopped just short of the brilliantly lit cages displaying the removed wild animals in various states of ill-temper, some snarling, some growling, some pacing and tail-lashing and not a few staring with manifest distaste at the *jeunesse dorée* who clustered around them with cries of admiration.

Petula and Henry had managed to wangle a police control rostrum from the county's Police Commissioner whose son and daughter were among the guests. They had directed its placement at the head of the drive, at centre of where the cars were being halted, and now they stood, a bottle of the Widow in a cooler and two glasses at their feet, so that they could refresh themselves *ad libitum* and still lean down to greet each new arrival from their unorthodox receiving dais.

On either side the two very black, grinning bartenders

Buck and Bud, wearing white mess jackets and gloves, shook silver cocktail shakers with marvellous gyrations and grinned, perspired, mopped and shook again while the footmen held out their trays of cocktail glasses to be filled and then moved off into the growing press.

Also in the van, lynx-eyed and forewarned, stood Sawby ready to move alongside each car as it stopped, and hold out his silver salver for the invitation cards. These he then slid off into the well-scrubbed paws of Poppy's son Pete who deposited them in growing stacks on a small table beside him.

It seemed only moments before the drive's wide sweep was as filled with guests as for any past Invitation Meet, with admiring clusters before every cage, making a harlequinade of floating chiffons interspersed with the magpie elegance of young men in tails. Cocktails were sipped at an alarming rate. The saucy French maids, in their startlingly brief skirts moved with their replenishments of cigarettes offering every brand from Gauloises and Gold Flake to Woodbines and 'Turks' and hastily crossing their long legs as daring youngsters purposely dropped their handkerchiefs and bent to retrieve them in order to obtain a full view of the leg exposure.

As if quite shocked by it all, prim daylight withdrew in favour of a twilight which rapidly retreated into night until the ever-swelling company became encircled by the darkness of trees as they stood in one great pool of lights.

Heads turned as a silver Royce purred up. Henry standing in the midst now of an uproarious group, snapped open his grandfather's half-hunter, saw that the hands stood at ten minutes to eleven, snapped it closed and slipped it back into his waistcoat pocket. A cheer went up. Lucy and Lucien had arrived. Cries of 'Lucy darling' were followed by a rush of young as if a wave were sweeping them forward to greet the disembarking and very famous couple. Lucy kissed her cousin, stepped back a pace and,

'Darling!' exclaimed Petula, 'such sophistication!'

Lucy's small feet were shod in gold, with orange chiffon harem trousers floating out just above them. Her narrow hips were tightly swathed in more folds of chiffon tied in strands which were thickly encrusted with jewel embroidery and knotted in front. On her fair curls curved a pair of orange aigrettes and the bloused chiffon top of her daring ensemble had big, billowing sleeves, through which the outline of her small high breasts was a trifle more than indicated.

Lucien begged leave to present his 'friend'. 'Teddy Mount-Gordon, my cousin Mrs Henry Lorme...'

Petula submitted to her hand being kissed, then saw to it that Bud and Ben shook fresh, 'Manhattans was it, Lucy and Lucien? Yes, and a Bronx for Mr Mount-Gordon.'

'So *formal*,' he exclaimed, '*my* friends *always* call me Teddy, please, *please* just for tonight's *pluperfect* binge can I not be Teddy to our *reigning* beauty?'

Sue-Ellen, wandering up with Ninian in attendance, heard enough to have confirmed for her the source of Lucien's latest mannerism. Then Petula, at an urgent nudge from Henry, made her excuses saying, 'Now do excuse me, but I simply must fly. You're at our table for supper so we shall all meet later.' Then, catching Henry's hand, she ran to the narrow path which had been left between the white lions who had worked themselves into a teeth-gnashing spate of tail thumping while the white puma sat in rigid disapproval like a Scottish spinster from a Manse, looking out over their heads with an expression of frigid disdain.

Over the babble and the crying of names, over 'Baba love,' ... 'Paula my darling,' ... 'Noël what fun!' ... 'Adèle I thought you were in the States' ... and little bobbings as the two young Princes weaved among them, escorting their Penelope and Poppy, came the faint sound of a long, sustained blow on the symbol of their age – a saxophone.

The cries diminished. The invisible saxophone blew again, this time more strongly. Chatter sank down, and from somewhere an incredulous voice cried out, 'It can't be, they *are* in the States! ... but it IS I swear it...' and into the now complete silence, to the unmistakable Washboard Blues stepped the Original Dixieland Jazz Band, led by a smiling trio, Petula and Sue-Ellen with Henry between them. To sustained, almost hysterical applause the trio led them round in a complete circuit and almost hypnotically, princes and their little, pretty girls, debutantes, ex-debutantes, even the breathless and matchless beauty who had recently

married young Duff Cooper fell in behind as if the coal
black musicians were in truth a modern version of the Pied
Piper and the sophisticates of current society the little furry
creatures who pursued them. . . .

With the circuit completed the guests needed no telling.
Up, up went the band, who had changed their playing to
their own special rendition of Dixieland, to the top of the
steps with the cheering guests following, until they crossed
the hall and began the march towards the lights which
winked right on cue as the leader came in sight of the
ballroom and 'The Forty-Four Nite Spot' flashed its welcome exactly as all had hoped it would. The party was
coming in. The lights sprang up in a dazzling blaze. The
musicians climbed to the platform, still blowing furiously,
and into the wide entrance the first of the guests halted to
cries of, 'It's too, too utterly. . . .' 'It's divine . . . how
rivetingly witty and gay. . . .'

They began filtering through. The tables filled up, then
favours were undone and exclaimed upon as fresh cocktails
were circulated.

As all this was happening a small figure on the second floor
flung seven knotted sheets over the sill of the corridor
outside the nursery wing. The sheets snaked out in the
darkness, for now exterior lights were being extinguished
leaving only the animal cages to stand out against the
surrounding darkness. The small figure appeared, un-
noticed on the window sill, climbed out, waved one leg,
wrapped it around the sheet . . . and Rupert de Lorme slid
down, landing safely by his Plum-taught knots and completely undetected. He had decided to participate in his
eldest brother's party.

No sooner had he landed than he burrowed into the
nearest shrubbery. He did this undetected, under cover of
the excitement as the Dixielanders marched into view and
every eye was fixed upon them. Crouched under the ever-
greens he scrabbled his hands in the wet, peaty soil and
carefully smeared his face. Then, skirting the celebrants
who were now starting their ascent into the Castle, he
worked his way cautiously towards Sawby's stepson. His
objective was the small table on which the collected invitation cards were now piled very high indeed. Rupert

waited. The lights began to blink out. Sawby had long gone,
and now Pete, forgetting his last injunction, remembering
only that Sawby had told him, 'There's a bite to eat and
drink in the Servants' Hall for you so cut along there sonny,
but don't forget those invitations,' cut along, rapidly. Once
he had vanished round the end of the Castle's façade,
heading for the servants' entrance, Rupert put out a now
grubby paw, grabbed a pile of the cards Pete had left behind
and began running in the direction of the main gates. As he
came in sight of them Rupert saw that a cluster of people
were still on the farther side as the two watchmen closed
those gates in the face of several pleading young men.
Rupert waited again. The men turned away and began
plodding back to their braziers. Rupert thrust his face
between the wrought iron. 'Anyone want a genuine invitation?' he demanded.

The group rushed forward.

'Cost you two guineas each,' Rupert said warningly, 'an'
I've got ten for sale.'

Several fell back; but a group of five young journalists
who had been astute enough to wheedle the price of hired
dress suits out of their editors, plus the price of railway
tickets for the girls they had brought with them, now
crouched against the gates, paid over the guineas, and
received the whole packet of returned invitations in
exchange.

'You can choose,' said Rupert, 'it doesn't matter giving
you extra, the butler would throw you out if you weren't all
togged up. There's a name on every one by the way and
sometimes two.'

After a struggle with the gates one of them shinned up,
climbed over and performed the office of re-opening them.

'I'm off now,' Rupert told them. 'Goodnight,' and so
saying, listing a trifle to port with twenty-two guineas in his
left-hand pocket, he vanished into the darkness and began
working back the way he had come. Once there he set off in
an entirely different tack. He had made his profit, which no-
one could ever find out, now he was about to amuse himself
before making his way upstairs again.

This time he inched round the left of the great façade,
coming at length to the blaze of lights which were spilling

out onto the topiary, along the main herbaceous borders and reaching to the crescent rose gardens beyond. Rupert scuttled against the wall like a small land crab until he reached the band's marquee. He had been sufficiently angelic during the day to ensure being shown everything before he was taken back by Ninian to Nanny Rose. Therefore he knew *which* band would be playing, and when and where they would be during their respite.

He did a further bit of scrabbling between the back of the marquee and the castle wall. He tugged out a large bag, fished in it and stuffed some of the contents into his overworked pockets. What would not go in he clutched and hurried to where he had carved a neat, small hole with his penknife, sufficiently low down for him to peer through. The legs within wore the tell-tale red socks which he had marked down as belonging to the Dixielanders. He watched the feet intently, saw them converge upon the back exit, and drew back in the nick of time as they streamed out into the warm September air.

The Dixielanders had decided upon a breath of fresh air before returning to the platfrom. From inside Rupert could hear the sounds of Ambrose's band playing a two step. He counted the emerging men carefully. They all wandered off down the grass path between the herbaceous borders talking, laughing ... now! Rupert darted forward, dashed in, and thrust something from his paws and pockets into each Dixieland Jazz Band Instrument, ramming all down hard. Mission accomplished he shot out again, strolled round to the Blue Drawing Room whose windows he had opened earlier, climbed in and began creeping towards the main staircase. A huge bubble of sound burst over him from the general direction of the ballroom; but the main hall was totally deserted. He fled up the stairs, rushed the second flight, panting by now, to stand heaving a bit outside the nursery wing door. As he had expected, the sound of voices, just two very familiar ones, came from the kitchen where Nanny Rose and the rapturous Nurserymaid were preparing the cocoa for their midnight orgy. Very well pleased with everything, Rupert tip-toed to his now un-locked room, shoved the bundle of sheets he had retrieved en passant to behind the wardrobe and in moments was between the

sheets, peat-streaked face and all with the twenty-two
guineas safely cached up the bedroom chimney. He slept the
sleep of one who has accomplished something very
praiseworthy.

In the ballroom Ambrose had replaced the Dixieland
Band as supper was announced. There was a surge towards
the buffets, and a surge back again with loaded plates. Some
ate and drank, some rushed onto the dance floor. In between
they returned to swap partners, nibble a few mouthfuls and
smoke a great many cigarettes.

To the tune of 'All Alone', first sung by Alice Delysia,
Ambrose's stint ended in a bout of generous applause, which
was as nothing to the uproar which greeted the re-
appearance of the men from New Orleans.

Up went their instruments to their grinning water-melon
mouths ... and they blew ... and blew ... A ripple of
laughter stirred, rose to a roar as first one and then another
registered stupefied horror as no sound emerged from their
gleaming instruments. Then someone shouted, 'Look inside,' after which the laughter became a gigantic howl as
yards of cotton wool were hauled out and dropped to the
platform ...

Gallantly they began again. A cheer went up as the sound
came blaring out; but in all that company of young, four
faces were lit by anger as four pairs of eyes met and Ninian,
Sue-Ellen, Henry and Petula mouthed, 'Who?' Ninian
muttered, 'God alone knows *how*, but I'll lay a pony to a
pice that's Rupert's work.'

Petula nodded, 'Must be,' she agreed. 'No Nin *do nothing
now please*, the cabaret is due to start any minute. They're all
being regaled in the White Drawing Room ... look, they're
coming now!'

The winking lights in the wide entrance had been switched off and the corridor lights too so that the little group
who waited there were in complete shadow. Four footmen
came across carrying four chairs above the guests' heads.
Lucien, young Mount-Gordon, Andrew, Ninian and young
Charles all moved their chairs to make way. The ballroom
switch was pulled, leaving them all in total darkness.

Simultaneously the Dixielanders drew back, Ambrose
came forward and by the time the manoeuvre had been

completed five very famous people, the darlings of these very bright young things were seated at the young Lormes' table.

Up went the platform lights. Ambrose stepped down into the centre of the ballroom into the beam projected by the Castle electricians' special spotlight.

'Your Royal Highnesses, My Lords, Ladies and Gentlemen,' Ambrose announced, *'it's cabaret time at the Forty-Four!'* He paused for the roar of applause then said, 'For your delight we are honoured to present, Miss Adèle and Mr Fred Astaire, the Western Brothers and Mr Billy Mayerl who has very kindly consented to open the performance for us by playing in his inimitable fashion "Kitten on the Keys".'

Billy Mayerl rose from the Lorme table, the spotlight caught and held him as he crossed the floor, climbed to the piano and began to play.

It had certainly become a night to remember. When last of all the reed-slim Adèle, whom they all adored, took the floor with her brother they gave them a standing ovation before they began to dance. When they had danced the galaxy of youth stood on the tables, cheered, filled the great rooms with cries of ' 'Core' . . . ' 'Core' . . . and simply would not let them go.

At length a dozen young men rushed the floor and carried them back to their hostess's table shoulder high. As she slid to the ground Adèle saw that the Royals had joined the party. Curtseying as only she could, she had a Prince to draw out her chair as she rose again, and his brother to hold out a fresh glass of champagne as the room toasted her.

At a nod from Henry, Ambrose began to play 'Where do flies go in the winter time, Do they go to gay Paree?' and with a great scraping of chairs everyone crowded onto the floor.

Henry, dancing with his Petula, at last bent his head to catch her murmured, 'I think it *is* a success darling don't you?', met her shining eyes and just nodded. 'A riot,' he agreed, 'don't look now but I think something is going with Andy.'

Andrew and Victoria were dancing cheek to cheek. They both looked as if they had suddenly been transported to heaven and had no compunctions whatever about displaying their rapture.

'Oh I am glad,' Petula cried, 'let's go and congratulate them.'

'You'd need wings my love,' Henry regretted, 'there ain't enough room to move now. It'll have to wait, but I'm jolly glad all the same, Victoria's a ripping lass and it's altogether a bang on do.'

As the night wore on the Dixielanders came back to blow them 'It ain't gonna rain no mo', to which voices were joined until, as the first faint promise of dawn touched the sleeping gardens, Ambrose led his band into a belated 'At three o'clock in the morning . . .'

It was five minutes to seven when the last roaring Bugatti shot away down the drive. 'Even the Royals,' as Petula said gleefully, 'didn't leave until five o'clock.' To which Henry added, 'Despite the notice faithfully posted outside the Guard Room at St James's Palace slap on eleven thirty p.m, every ruddy night "His Royal Highness has retired for the night and is sleeping peacefully". Ha, bloody ha!'

CHAPTER 7

How Far to Babylon?

When the Castle Rising inmates tottered down the staircase between three and four o'clock the following afternoon they were somewhat the worse for wear. Despite this, a Council of War was set up in the Library where one and all rejected Sawby's solicitous suggestion of black coffee in favour of a curious assortment of what Henry called 'corpse-revivers'. These ranged from prairie oysters to three aspirin and a Bass, with only the heir standing out for a 'King's Peg' and being deemed 'stinkin' old-fashioned' for his pains.

Belowstairs an argument was in progress between Sawby and Mrs Parsons who were also feeling fragile. In consequence their tempers were short and their hands none too steady; but it was left to the irrepressible George to demonstrate the ultimate in hangovers. He encircled his neck with a not over-clean table napkin, clasped one end around a glass of Guinness and used the free, shaking hand to raise the beverage to his lips by the napkin's farther end. ' 'Ef you 'adn't partook of them cocktails,' Mrs Parsons told him spitefully, 'you wouldn't 'eve to rekorse to such sordid hantics.'

Then an unusually fraught Sawby asked, 'Do I take up the morning papers or do I not? That is what I want to know.'

'Since wen 'as you ever bin backward in comin' forward?' Mrs Parsons snapped querulously. 'Anyway wot else? They're bound to 'ear an' see afore long ain't they?'

Poppy suggested soothingly, 'Get it over Albert do. Then we can all 'ave a bit of peace.'

The man rose with a sigh, gathered up the sheaf and made his way slowly to the Library which was strewn with near-corpses.

'Yes Sawby?' Henry looked up from mixing his wife a second prairie oyster.

'The, er morning papers sir. I don't think they will please you, but I felt it my duty to bring them.'

'What on earth!' Henry exclaimed, 'OhmiGod, my head!' Sawby withdrew with greater haste than dignity. Closing the door behind him he heard, 'God's Boots, look at this!' and shuddered as he made his way back across the hall.

The fruits of Rupert's first business venture were slapped across the front pages of the morning papers which were now being passed from hand to hand with accompanying cries of consternation.

'Listen to this!' young Charles rattled the *Daily Mirror*, 'High Jinks in Stately Home. God give me strength, it's all here!'

He lowered the paper, 'How could they have found out?'

'Oh,' moaned Petula, ' "Who Stuffed Cotton Wool into the Negro Jazz Band's instruments?" and "Prince of Wales dances Turkey Trot with Miss Adèle Astaire".'

'The *Daily Sketch*,' contributed Ninian, his voice half-strangled with fury, 'says "Wild animals celebrate wild night with Peer's son and heir. Castle Rising transformed into London Night Club".'

It was all there, sometimes hugely garbled, but basically factual, though the facts were carefully, even cleverly presented to make the dance seem like a cross between a bacchanal and a Borgia orgy.

'Why?' asked Andrew wearily, 'didn't they go the whole hog and call it a Debauch I wonder?'

'Because,' snapped Sue-Ellen, who had never before been heard to snap at anything, 'that would have made this muck actionable.' She threw her paper down. 'I refuse to read another word. I just want to know how they got such detailed information.'

Petula looked piteously at Henry. 'Darling whatever will the Royals think?'

'God alone knows. We'll be barred from Court, the Royal Enclosure: *personae non gratae*, that's us from now on. If I could get my hands on the stinker who is responsible I'd strangle him.'

'No single stinker,' Ninian pointed out, 'have a heart chum. What one journalist could have supplied such details to at least four different papers?'

At least the yellow press reports worked one near-miracle. Hangovers were sunk without trace as they wrestled with the full horror of the situation. Then into the room stepped Edward with an envelope on a salver. He held it out to Petula who took it in silence, remembered – just – to say 'thank you', and then ripped open the envelope.

'This is all we needed!' she groaned holding it out to Henry.

It went the rounds, silencing comment by the awfulness of its contents. 'Expect to dock Sunday morning. Hope you had a splendid party. Love to all.' The signature was simply 'Aynthorp.'

Ninian stood up. 'And where might you be going?' Sue-Ellen demanded.

'Siberia,' said Ninian, 'coming?'

About an hour later Petula pulled the bell and asked for Sawby. When he came she faced him with a rueful little smile. 'This is a nice ending is it not, Sawby, after you all worked so hard?'

'Terrible madam,' he agreed.

'Whom do you imagine could have done such a thing?'

Sawby hesitated. 'Well madam, I too have a mystery. My stepson Pete brought me all the invitation cards. My footmen report that three hundred and ten seats were occupied at the tables in the ballroom. Yet there are only three hundred names on the cards and I can assure you madam every one gave me their invitations.'

'Gate crashers!' they cried in unison, 'well thank the Lord it wasn't any of our friends.'

'But how did they gain an entrance, madam? *No* one tried to come without their invitation. I can assure you of that.'

'Do you know by any chance who was responsible for the cotton wool in the band's instruments?' Henry was off on a tangent.

'No sir.'

Henry spoke again. 'Sawby, we rang because his lordship and her ladyship are coming home. The cable says they dock tomorrow morning. Can you please arrange the necessary cars so that they may be brought here for our execution.'

Sawby's mouth twitched but he managed to control himself.

'Yes sir. If I may presume sir, I consider the newspapers have been most unjust.'

'But will his lordship?' Charles gloomed.

Sawby waited. 'There was one other thing sir,' he ventured.

'Yes?'

'There are seven sheets missing from the Nursery laundry this week.'

'*Seven sheets!*'

'Yes sir, and furthermore I happened to be in conversation for a moment with Plumstead. He remarked, casually, that Master Rupert had been receiving instruction from him as to the way to tie the strongest knots. I do not suppose there is any association between these matters but I thought perhaps I should draw them to your attention.'

The silence which followed his departure was of considerable duration. Finally Henry, rumpling his hair into total disorder, said, 'I always felt that pox-stricken boy was behind it somehow.'

'Henry!' shrieked Petula, 'what a dreadful word. Kindly apologise.'

He obliged in a desultory manner and returned to his moutons, 'Can any of you tell me *how* the little b.... beast did it?'

Ninian rose looking grim. 'No, but I think a thorough search of his room might not come amiss. Hen have I got permission to give him a sound thrashing if he is the culprit?'

'No. We can't Nin. We must wait for the old man. We can lock him in, put him on bread and water, but I don't think we can lather him, especially after all he's been through fairly recently. By all means go and search his room, though on second thoughts I'll come too; Andy you should be in on this as well.'

As the three brothers vanished Petula heard Henry say, 'At least this'll put us in the clear with his blinkin' lordship if it is true.'

During their absence Victoria walked in and shortly after she had been supplied with a reviver, Sir Charles and Lady Constance appeared.

'Dears I thought you would be in need of consolation,'

said Constance gently. 'I suppose you have no idea who was responsible for all that rubbish in the papers?'

Petula took it upon herself to explain where matters stood at present, and to their utter astonishment Constance immediately dissolved into peals of laughter. 'Oh my dears,' she paused, wiped her eyes and then surrendered to a fresh gale of laughter. 'If you could see your faces,' she choked.

For answer Petula handed her the cable. 'I think,' she suggested, 'this might dampen down your mirth. They'll be here in the morning.'

Sir Charles helped himself to a drink, sat down, crossed his legs and asked permission to smoke a pipe. When this was tamped down and drawing satisfactorily he spoke. 'If it *was* Rupert I would suggest you cease actin' like tragedy queens. If you are sensible you will now order a substantial meal, eat it, sleep on this affair and when you have faced the music with Christine and Gyles we will start a little leakin' campaign of our own. I should think the Palace would have somethin' to say about it too. Gyles still has friends at Court. Moreover there are plenty of witnesses to the fact that last night's dance was not a drunken orgy. You are all over-reacting.'

He paused and into the pause the three brothers erupted. Henry held a knotted string of grubby sheets. He flung them down onto the carpet, exclaiming, 'Behind the wardrobe in that little swine's bedroom.'

This set Constance off again. 'Oh dear,' she cried when she could subdue her mirth sufficiently to speak, 'you said that like "dead and never called me mother!" This is pure melodrama, do stop it, my sides are sore.'

Henry eyed her balefully. 'So you think it's funny?'

'No, love I do not, but you all are. Tell me did Rupert 'fess up?'

''Fess up is it,' Ninian was almost beside himself with rage, 'he refused to say a word, just closed his lips and looked defiant. Nanny Rose has locked him into his room and says she'll keep him there until the old man gets back. He actually blew a raspberry at us from behind the door after Nanny had turned the key.'

The melodrama continued. The next arrival was the irascible Duke of Barton and Sale. He marched in, surveyed them, greeted the Danements, said 'Ah Henry,' and to their astonishment, sat himself down with a thump and enquired in what passed for a reasonable voice from him, 'Any truth in this garbage the papers have put out?'

'None, sir.'

'Normal behaviour, eh? Just high jinks.'

'Yessir.'

'It's the truth, sir.'

'Damned disgraceful then. I shall tell yer father. Victoria here ... she's always bin truthful ... she said there was nothin' in it. How did the lepers gain admittance?' And thus the whole tale had to be re-told once more.

The Duke clamped an eager hand around a large brandy and soda and listened with only a few grunts to punctuate the report. Then he delivered himself of this verdict.

'I shall take a hand in this. It's monstrous! D'you mean to tell me that some sewers from Grub Street, masqueradin' one supposes in dress clothes, got in, ate yer food, drank yer wines and then wrote this calumny?'

'Yessir.' Henry was again head-rumpling furiously. 'Come to think of it, there *was* a table of ten in the corner by the band, I *thought* their faces were unfamiliar; but then I was pretty hard pressed at the time. Adèle had just taken the floor. In the excitement I forgot all about it.'

'Pity,' the Duke regretted, 'you could have scragged the lot of them. That would have been *most* satisfactory. However, I came here on another matter,' he looked across at Victoria who was watching him intently. 'I understand you Miss and young Andrew here have somethin' to say to me. Better cut along to the Gun Room. I'll follow. No go along, don't stand there ditherin', do as I say, go on shoo!' Incontinently the pair fled.

He frowned at the library group, bringing down his tufted eyebrows ferociously. 'Sooner or later,' he informed them, 'I'll have those fellers' lights and livers for this, you see if I don't! But now,' he jumped up, 'if you will kindly excuse me I have other fish to fry.' So saying he marched out in the general direction of the Gun Room.

Half an hour later Victoria and Andrew rushed in, both talking at once and therefore wholly incomprehensible. When they had calmed down a little the gist of their much dreaded interview with Victoria's irascible guardian emerged.

The Duke had bestowed his Dower House upon them together with his blessing. He had been uniquely benevolent. Finally he departed on a shout of 'I'll see yer aunt gives a luncheon when the Aynthorps return, to settle all the details.'

Anent their future home, Victoria reported her uncle as having said, 'the dam' place has stood empty since yer mother took off to chivvy her father wherever the old sod is now'. She added gleefully, 'Uncle has promised to pay the piper for restoration and redecoration so we're off tomorrow to explore everything from attic to cellar and plan colour schemes. I haven't been inside since poor mummy died; but all the furniture is still there so we're bound to find some ripping stuff. Mummy had great taste.'

Andrew stood about beaming fatuously until Victoria paused for breath. 'You don't know the half of it,' he burst in, seizing Henry and dancing him round the room. 'Dookie's given us extra acres and told us something even Vikki didn't know ... ow you silly sod that's my foot!'

The brothers separated in disorder.

'Feller's potty that's what!' gasped Henry collapsing into a chair.

'No I'm not,' Andrew continued, hopping on his undamaged foot, 'I've got me a ruddy heiress. Three thou' a year! Ain't that something? With the best girl in the world thrown in! Now the old man will have to top that or I'll never be master in me own house. Oh glory be and Dookie says he's taking over the wedding, fids fids I gloat! Hen what about a drop of the hair of the dog?'

Henry reached for the bell, pulled it and delivered himself of a pithy comment.

'I'll tell you somethin',' he volunteered, eyeing his wife thoughtfully, 'the dramas in this house are becomin' a trifle extreme. In fact in the unlikely event of you pre-deceasin' me I would like you to put on my tombstone, "never a dull moment". Pity there won't be enough room for some addenda though.'

'What would you suggest?' Petula twinkled.

'The limelight at Castle Rising was always part-worn

through bein' snatched from hand to hand' he said promptly. 'May as well face it Pet, we're a bang up lot of screamin' extroverts. Still it's stimulatin' . . . ah Sawby can we please have a couple of nice cold bottles of whatever champagne is chilled, ready and appropriate. Mr Andrew is about to become engaged to Miss Victoria.'

The small boy who was currently locked in his bedroom in the nursery wing was in the forefront of all their minds, even during the hustle and bustle of what Henry described with his customary *lèse majesté* as 'tiddlin' up the old place for the arrival of the reignin' monarch and his spouse'.

There was the same frenzied activity on the estate. Andrew had ruled a thorough clean out of the Aynthorp Enterprises buildings. Sue-Ellen was chivvying her men who rushed about with barrows of fresh straw, shovelled up accumulated piles of droppings large and small onto carts; emptied, cleaned and re-filled water pools while the instigator of all this chewed the end of her pen as she strove to make columns of figures agree.

Petula had a conference with Mrs Peace in her housekeeper's room, then rose and followed that autocrat of castle management when she detached and laid aside her pince-nez and gathered up the lists which were her passion, in preparation for an onslaught upon the housemaids. They were dusting, sweeping and polishing in Christine and Gyles' suites. Pearson was systematically working through Christine's closets, checking that every garment was in perfect order. Through the opened, connecting door Pine could be seen brushing Gyles' suits with Boots crouched nearby polishing hunting tops, Newmarkets and patent leather slippers as if his life depended upon his being able to see his wizened reflection in every pair.

Two kitchenmaids were detached at Mrs Peace's request from the octopus hold of Mrs Parsons and were now taking great bowls of flowers from the van drawn up outside the main entrance, climbing upstairs with them and handing them to Victoria who put them in their appointed places.

The most senior footman, Edward, worked his way cautiously between them carrying his handled box from which he extracted ink for the inkwells on the two desks, fresh blotting paper, writing paper, postcards, envelopes and stamps. These chores completed he tidied the great piles of waiting correspondence and stood back to admire his own handiwork. On his way out he managed a sly pinch at kitchenmaid Eliza's plump behind. 'Ouch!' she exclaimed, and scuttled away as she saw Mrs Peace rustling towards her, chatelaine rattling from the black belt which encircled the waist of her hour-glass figure. At the sight of her, whipped cream walnut hair style, high collared black dress fastened with the customary hair brooch, pince-nez in hand, everyone redoubled their efforts.

Below stairs Chef André worked on a new creation in honour of the home coming. Sawby stalked through carrying a cobwebby bottle of vintage port as if it were a sacred chalice, declaiming as he progressed, 'Remember now, everyone at twelve-twenty sharp upstairs into the hall.'

Mrs Parsons promptly seized upon this theme and embroidered it. 'Clean nails and tidy 'air naow, an' woe betide any of yer as doesn't look spotless from 'ead ter toe. I'm orf upstairs to change meself. By the time I git back you'll all be ready or I'll want ter know the reason why. Daisy stop chattering you're giving me a n'earache girl.'

Lumbering up the back stairs she encountered Mrs Peace, coming down.

'Ah there you are cook,' said she magisterially, 'I have informed Mr Sawby he must have all the staff mustered in the great hall for inspection at twelve-twenty precisely.'

'Queen Anne's dead!' thought Mrs Parsons. Aloud she muttered 'Yes'm,' standing aside to let the housekeeper pass. When she had done so she muttered, 'Stuck up ole cow!' under her breath and panted her way upwards, for Mrs Peace was the one person capable of intimidating her and she valued her place too much to attempt open resistance.

At the appointed time she returned to chivvy everyone aloft through the green baize door. Sawby then lined them up, the women on one side, the men on the other, with Mrs Peace at the head of the female line and himself facing her.

Henry and Petula strolled from the White Drawing Room across the hall and out through the opened doors as the butler and housekeeper went down the line looking for trouble and occasionally finding it. There was a little fidgeting, Mrs Peace hissed, 'Stand still *if* you please,' and the bonnet of the Royce appeared round the bend.

Sawby broke ranks to go out and down the steps just in time to hold open the door as Grantham drew the car up. 'Welcome home my lady, welcome home my lord.'

They had all heard it so many times before. They would hear it many times in the future, nevertheless it was very agreeable. The Aynthorps dismounted. Christine put her arms around Petula and kissed her, Gyles, doing likewise, said approvingly, 'Charmin' frock m'y dear, you look prettier than ever.' Father and son shook hands and the four moved up the stairs together. At the door Henry and Petula turned away. Then the Aynthorps went down the lines with a handshake and a kind word for each of the staff. The women bobbed, the men bent their heads respectfully and then it was all over.

Moments later they were surrounded by family in the White Drawing Room while Pearson stood waiting to take Christine's hat and gloves. This serene and welcoming atmosphere persisted through the ritual madeira sipping and on through the ensuing luncheon. A special word of appreciation was duly sent to André for his new creation. It was only when they were all back sipping coffee, when Sawby spoke his ritual, 'Will that be all my lady?' and received his quittance, that, behind closed doors Gyles said quietly, relaxing in his favourite chair, his cigar drawing satisfactorily, a ballon in hand, 'Well now, what really happened to Rupert?'

'Do you want it in broad outline or from beginnin' to end sir?' Ninian asked.

'The latter, if you please. I gather it was grim.'

'It was,' said Henry with considerable feeling.

The young ones looked questioningly at each other. Finally Petula ventured, 'Well the first we knew of anything amiss was Nanny Rose appearing in tears saying Rupert was missing.'

Having thus broken the ice they managed to share the story between them. It was listened to in silence except for a small cry from Christine when they reached the point of Ninian's discovery at the bottom of the landslide. She went very white but gestured to her son to continue. Only when they had done did the Dowager elect to take the floor.

'Nor,' she said drily, 'is that all my dears. Are you sure you want to hear the rest so soon after your return?'

All this drew was a 'Pray continue Mama' from Gyles, so Henry and Petula shared the telling of the second episode between them and Ninian wound it up for them by adding, 'Frankly sir I was all for giving the young s . . . er sinner a good latherin'; but Hin and Andy thought we had better wait for you. So we just confined him to barracks where he has been ever since, except for a short walk this morning. I am told he is extremely cross.'

'Indeed?' Gyles' tone was chilly.

Christine burst out, 'Gyles pray do not be too hard on him. Remember he is such a very little boy.'

'I grant you six is no great age,' Gyles agreed evenly, 'but you must confess our son is lucky to have survived. Slidin' thirty feet and more down knotted sheets!' despite himself the corners of his mouth twitched. 'Let us just agree that Rupert possesses a most inventive disposition, combined with a precocious capacity for formulating plans and then executing them with, from his standpoint, complete success. I am therefore inclined to assume that he is old enough and fiendish enough to warrant some fairly stringent disciplining. I would welcome comments from you chaps if you have any.'

'To your "fiendish" sir,' Ninian responded, 'I would add fearless. Plus the fact that when his temper is up he is not only unpredictable but downright dangerous.'

Gyles nodded. 'Henry?'

Inevitably Henry's hand flew to his hair despite his wife's protest 'Darling do please leave your hair alone for once.'

At length he stammered, 'I'm worried. No school would take him. 'Tanyrate if they did he'd be sacked within a week.'

Gyles turned his head, 'Andrew?'

'Foxed sir,' he regretted, 'I mean, well, grandfather could erupt but he never physically attacked anyone when his paddy was up, except on that famous occasion when he took a horsewhip to that evil old chimney sweep for what he had

done to Boots.[1] I'm mild tempered for a Lorme, but if it
'ud bin me I'd've killed the brute! I'll say one thing more.
Please don't lather him sir. He's as hard as flint for such a
little 'un. Lathering only makes him worse. He simply bides
his time and then does something else awful in revenge just
as soon as an opportunity arises.'

Instinctively he glanced down at the mark on the back of
his right hand where Rupert had stabbed him with a fork at
the nursery tea table.

As was his custom John Newmarket listened but in complete silence, as usual. Then to everyone's surprise he now
spoke up.

'The little lad's got to be schooled Gyles, like an unbroken
colt of particularly devilish disposition. What you need is a
feller who can drive the salient points of all this home to him
that disobedience in *anything* automatically spells acute dis-
comfort but always excluding the whip which is the last
thing which should be used in my opinion.'

Gyles regarded the ash on his cigar thoughtfully. 'I think
you are right old boy,' he conceded. 'The vital question is
where do I lay hands on such a paragon?'

Setting aside Rupert's abnormal behaviour it was a
normal homecoming filled with accumulated problems and
anxieties for them both. For Christine there was a vast
amount of correspondence containing the usual percentage
of bad news, accidents and illnesses to friends, two deaths,
one broken marriage and the dire information that yet
another family was being forced to sell up. Additionally her
post contained innumerable requests for fittings; the dates
of divers committee meetings all of which she disliked
intensely; bazaars to open, fetes to attend, invitations to
christenings, marriages, and a lengthy letter from an nona-
genarian great aunt who still persisted not only in crossing
but also recrossing each page, forgetting that paper was not
nearly so valuable as when she had learned this curious art.

Christine put down her paperknife resolutely. 'No more,'
she thought, 'enough is enough,' and a wave of home-
returning depression engulfed her as her mind went back to
her small son.

[1] Book 1, *The Lormes of Castle Rising.*

There was little now which she did not know about the family into which she had married. She knew the histories of all their delinquents too, having listened and learned from her mother-in-law, the Dowager, and from the little Countess Marguerite who was steeped in family lore and had even translated early diaries from the original black letter into both English and French. These two old gentlewomen shared Christine's unease concerning Rupert's future and made comparisons between this little boy and the past wickednesses of earlier de Lormes. They likened Rupert's craving for adventure to that of an earlier Rupert of the Restoration period. He kept his contemporary older generation on perpetual tenterhooks by his amorous escapades and perennially terrified lest any of them should reach the ears of the Long Lad who was Rupert's King, master and, besides, frequent companion in matters of dalliance. Sometimes they compared Christine's little son with the even more awful 'Patch' de Lorme. He took to the skull and crossbones, lost one eye in a brush with the Spaniards, narrowly missed being hung from their yardarm and undeservedly died in his bed surrounded by legitimate progeny while his numerous bastards ran wild throughout the country. The exploits of scandalous de Lormes continued to haunt Christine long after the sound of the first dressing bell which brought Pearson to her boudoir. As the woman brushed and dressed her hair Christine recalled the dreadful stand and deliver Gervaise de Lorme who should most certainly have dangled from a gibbet; but de Lorme luck held for him too, aided as he was like all his kind by the automatic closing of family ranks and the subsequent expenditure of vast sums of Lorme inheritance to keep all secret. No matter how far she raked back over those colourful sinners who recurred and recurred throughout the family history, Christine could not call to mind a single instance of murderous temper. Yet Rupert had the makings of this as witness, she reminded herself, poor Henrietta's scarred cheek and Richard's hand.

Christine then tried to remember something she had heard about a man who was engaged on child reform. She worried away at this elusive recollection until Gyles strolled in from his dressing room.

'Gyles,' she appealed, 'who was that man we met who specialised in child reform?'

'D'you mean the feller at Lucy and Lucien's dress affair? for if so I do have some recollection of him. He was with his sister as I recall. She was the wife of the playwright Somerset Maugham. Wasn't their name Barnardo? and does he not run some sort of homes for orphaned children?'

'That's the man!' she nodded. 'Most of his children were of the Artful Dodger class. Now what was it he told us?'

Gyles reflected then, 'Give me a child before it is seven and I can undertake to do something with him no matter how dreadful his background has been; but after seven ...' he just shrugged his shoulders. 'I take your point,' he added, 'I might make a contact eh? just as a matter of interest, perhaps offer a donation, and even, if things turned out promisingly enough, find out obliquely if he knew the sort of chap we were lookin' for.'

'Exactly.'

'Tricky,' Gyles mused, 'but not impossible. It will need a good deal of working out first though. Now come along my love let Pearson dress you please. If we go on like this we shall be late which is unthinkable.' He turned to go but Christine called after him, 'What was it you came in here to say Gyles?'

'Only that I have a matter of business to discuss with you, but it will have to wait until mornin' now, since the Danements are dinin'.'

Gyles was pursuing his chosen policy of retrenchment through expansion. In the furtherance of this aim he had recently decided to invest in pedigree cattle. While outward bound to Australia he wrote home to Scotland ordering a hundred head of in-calf pedigree Ayrshires. This was to be his nucleus. He had the necessary acreage for grazing and was confident that with the contacts he and Andrew had already made there would be no difficulty in selling profitably. First he would do so off the hoof, but his long term plan was to employ master butchers – probably through André – so that he could offer cuts of beef which were virtually unobtainable from the standard English method of dividing carcases. He lay on deck, a panama hat tipped over his face, seemingly drowsing in the sun as the great ship churned up her enormous wake. He was actually envisaging a time when Aynthorp Enterprises would have a chain of Home Produce Shops in strategically placed towns throughout England, all of them stocked with the products of Aynthorp Enterprises. A slight chuckle escaped him at the thought of an Aynthorp in butchering. Finally he wrote to Charles Danement who cabled back 'Increase order by forty for me'.

When the three Danements arrived for the reunion dinner party Sir Charles managed to draw Gyles to one side for some preliminary questioning. He raised the subject again at the dinner table at which Christine became thoroughly put out not only by the pair of them but also by her own sons who seized on the topic avidly. She frowned. Cattle were not a subject for dinner table conversation! Petula fidgeted, restless with boredom. Eventually Claire protested. 'I declare,' she exclaimed crossly, 'that even though you men may find pregnant cows a simply riveting subject *we do not.*'

Gyles apologised, peace was restored; but the moment the door was closed on the women the men closed ranks and put Claire's pregnant cows back on the agenda as Gyles poured himself some port and circulated the decanter.

'I'm bound to say Gyles,' Sir Charles spoke ruefully, 'forty pound apiece for in-calf heifers is mighty steep, however if you undertake to handle the sales end I'm comin' in.'

'We might have a few goats too father,' said Andrew hopefully, 'we could easily flog goat cheeses on the stalls to begin with.'

Gyles leaned back in his great carved chair. As he did so he fancied the portraits of his ancestors on the walls looked down on him with affront and disdain. He almost heard the word 'trade' being ejaculated scornfully. He began to speak.

'Let me recapitulate a little if you please to put you squarely in the picture. If somethin' constructive isn't done we're all goin' to be in a pretty pickle in a few years' time. I initiated "AE" as you so vulgarly term our company, as an eventual means of arrestin' some of the rot; to lay the foundation, in fact, for future drastic retrenchment. I envisaged two alternatives as prices rise and expenditure increases, *if* we are to keep pace with our past pattern. On the one hand we could sell land, a bit at a time until – and mark you in the foreseeable future this is what I predict – we should be compelled to sell up altogether. It's happenin' now with some of our neighbours who have bin where they were for many centuries. Sons come home expectin' to pick up where they left off. Not a bit of it! Funds are simply not adequate. The lucky ones are kitted up and packed off to Burma to tap rubber, or Assam to grow tea. Chaps who found the market flooded and thought to make soldierin' their career learned that their people could no longer afford to give them the allowances they needed to keep their end up. Still farther down the scale fellers started poultry farms using inadequate gratuities or pensions to launch 'em. To be undercapitalised is to be undermined from the onset. No go in fact! He broke off and looked at his four sons. 'If I had no means where would you chaps be today pray tell me?'

The ensuing, startled silence was almost laughable. Gyles and Sir Charles exchanged glances. Young Charles muttered, 'Up the creek without a paddle!' It was left to Richard to say gloomily, 'Workin' in some Zoo at four pounds a week I suppose.'

Gyles nodded. 'Now let us hear from Henry. You have a wife and two children to support remember.'

Henry savaged his copper head before acknowledging, 'I'd try for a job as land agent I suppose with some flamin' war profiteer.'

'Ninian?'

'Get a job in a racin' stable if I could. Trouble is I only know about horses and soldierin' and in my regiment I couldn't last a week on m'y pay.'

'Exactly,' Gyles replenished his glass then launched the decanter once more. 'Andy here is in the same case as the rest of you. Thank you all for establishin' m'y point. Now it's over to you Charles I'm talkin' too much; do the older generation stuff for me.'

'Easily,' Sir Charles' mouth was wry, 'I'm one of 'em. Risin' prices and insufficient capital have forced me to sell up one farm already. What's more boys yer father and I have half a dozen friends in the county who have also committed

the heinous sin of sellin' land. Furthermore some of 'em
have had to pack up altogether. Then what happens?' He
looked around him, obtained no response so resumed,
'Fellers of my age are too old to chance their arm fruit
farmin' in Africa. They clear out just the same; but to the
French Riviera where they buy villas which resemble iced
weddin' cakes and spend their time playin' bridge under
awnin's on the beach at Monte, aching with nostalgia for
the things they've left behind. They shoot clay pigeons
instead of partridge and pheasants; play tennis when they
should be huntin', and fish an occasional trout from the
streams above *Piera Cava* instead of workin' their own
rivers. Grr.'

'Which brings me to the crux,' Gyles added after a telling
pause. 'I am all for stayin' and fightin' to hold on to what
I have in trust for you. I decided long ago that to ensure
this castle is properly maintained, staffed, and above all the
entailed capital intact by the time I take the swan's path,[1]
everything must pay for itself. As a long term policy this is
the only possible way it can be done. I worked the problem
out in relation to our old way of life. We had pheasants and
partridge, the occasional snipe and woodcock. We shot 'em
for pleasure, and gave rather splendid shooting parties. The
bag graced our tables, the surplus went to less fortunate
friends, the local hospital and other deservin' causes. Now
I sell the surplus, havin' found a suitable market. We're
currently breedin' apace to increase revenue. We have
added flocks of guinea fowl, duck and geese to sustain the
market when game is not in season and thus we justify the
retention of the staff concerned. That little section *is* now
self-supportin'. Presently it will begin to bring in extra
revenue so we shall then, hopefully, show a profit. You don't
need me to give you other examples, you know it all; but
what we have done already is as nothing to what we shall
have to do to keep pace with inflation which, I may add, has
come to stay. Never again will the working man pay
tuppence for a pint of ale and threepence for a packet of
cigarettes. If you want an example nearer to home the black
stockings worn by the maids which cost us ninepence a pair

[1] *The Lormes of Castle Rising.*

before the war are now double the price, while the liveries for the men have gone up by thirty-three and a third.' He became reflective at this point. 'I once read a definition of wealth which vastly commended itself to me, "wealth is a high wall round a quiet garden shutting out the cries of noisy people". Given the first premise – that our privacy is safeguarded – I am now prepared to commercialise in every way possible to achieve my objective.' He broke off as the door opened disclosing Sawby.

'Well Sawby what is it?'

'A message from her ladyship my lord. She has sent me to ask if you could please join the ladies in the drawing room.'

'Ouch,' exclaimed Henry, 'you're in for a wiggin' sir. We've been in here an hour already. Just sum up for us before we go.'

'No,' Gyles refused, 'you do it. Dammit you're the heir.'

Henry flung him a reproachful look, hesitated, then took the plunge.

'Alright then. As I see it we become tradesmen, capitalising on our existin' assets, boostin' them to the top of our bent in order to keep not only the servants and estate workers but also us, your sons. We hang onto the old life for just as long as we can by makin' this great place earn its keep. *Toujours fidèle* in fact to a way of life which I for one think is just about perfect. Will that do sir?'

'Yes,' said Gyles rising, 'that will do very well. Now let us join the ladies.'

CHAPTER 8

Johnathan Brownrigg

The women of Castle Rising had reached the shoulder-shrugging stage concerning what Petula called 'those dreary cattle'.

Even when such topics had been exhausted, other anti-social contributions were made by the men with wearisome frequency. The Lorme ladies were compelled to listen with as much reluctance as they dared show while Gyles pontificated on the prime cause of trouble – the government. As a result of their bungling, so he assured everyone, a disastrous situation had been created both for farmers and for landowners who had obeyed the war-time call to sow more wheat in order to compensate for the fall in the imports of foreign wheat reduced by one third when the sea lanes were menaced by German U-boats.

Every available acre then went under the plough in order to make up those wheat deficiencies. Men like Gyles and Charles Danement took the financial strain for their tenant farmers by meeting the cost of seed, up-to-date farm machinery and the new fertilisers. Henry scandalised his wife by referring to the salesmen of these last as 'tin shit merchants'.

In those troubled times during the recent war, with his own son at sea and he a widower, Charles Danement had closed up his Manor House, except for the quarters he allocated to two aged and homeless folk bombed out in an early Zeppelin raid who were only too thankful to act as caretakers. He moved into the Castle and from there somehow contrived to run both estates in concert with the equally overworked Gyles. Then land girls replaced the men who had volunteered. These too were housed and fed within the Castle by ex-suffragettes like themselves. It all worked astonishingly well except that it soon became plain to everyone that three women, working very long hours indeed, still only just managed to encompass the work previously done by two men with shorter working hours. On top of all this the difference between the volunteers' pay packets and their service pay was made up by the two landowners at a time when wages everywhere had already begun the upward rise which was to be a permanent feature of post-war life.

The Armistice was signed at last. In 1919 there was a fine, hot summer and farmers everywhere were able to gaze with justifiable pride on the fat heads of golden English corn which ripened into a bumper harvest. In 1920 the crunch came again when the government did its lunatic worst by removing the embargo on foreign imports.

As foreign grain poured in once more, so of course the price of home produce plummeted, resulting in panic among the unfortunate farmers. In many instances those who had not been helped by the owners of the big estates had slaughtered their cattle and sheep for food, taking whatever prices they could in order to use the money – ironically referred to by many as 'cloven hoof money' – for re-equipping as best they might in order to achieve a turn over to arable farming. They found themselves now with nothing left in their old woollen stockings or post office accounts let alone on the credit side for the very few who had banking accounts. They then faced yet another turnabout.

Gyles and his kind did what they considered as no more than their duty; they financed this second switch-over, doing so on a 'settle gradually without crippling yourselves' basis. This was when Gyles and Charles developed a positive fixation over investments in pedigree cattle. They knew that Aynthorp Enterprises were selling from present stock as much butter as could be churned and put up in pats with a fleur-de-lys stamped upon each pat. They knew too that the same could be said of cream. *Ergo* they must clearly increase production and while doing so, must maintain the very highest yield quality by investing in pedigree stock.

One enthusiasm led to the next. They became convinced that similar sales would result from producing old English cheeses so as Andrew had suggested they decided to buy goats and emulate France in the production of goat cheeses. They already knew that the Castle's first business venture could clear all prime beef especially if it were butchered by skilled men, thus ensuring much better prices. Charles Danement declared his intention to build smoke houses so that he could undertake the smoking of venison from Gyles' Scottish deer. Gyles would then buy back from him through 'AE', as the boys called their company, selling it to the hotels and restaurants whom they already supplied with eggs, game, poultry, cream and butter. One other thing Gyles then proposed to Charles; that he should also smoke 'Aynthorp Salmon' from Clangowrie waters.

Their menfolk were well and truly 'gone away' on these new hobby horses and petticoat rebellion was imminent when Gyles astutely enquired of his wife if, despite all she had to do already, she could possibly give 'another of our traditional shootin' parties, with shootin' luncheons accordin' to the gospel of m'y late father.'

Christine's face lit up at the proposal. It was left to Petula to exclaim, 'And is everything to be exactly as it was in darling Grumpy's day?'

'Exactly so my dear,' Gyles smiled, inwardly congratulating himself upon the astuteness of a move which had been deliberately engendered as a sop to Cerberus.

'I thought,' he explained, 'that we might ask old Cubby, Ted Fotheringham and of course Podge, always provided he doesn't go berserk and shoot another beater in the gaiter. Make it a small house-party my love if you please and give old André his head over the dinners. I am beginnin' to think that below stairs is becomin' a trifle restive in their stalls. We aint done any proper entertainin' for quite a while.'

This greatly reduced the rebellious atmosphere both above and below stairs as Above launched its collective self upon a lavish spending spree, an exercise in which they all rejoiced, particularly on those auspicious occasions when the expenditures seemed justified; while planning, polishing and predicting replaced grumbling in both Servants' Hall and Steward's Room.

In the middle of all this Stephanie was rushed into the Convalescent Wing of the war-time recuperation nursing home trailing in her wake a white-faced and speechless

Harry. She was already well into her first pains, long before the happy event had been predicted.

Henry's contribution was a muttered comment to his wife as he prepared to drive down to the village to collect Lady Constance whom the Manor reported had gone shopping. He said, 'About time too, if you ask me that poor girl had the largest bun in her oven I have ever seen. If she'd've gone on any longer she must surely have burst,' after which he flung himself over the door of his car and set the vehicle screaming down the drive.

A few hours later Dr Jamieson remarked to Constance as he washed up, 'It is a curious thing my dear, but you know my dear father always declared that in all his forty-nine years as a hard working GP he had never delivered a seven month old baby which was not the first. He should have been here to see his record broken for I'll undertake this child is well ahead of its time and the parents already married for several years, eh?'

In a surprisingly short time he delivered Stephanie of a sturdy son. Furthermore there were no complications which prompted him to murmur as he held up the newcomer and slapped him, 'Easiest delivery I've had between these ancient walls for a great many years.'

Dead on cue the scrap yelled in confirmation.

Again, after an astonishingly brief interval, the family were admitted to see Stephanie propped up in bed, backed by an immensity of pillows, looking almost pretty, with the sleeping babe in her arms and her now normal-coloured spouse beaming fatuously down upon them both from his vantage point at the head of the bed.

'Have you decided what to call him love?' Henrietta asked, her tears falling like summer rain.

'Of course Mama,' Harry smiled. 'Sinclair.'

He was rewarded by such expressions of wonder and delight by the grandparents that Harry swallowed convulsively, finding himself in peril of disgracing himself with an unmanly display of emotion. This was mercifully unseen as all eyes were upon Grandpapa Sinclair who proceeded to entangle himself in a welter of stuttering transports.

That night, as long established custom decreed, the baby was toasted, even so this simple ceremony was not enacted without the gravest misgivings by all present, for tradition also required that the youngest male in the family propose the toast. This meant Rupert who was led down in the custody of the man whom Rupert's brothers referred to as 'Rupert's Keeper'.

After his conversation with Christine Gyles had absented himself for just long enough to visit Doctor Barnardo. The invitation, when it came, was warm but to Gyles' surprise the meeting was not to be at any of the good Doctor's Homes but at his own estate which Gyles was surprised to find was also in Essex. During luncheon he soon learned that the Doctor needed no spur to talk about his orphaned children. Then when the two settled in a small study overlooking a pleasant lawn Gyles found no difficulty in speaking of his own predicament. In so short a time the reserved Gyles felt no qualms at recounting Rupert's peccadilloes to a man in whose discretion he felt absolute confidence from the onset.

Promising nothing, but undertaking to see what he could do to help, the Doctor saw Gyles off with renewed thanks for the very generous cheque which he had left behind him for the orphans. All was duly reported to Christine and within a few days a letter came suggesting Gyles interview a young man called Johnathan Brownrigg who had just come down from Cambridge with two blues, for Rugby and Boxing, together with a First in English. The Aynthorps promptly instigated enquiries of their own via the inestimable Trusloves, father and son who had been the family's lawyers for many years as their forbears had been.

Gyles found old Mr Truslove had become very frail, though he still held tenaciously to the reins. Gyles thought amusedly that even a suggestion that the old man might well hand over the reins to his son and replica would very probably have killed him.

He spent an hour with them both and drank some very distinguished sherry in their company. Driving home he reflected on how apt had been his wife's nickname for them, 'The Pelicans', inspired by their twin habit of poking their attenuated noses forward with pecking movements as they pored over whatever papers were spread before them. Both wore spectacles. Both pairs had a marked tendency to slip forward down their long beak-like noses and both, while looking as if they had been born old and thin, were as astute and discreet as it was possible for a pair of dry old legal birds to be. The family had a great fondness for them and owed them much for their unswerving loyalty and invaluable assistance over the years.

Gyles duly supplied this pair with Dr Barnardo's letter, recounted Rupert's wickednesses yet again, listened to their 'tch ... tch' comments ... and left the rest to them.

When they asked him to visit them once more they made their report. Johnathan Brownrigg was the only son of an impoverished widower cleric whose wealthy brother had undertaken to pay the piper for the boy's education. His generous Uncle Tom put a limit to his generosity when he sent for the young man and stated, 'With a gentleman's education behind you, brains, brawn and good blood to aid you, I feel that I am justified in telling you that from now on you must stand upon what I perceive are your two rather over-large feet. I believe though that I can possibly qualify this by also telling you that if you do well there might just be more coming to you ... one day.'

The Aynthorps sent for Mr Brownrigg in order to advance to him what they considered was a monstrous proposition and certainly one which no young man in his right mind would entertain. Therefore more in desperation than in any hope of acquiescence they asked him to family luncheon which was something of an ordeal in itself. He appeared unruffled by it however, displayed manners which pleased them greatly and was duly led away thereafter to Gyles' old office, while the drawing room party passed first judgements on their guest over coffees and *tisanes*.

The Dowager spoke first, pronouncing him 'Charmin'.' Christine merely stirred her coffee thoughtfully, but remained silent, while Henry contributed, 'One can't deny the feller has a dashed easy manner and for my money he's no fool either.' After a pause he added, 'Excellent in a tight corner too I should imagine, hands like hams and shoulders like a prizefighter.'

In the old office Gyles invited his guest to put on a pipe if he wished. When both pipes were drawing satisfactorily he then went directly to the heart of the matter, describing with complete accuracy the tally of sins for which his six-year-old was answerable. When he had done.... 'I'll take him on sir, if you think you can accept me,' said Johnathan eagerly.

Gyles looked startled. 'My dear chap ... are you sure?'

'Oh yes sir, you see I am going into teaching, hopefully at my old school.'

'Which was?'

'Harrow, sir. Headmaster's House.'

'Good Gad! How fortuitous. I was there meself long before your time. But why teachin'?'

Mr Brownrigg almost obscured himself in clouds of tobacco smoke before managing rather shyly, 'I'm interested in people, sir. My pater was a great friend of Dr Barnardo who runs those homes.'

'Was he now?' Gyles had no need to stimulate interest. 'Capital feller who has done an uncommon amount of good in my opinion.'

'Yessir. He said something once which caught my attention ... "give me a child before it's seven and I can do almost anything with it ...".'

'You ain't got much leeway with my son,' Gyles pointed out drily.

'I know that too, sir; but I have some, and, well some rather special stock to work on wouldn't you say?'

Gyles looked doubtful. 'We don't always breed true,' he reminded him quite reluctantly. 'There have been some shockers here and there down the line.' His voice trailed off. He had a sudden flash that there was more behind this than had been said; but for once was a trifle at a loss as to how to continue probing. He managed, 'To put not too fine a point upon it Mr Brownrigg there have been some pretty ripe bastards in my family down the centuries.'

'I, er, have heard talk of it, sir.' The young man nodded.

'Have you biGod ... then may I, without offence, be permitted to enquire if you are not also hedgin' slightly with me?'

The other laughed. 'You are sir and I am,' he admitted. 'One is, er, diffident you must allow but, well it's really very simple. You see I have a hunch that I shall finish up in the Church; but frankly I find so many clerics whom I believe are failing because they lack a proper understanding of human frailties. No man can hope to bring God to His people, or His people to Him, if they lack balanced experience of the human race. I intend to find employment first in the specialised field of what people are all too prone to dismiss as unmanageable children. *If* I can succeed in taming a few of them I shall feel more grounded for tackling older ones. In fact this egotistical man's project' – he inverted his pipe stem and prodded himself in the chest – 'is then, but only then, to have a shot at older ones whom I still believe can be salvaged despite my admiration for Dr Barnardo's ruling.' He smiled deprecatingly, 'I hope that doesn't sound pompous and silly sir, nor the fact that I intend doing a stint in one of HM's prisons later on.'

Gyles shook his head. 'No it does not, but can you also explain to me how Harrow fits your plan?'

'The principle of learning to walk before I run and an exercise in the Aristotelian proposition. If you can tell me any surer way of finding out what I'm made of than by trying to control, teach *and* win the friendship and respect of that Machiavellian cross-section of humanity lumped together as public schoolboys, I should be glad to know of it. They are clear-sighted, devious, deceitful as part of their essential protective colouring at the same time but, in the main, they are painfully accurate in their judgements. So if I can win them I might just have the courage to make an attempt upon men's souls.'

'If it's any criteria,' said Gyles gravely, 'put me down as one of your supporters. Now let us understand very clearly. My son Rupert is a small fiend and I dread what his uncontrolled temper may bring him to if this is left to develop. Should you tame him at all, thus givin' the women of my family a measure of tranquillity; and should you be able to reduce the amount of damage he wreaks on himself as well as everyone else once that shockin' temper is up – which is whenever he is flouted – you can truly claim to be walkin' in the steps of the Master in my opinion. It would be nothin' short of a miracle in fact. So, let us get down to details. I offer you six hundred a year, comfortable private quarters, the daily pleasure of winin' and dinin' – for we have a superb chef . . .' He ran on, sensing that it was expedient to give this young man time to reorient himself after such revelations which he felt were very rarely given. 'Mark you, I know well enough the blighter is savin' from what I pay him in order to retire to a small restaurant in France; but while he lasts, dinin' can be an experience. Oh, there is another small thing, do you by any lucky chance shoot?'

'I do sir. A pal of mine at Cambridge used to invite me. I could never run to good guns, but he supplied me.'

Gyles nodded approvingly. 'Then pray number among your more arduous duties comin' out with us to help decimate our birds. We're strong on pheasant and partridge, bag an occasional snipe and do quite a bit of duck shootin' around the marshes hereabouts.'

'*Scilicet atque Ossae frondosum involvere Olympum,*' Johnathan quoted smilingly.

Gyles nodded. '*Inceptis gradibus plerumque et magna professis. Purpureus late qui splendeat. Adsuitur pannus,*' he responded. Then, breaking their mood with a brisk, 'Then that's settled,' he rose, crossed to his desk and asked as he sat down, 'When could you join us?'

'When you wish sir.'

Gyles scribbled for a moment, ripped out a cheque and proffered it.

'Travellin' expenses,' he explained, 'and a little bit on the side to repair any gaps in your wardrobe. No pray do not thank me. The bargain is all on my side I do assure you. Come along now, we will go to tea. It will give you another chance to get the hang of this family of mine.'

He glanced down at his Borzoi who had arranged herself over Johnathan Brownrigg's feet.

'So ho,' he chided her, 'faithless! Like all women. You like him my girl?'

Diana gazed thoughtfully at her master then turned her beautiful head and licked the hand which gentled her.

'I see,' Gyles nodded, 'but will you release him now please. Tea!'

It was after tea on this day that Stephanie went to the convalescent wing. When the tea equipage was retrieved by Raikes and Edward, Christine invited Johnathan to stay the night, assuring him that Pine would supply him with whatever he needed.

'I only hope,' she added, her eyes on his massive shoulders, 'that Pine can fit you. He has never failed us yet. Now
would you care to come up to the nursery and meet your
hair-shirt?'

They climbed the staircase, chatting easily. Christine
asked if she might call him Johnathan, was rewarded by a
shy smile, then, as he held open the door of the day nursery
both were assailed by pandemonium. They went in.

Rupert was struggling on the Nursery floor. He was
locked in combat with his brother Richard – six fighting
fourteen – the tea table was in chaos, the smaller children
screaming and Nanny fielding falling crockery while Doris
tried to quieten the brood. The carpet was a shambles
of broken cakes, overturned jam dishes and broken
biscuits.

'With your permission, Lady Aynthorp,' murmured
Johnathan striding into the tangle of flailing legs and arms.
He plucked Rupert up, held him aloft, shook him like a rat
and then stopped, holding him dangling, yelling abuse and
flailing unsuccessfully.

'When you shut up,' Johnathan told him, 'I will release
you. Understand please that I am very strong so can dangle
you like this for simply hours.' He shook Rupert once more.
The remainder of the nursery folk silenced and stared.
Christine stood quite still in the doorway. Rupert continued
to howl and flail.

'Shut up at once,' ordered Johnathan, 'or you will be very
sorry.' Rupert yelled on. 'So with your permission Lady
Aynthorp?' Johnathan murmured again, moving towards
the door. Christine stood aside at once to allow this astonishing young man to pass, her mouth twitching as he went by.

Down the staircase went the diminishing shrieks, across
the hall to where Johnathan wrenched open the doors with
his free hand and ran Rupert, still dangling, down the steps
and towards the stables where he had seen Plum filling up a
large horse trough from a hose just before luncheon. He
strode over to this trough.

'Cool down,' he advised, plunging Rupert into the cold
water. When he came up spluttering, incredulous,
Johnathan asked cheerfully, 'Feeling better?'

'Shit on you, you stinking bastard,' Rupert spluttered.

'From a count of three you'll be dunked again,' he warned catching him by the arm as he tried to climb out.

'Now, one, two ...'. On the count of three Plum stepped out of his lair in time to see the bright head vanishing under the water as 'three', shouted Johnathan and pushed him in again.

As the child surfaced, 'I'll dunk you like a doughnut into coffee,' Johnathan told him hauling him into the air again dripping and coughing.

'I hate you!' Rupert shrieked.

'Don't give a hoot about that. Want some more? Right,' and down he went again. On the fourth emergence Rupert wailed on an entirely different note, 'Lemme go you stinking beast ... lemme go. ...'

It took seven dunkings, watched by Plum who stood straddle-legged with his eyes gleaming. Ultimately a dripping, choking surrender saw Rupert carried into the harness room, enveloped in a noisome old horse blanket and rubbed down with such vigour that he was completely floored at last.

Then he stood, sullen, head-hanging, panting. 'Who ... are ... you anyway?' he managed.

'Sir,' prompted Johnathan.

Rupert hesitated, then, 'Sssir,' came out at a mumble.

'I am your new tutor. My name is Johnathan Brownrigg and what you have just experienced is only a tiny foretaste of your future experiences you dirty-mouthed little boy. If after this you do not behave, or, conversely *if ever* you dare behave as you did just now in the Nursery I shall make your life pure hell. I will chuck you into horse manure, dunk you into ice cold water, wallop you until you cannot sit down. I promise you I will make your life awful unless you choose to behave like a civilised human being and not a wild beast. So *you* just make up your mind which way you want it to be. I don't care one way or the other. It is just part of my job you see, so, either you treat with me or you take the consequences. It is your choice.' He nodded to Plum, said, 'Thanks a lot,' and grinned at him as he began hauling Rupert back the way they had come.

That night, after little Sinclair's arrival, when the summons came for the youngest Lorme male to propose his health Gyles still hesitated.

'Oh please sir,' urged Johnathan, 'let me try.'

'Cut along then,' Gyles agreed. Johnathan did so.

He returned with Rupert, hand held in a grip which gave him the message – eloquently – that struggling would merely prove very painful. The boy had been bathed, changed and hair brushed until the 'Lorme' colour shone like burnished copper. He was neat, tidy, subdued. He also managed to look very small and defenceless. Johnathan ignored this. Nor did he think fit to tell the assembly that a few moments before he had sat on the little termagant in order to teach him what he must do.

When Rupert had completed the ritual, clearly thinking he had won a bisque for his good conduct, 'Papa,' he said pleadingly. 'Please Papa . . . I promise I will try to be a good boy . . . but do I really have to have this cruel, awful brute to look after me?'

Gyles looked down at the beautiful scrap of humanity which he had sired. He hardened his heart. 'I very much regret the answer is "yes", my son. By the way, you will remember that in future you always say either Mr Brownrigg or else address him as sir. Never again let me hear you call a stranger in my castle a cruel, awful brute. Oh, and one other thing; it may interest you to hear that Mr Brownrigg is really a very charmin' feller. He is in fact two fellers as far as you are concerned, turnin' in a flash into your cruel, awful brute the very instant you misbehave in any way; otherwise bein' a most interestin' and kindly companion. Do you understand?'

'Yyyyes sir,' Rupert stared at the floor disconsolately.

'Now kindly say goodnight to everyone and then go straight up to the Nursery or I shall refuse to answer for what Mr Brownrigg will do to you; except I can undertake it will be horrible.'

Rupert hesitated. He turned to look pleadingly at his mama; but her face was turned away. He looked back at his papa who had begun drumming a trifle impatiently upon the table top.

'Now Rupert,' said papa very quietly. Everyone else was examining the patina of the dining room table as if they had never seen the like of it before. Draggingly, disbelievingly, yet having had sufficient experience of Mr Brownrigg being 'awful' not to take any more risks for one day, Rupert went from the room and began climbing the staircase, a small, pathetic figure which tore at his mother's heart strings as the little devil meant it to do; but she made no move and Rupert continued straight on up and into the Nursery. What happened thereafter was told to the senior servants in the Steward's Room by Nanny Rose.

'He come in, dragging his feet he was. Then he stood for a minnit looking at me. He pulled one of those awful faces, then he said, "I'm going to bed, anything's better'n being with you lot in here." He undressed hisself too. Of course I found his clothes was flung any which ways; but there was no more trouble with him that night. There was in the morning though 'cos Mr Brownrigg – ooo ain't he handsome – he come in jest as I was opening up. He asked me – ever so serious – to tell 'im exactly what happened. So I did. He thanked me, so polite too – then he marched into Master Rupert's bedroom, who was dressed by that time. Would you believe it? He made that child take all his clothes off again and fold them neatly on his chair. Then he made him dress again. He did it three times until Master Rupert was near to tears. Then he come into the Day Nursery with him and asked if he could stay to breakfast; but afore Master Rupert could get to his chair he made him apologise for what he said to me. Then he said ever so quietlike, "Until you and I can trust Master Rupert I shall not leave him lest he misbehave; but each week I will let him have one meal without me in here. If he does anything naughty then I shall throw him back into the horse trough, take him out and chuck him back again at least ten times."

'Then in a changed voice, ever so nice and gentle, he began talking to the other children. But he went back to the old stern voice when Master Rupert reached for a hot roll, and you all know how much he loves them rolls. Mr Brownrigg said "No rolls for Master Rupert please Nanny until I say so. Just give him porridge and milk with no sugar please." You should a seen Master Rupert's face. He pushed the porridge I set before him away, saying "I don't like porridge." Mr Brownrigg was on to him in a flash. "Alright then, let's start the day," says he getting up and leaving his own breakfast, "Nanny will give you the porridge for

luncheon won't you Nanny?" So o'course I says, "If you say
so sir." Then he dragged Master Rupert orf and ran with
him all the way down the drive right to the main gates and
back again. He did that three times. Mr Plumstead told me
'cos ee was crossing the Park and heard wot happened as well
as saw it all. Master Rupert gasped out "Alright I'll be
good", and stood heaving and panting until he got his breath
again. Mr Plumstead said as how Mr Brownrigg wasn't even
breathing heavy.'

'I wonder wot 'appened next,' said Mrs Parsons longingly.

'Boxing,' supplied Sawby shortly, 'with Mr Brownrigg
on his knees. He's a Cambridge blue. By the time he'd done
Master Rupert was flat on his back, but he gasped out, "I'd
like to box like you" and he said "sir".' He paused, reflected
then added, 'If I was a gambling man Mrs Parsons I'd offer a
hundred to one on the tutor.'

Johnathan's policy was very simple. First he wore the
child down physically. Then he talked to him and by this
gradually won his interest. At luncheon on that first day
Rupert polished off the cold congealed porridge and asked,
'Can I have something else please, Mr Brownrigg?'

He was given pudding. He ate three helpings. Then came
lessons which went on until tea was ready. By the time
Rupert had drunk his tea and stuffed himself with three
boiled eggs and dry bread he fell asleep at the table.

'All yours Nanny,' said Johnathan rising, 'but may I carry
him through for you?' And he picked him up gently, said
'Goodnight and thank you for your co-operation', to Nanny
Rose and after she had undressed Rupert he went off to
change for dinner.

That night Johnathan asked for and obtained an audience
with Gyles, privately. He requested permission to stay on
without collecting his personal possessions for a while, and
having obtained it he joined Henry for five hundred up in
the billiards room, beat him easily and then retired for the
night. The family metaphorically held its breath.
Meanwhile Gyles arranged for Grantham to collect Mr
Brownrigg's baggage.

On the third day Rupert actually asked him about his
boxing blue and made valiant attempts during the next
session to feint in imitation of his tutor. Then he asked if Mr

Brownrigg could climb. He was very thoughtful for a while after being given the details of his tutor's mountaineering experience; deeming it fruitless to challenge with his own tree-climbing, in the light of these disclosures. For his part Johnathan was elated by the boy's retentive memory, this he promptly taxed; but always with the rider 'I don't for a moment suppose you can remember all this' and exulting when a few days later on questioning him he found Rupert remembered every detail. He soon discovered that the boy was his for just so long as he could maintain ascendancy in everything. Then one fine morning when they went riding together Rupert gained the ascendancy – for the first time.

They sat on a piece of picket fence afterwards, one very small figure in jodhpurs with a velvet cap pulled down over his curls, and one very large man similarly accoutred from the funds contained in Gyles' cheque.

'You ride well,' Johnathan told him experimentally.

'I know,' said Rupert simply.

'Hands a bit hard but then that's your nature, you can overcome it if you try.'

'I like the feeling of power,' Rupert murmured.

'You'd be a better horseman than I am if it wasn't for those hard hands,' Johnathan said regretfully.

Something flashed in the child's eyes. 'Yours are pretty hard at times too ... sir.' His eyes darkened as he spoke, clearly anticipating trouble; but Johnathan decided to take him seriously.

'Agreed,' he said placidly, 'but then no one handles a wild stallion as they would a delicate young mare.'

'I see.' Rupert thought for a bit, kicking his heels against the fence. Then to Johnathan's astonishment he said, 'I suppose no one can be best at everything. I shouldn't worry if I were you, I have been thinking and I believe it is only that you haven't had much practice. Hen's a ripping horseman – better'n me I think, but don't ever tell him I said so ... er, please ...' After more thought Rupert said regretfully, 'You do so many things well don't you?'

Johnathan said quickly, 'It's not important. What matters is trying to do whatever it is better each time and above all being sporting about losing.' He spotted interest in the wide brown eyes. 'My mother did something to me once when I was very small I remember!'

'Much smaller than me?'

'Oh yes, about two and a half I think. I fell down as I ran to her over gravel. It skinned my knees and I hollered. She was shocked. Do you know what she said?'

'What – sir.'

'She said, "Stop crying Johnathan do. Apologise to the path *immediately*; how do you know you haven't hurt it more?"'

'This was such a remarkable idea that I stopped yelling at once. It is a silly story; but there is a principle behind it. It is in the Winchester College tag "Manners Maketh Man".'

In the end this constituted a lesson which grasshoppered from apologising to gravel to the conduct of aristocrats as they travelled in tumbrils towards the guillotine in the Place de la République in Paris, and ultimately to a dismounting from the picket fence for a slow stroll down to the lake to feed the swans. There they settled together on the seat beside the water and Johnathan explained that so many of those aristocrats whose heads fell into the dreadful baskets bought much of it upon themselves by heedlessness. Thus he not only held the boy's attention, but was able to amplify still further; drawing a parallel with landowners of today whose good manners failed them to the extent of neglecting their less fortunate dependents. He was even able to show that not only was thoughtlessness the father and mother of neglect, but also that Rupert's father, his employer, was such a splendid fellow, like *his* father, Rupert's late grand-father, who really had been what a man called Chaucer had called 'a very parfit, gentle knight'.

When luncheon was over Johnathan was given the morning's facer anent Justin Aynthorp with the observation from Rupert, 'I bet he hadn't got a wicked temper like me.'

'But he had,' Johnathan assured him, 'so has your father; but both have learned control,' hearing as he spoke the feet of Ananias thundering but committed to what he normally regarded as a very grave offence, that of making the ends justify the means.

At dinner that night joining the new-come guests already

assembled for the shoot Gyles asked him, 'Feel you could leave Rupert tomorrow and join the guns?'

He hesitated, asked leave to discuss the matter later and after some considerable heart-searching told Gyles, 'I have to start sometime sir,' he said, 'but it's very early days. I will only take the risk if you say so.'

'You must do as you think fit,' Gyles replied, 'let's leave it until the mornin'.' After which he became convulsed when Johnathan recounted the exchange over the vital matter of Lorme tempers.

In the schoolroom the next morning Johnathan leaned back in his chair and appeared to be studying the ceiling.

'Thought I might go shooting today,' he told the ceiling.

'Can I come too?' asked a small, eager voice.

'Well now,' Johnathan transferred his gaze to his pupil. 'There's a problem. It's that temper of yours. You know how it flares up without warning don't you?'

'Oh but I promise to be good sir, honestly.'

Johnathan frowned, 'Even supposing one of the guns chooses to tease you? You see if you said "shit on you", as you did to me when I was a stranger or called a guest a bastard I should be the one to be disgraced. They would just dismiss you as a scandalously badly brought up little boy and I might even get sent away by your father.'

'I swear I won't sir, truly I won't.' Rupert urged him.

'But how can I be sure?' Johnathan debated aloud. 'I think I could be, if you agreed to stay here, work all morning and have your work ready for me when I get back. It would give me much greater confidence in taking a risk with you this afternoon.'

'What's the work I have to do?' Rupert countered.

'Very dull.'

'What kind of dull?'

'Go down to the stables, ask Mr Plumstead's permission, say I sent you and get him to let you muck out with one of the stable lads. Come in, clean up and eat your luncheon like a Christian. If both Nanny and Mr Plumstead give you a clean slate then you can come out with me this afternoon. You see that would give me the all important confidence . . .'

Rupert wriggled. 'Plum hates me,' he said uneasily, 'he

thinks I am the worst of all the Lormes. He says I'm a bad boy who'll come to a bad end.'

Johnathan rose. 'Prove him wrong then and you're on. Yes or No?'

Rupert slid down. 'Alright, you're on. Is it a promise?'

'Yes,' said Johnathan, 'cut along quickly before I change my mind.'

Rupert cut, Johnathan went to have a word with Nanny Rose then he hurried off, but not without considerable misgivings. And he was not the only one who was uneasy that morning.

CHAPTER 9

The Art of Shooting Partridges

Anne de Lorme was among the loaders. She had known this for some days which had in no way diminished her reluctance despite all that Gyles and Henry had done to teach her and make her like what they called the 'Art of Killing Partridges'.

This rather callous definition merely increased her distaste for what remained for her a cruel sport. This young girl's concept of art was Italy, the Renaissance and Leonardo da Vinci's sepia drawings of flying machines and flowers. It was also Spain's traceries in wrought iron, the pink lace of Palma cathedral and El Greco's painting of his own hand on the wall of a villa outside Toledo. Likewise it was Paris, the Louvre's Corots and *'La Victoire de Samothrace'*; though never religious paintings in galleries through which she hurried, loathing the dripping blood, the tortured faces and bodies almost as much as she did what she thought of as 'Rubens' roly-polys'.

Once, after a protracted session among these she had stripped off her own clothes and stood naked before a cheval glass. Her reflection gave her back long, slim thighs tapering down to extremely slender ankles and narrow feet. She thought her mount of Venus spoiled it, so pressed a slender hand over it to try the effect without it and hastily withdrew the hand as a most curious sensation shot through her. She looked upwards to her small, pointed breasts on which the nipples had hardened for an instant at her hand's contact below; then she reached for a hair brush from her coiffeuse and began brushing out her light, wavy hair. The relief this inspection gave her, as she accepted 'I'm no roly-poly!' was immense.

The reflected appearance of her own willowy grace and some other undefinable feeling she could not explain caused her to replace the hair brush and pull on her wrapper hurriedly as the thought came unbidden, 'What would Charles think of me if he saw me like this?' This led her to speculate upon a comparison of herself with Sue-Ellen whom she envied so desperately. She pushed this from her too, wandered to the windows and began staring out at the misty blue twilight scene.

Art, her thoughts reverted, was Degas and that controversial painter called Picasso and Angelica Kauffmann's ceilings and those miniatures by Fabergé. In all these this immature girl perceived some extra dimensional union between the visionary and the interpreter; while Rubens among painters she dismissed scornfully as 'just painting sex!'

How could there, she brooded, be any possible relationship between the arts I love and the senseless slaying of soft, wing-whirring little feathered creatures who swung so joyously in the air, only to be brought down to lie twitching in the stubble . . . to be gathered and flung into the game cart which so shudderingly invoked for her the plague carts, tumbrils and pyramids of dead bodies killed by disease, execution or wholesale slaughter in battle.

As was her nature she over-dramatised; but nevertheless she genuinely could not see art in the wholesale killing her father and her eldest brother supported so enthusiastically.

She dreaded the conversations she knew would occur as the beaters worked the birds, who were really little family people, struggling vainly to become re-united with their own and manifesting such dire distress at being driven to desperation – while the cries of 'hold 'em up', 'bring 'em round', 'let 'em come singly that's when we get a bag . . .' merely confirmed to her the breaking up of vital, contented families into corpses.

Anne stood obediently enough watching, waiting, but inwardly feeling sick. She glanced questioningly down the line of guns, positions drawn for, taken up, the little numbered ivory pegs the men drew for their positions rebestowed in their box. She heard Henry remarking to Johnathan, 'Expect you know well enough, we number from the right. Then after each drive we move on two places so that one becomes three, three becomes five and five becomes seven while seven goes to two.'

She saw Johnathan nod; saw her father sitting easily on his shooting stick, relaxed but missing nothing; saw a hare break cover and heard the crack of a gun. She saw the wounded hare head on, running unevenly now, heard the satisfied, 'He'll die alright,' and wished she could be like Lady Deadlock 'suddenly transported, if not to heaven then anywhere but here.' Then behind her closed lids her eyes reminded her that young Charles was not there, that Sue-Ellen was loading for his father, that Ninian was bringing his gun up to his shoulder. 'Oh nice shooting, very nice indeed Nin,' came from Henry as she opened her eyes just in time to do her job for Andrew, hand him his second gun, reload, regurgitate the spent cartridges onto the stubble as a further shot sent feathers tumbling through the air. Then her father's voice declared, 'That's eighteen partridge, one hare, and your pheasant Henry,' as the line of guns stirred and on the far left the shooting began again. The covey surged forward. The air was filled with the acrid smell of spent cartridges; the lovely crisp autumn morning was fouled by it. The leading bird crumpled, fell almost above her, as the flurry of them twittered out their fears ... and crack, crack, crack sounded their death sentences.

She dropped on her knees beside the now dead bird newly fallen beside her. She stroked its pierced little breast where the spots of blood were gathered, then suddenly she could endure it all no longer.

She flung down the gun she held, made a choking sound and fled.

She ran steadily, not really knowing where she went except that she was now drawing away from the 'carnage' ... the broken families of partridges, the little lost babies and their slain parents even now being added to the tally....

Unromantically she crumpled on the edge of a mangold wurzel field, put her hands over her face and wept for those shattered families of defenceless little creatures.

Young Charles, plodding along the hedge line almost fell over her. He exclaimed, 'Hi! what's the matter? Anne dear, whatever is wrong?' and knelt down beside her.

Never was transition more rapid from hell to heaven. The

tears wet on her cheeks she looked up. The face under the pulled down cap was so close ... so unbelievably close ...

'So unnecessary ...' she stammered, 'such cruel waste of grace and happiness ... all shattered by those guns.'

He patted her shoulder awkwardly, proffered a handkerchief from his sleeve, helped mop her off, saying as he did so, 'Never mind, stop cryin'. I hate it too. It's beastly, though I daren't admit to it ... I saw too many chaps ... during the war, you see. There now that's better.'

She looked up, smiling through the tears now. 'You too?' she widened her drenched blue eyes. 'Bbbut men like it ... daddy says it's an Art.'

'Well it ain't,' young Charles settled down beside her against the hedge, 'at least not to me. It's just slaughter. Mark you I'm a hypocrite.'

'Why?'

'If I followed it through I wouldn't eat 'em and I'm potty about roast partridge.'

'Sso am I,' Anne confessed, 'specially when André does them with juniper berries and his splendid sauces. We're bbeastly too Charles, such hypocrites.'

Charles sat back on his hunkers. 'Look here,' he suggested, 'why don't we both cut and run? We can make *some* excuse, I'll think of one. Let's walk back through the Zoo, we may be in time to see the penguins fed. I'm a penguin addict.'

Anne let him help her to her feet, brushed the clinging twigs from her heather-coloured tweeds.

Then he smiled gently, 'Maybe we can put it out of our minds,' he persuaded her, 'dismiss it as a necessary evil – if not for us. Do you like penguins?'

'Yes,' sniffed Anne, having a good blow. 'I adore them. They waddle so deliciously, I think they're the clowns of any zoo, sad and comical like pompous aldermen with bulging tummies. I expect they eat an awful lot of fish though.'

The sun had come out and with it the beginnings of a smile touched her still trembling mouth, 'Dear Charles you are kind, thank you so much,' she stammered.

'Kind?' Charles raised an eyebrow at this, 'at getting the chance of a stroll with a very pretty girl instead of joinin' the murder squad, you must be out of your mind!' He hesitated as if discovering the fact for himself for the first time.

'You *are* very pretty you know, especially when you smile.'

'Not as pretty as Sue-Ellen,' the words were out before she could stop them.

'Different,' said Charles giving a vicious kick to an obtruding lump of turned soil. 'She's older than you and me. She is more mature, poised, elegant somehow even when she's scruffy.'

His curious tone of voice made her widen her eyes. Then suddenly discretion flung to the lifting breeze she said, 'But still you're in love with her, aren't you Charles?'

He frowned. 'I think part of me will always be in love with her,' he said slowly, 'but that's entirely different. She was three years younger than Stephen and old Stephen was years older 'n me – he'd have been thirty-three this year.'

'Then how old *is* Sue-Ellen?'

'She's thirty,' Charles said slowly, 'but it's not only that. It's, well, she's so much more worldly and experienced than me. My pater says I'm a late developer. I think he means I'm a clot; but that doesn't alter the fact that whether I am or not Sue-Ellen is five years older than I am *and* . . . oh well what does it matter, she's not for me. I've begun to accept that now.'

Inexperienced as she was, startled as she was, and fighting to control an almost uncontrollable excitement at the turn their conversation was taking, Anne still had enough of the female's in-built self-protection to let this last comment go unremarked. Instead, somewhat artlessly she pointed out, 'Ninian's only two years older than you,' flushed up and wished the ground would open under her feet.

'Different thing again,' said Charles moodily, 'Nin's the very devil of a fellow! His war was a very different proposition from my war too. Besides James's death aged him. Some of us thought he would never get over it . . .' he lapsed into silence and they walked on.

Presently Anne said softly, 'But he's still younger.'

'Three years,' Charles agreed, 'with him it will never be noticed.'

He ran on ignoring her gasp as if thankful to confide in

someone. 'I may as well admit, I've been whistlin' up back alleys to the moon. She probably won't marry Ninian either anyway. He's such a stickler for what's what, so that damned money of hers will stand in his way if I'm not very much mistaken.' He broke off, 'I say I am an inconsiderate chump. Here I was intendin' to try and cheer you up and all I've done is moan over ... my own silly obsession.'

Impetuously she squeezed his hand, he responded and they went on holding hands and holding an even longer silence as they crossed into the lane; but even this seemed to have become more comfortable.

Then be began to dramatise himself saying, 'I won't deny I've taken a rotten toss; but am beginnin' to realise how hopeless it all is for me. It's a terrible blow, but when a chap begins to understand how futile a thing is, well, it's best to admit and call it a day, don't you think so?' he peered at her earnestly.

'Oh yes,' she breathed, 'I do Charles, indeed I do.'

'You're very understandin' and sympathetic,' he nodded. 'It's bin a great help talkin' to you. What would you say if I went and fetched my bus? We neither of us want to face the music just yet and there'll be some deuced awkward questions to answer whether we go back to luncheon at my place or yours. Supposin' we put off the evil hour a bit and go for a spin. We could find somewhere to have a bite in a pub if you're willin'.'

'A pub?' repeated Anne, wanting to pinch herself to see if this were real or if she were dreaming. 'I've never been in a pub. Oh yes please.'

'Nin takes Sue-Ellen,' he said defensively, 'so why the devil shouldn't I take you? Are you game?'

'Of course I am,' she said eagerly. 'It's high time I did what I wanted for a change. If you like I'll come with you and we'll skip the penguins ... this time,' she added hopefully.

'Then what are we waitin' for?' he caught her hand again. 'We can always the see the penguins fed tomorrow.'

Unbeknown to either Charles or Anne, Sue-Ellen had been watching Anne surreptitiously, suspecting that the girl detested her participation in the shoot and wondering what she could do to help. When she saw Anne bent over the dead bird, she defected for a moment, had a hurried word with the gamekeeper who was hovering nearby, with the result that as they were moving on anyway, by the time Andrew took up his fresh position in the line a beater had taken Anne's place as Andrew's loader. The head gamekeeper gave brusque instructions.

'Git along now and say as Miss Anne suddenly felt unwell. Don't gawp man, git . . .'

Thus but for her own specious, 'Pity about Anne,' during the luncheon break, and a comment from Gyles to the effect that he thought she looked, 'Under the weather poor lass', the incident went unremarked except for a grunted, 'You're a shockin' liar madam,' from Ninian *sotto voce*, and her warning reply, 'Shut up, I'll explain later,' to which he nodded, returning to the enormous portion of beef steak and kidney pudding on his plate.

These shooting orgies were among the few pleasures which had remained unchanged over the years. Very naturally they were not held during the war, but Christine and Sawby had conspired together this time with the result that it might have been 1909 when old Justin ruled the roost and not 1921, with Gyles playing host in his turbulent papa's stead.

The marquee had already been erected by the footmen, the hay boxes lifted out from the dray which Plum had seen was repainted and refurbished after its years of disuse. George and Edward laid the long table with a running commentary on the 'drill' for the footwoman Raikes' benefit, which ended, 'We only serve madeira,' George told her, 'wait a bit and I'll fetch the dry. We offers it to Mr Sawby first for inspection, then *they* sit about on them rugs — get 'em shook out for me like a good girl and I'll be back in a tick.' He vanished into the marquee and Raikes obediently began spreading a pile of thick tarpaulins on the ground. She then overlaid them with the dark green dray rugs with the big 'A' embroidered in yellow wool on one corner.

George came hurrying back with the silver tray on which old Justin had always been given his 'madeiry'.

Once this was set out with the buals and malmseys in their respective decanters Edward called from inside, 'They're comin', get yer Guernseys on or you'll get stropped by 'is lordship same as we was by the old 'un.'

They dived inside. Raikes looked doubtfully at her knitwear, then unfastened and removed her apron, assumed the Guernsey and re-tied the apron over the top, straightening her white cap – which was without streamers for out of doors – crouching to peer into the bit of looking glass which hung by a nail on one of the tent poles. Finally, hearing voices she grabbed her pair of white gloves and hurried out.

At this moment Grantham's head appeared over the hedge denoting the arrival of 'the ladies'. In tweeds and tongued brogues they dismounted and came through the gate. In moments the men joined them, walking towards them with caps pulled down, guns broken and under their arms. Gyles stretched his length beside his wife saying as he tossed away his cap, 'Capital mornin', m'dear, splendid bag. Gad I'm as hungry as a hunter!' Then Sawby approached, bowed and asked, 'May I serve the madeira now milord?'

The almost exact re-enactment of the pre-war scene when her father-in-law was alive made Christine's eyes sting for a moment. She remembered him so vividly, and in her imagination almost heard the stentorian roar as he spotted, during Sawby's bow, the absence of any Guernsey.

'You'll catch your death of cold man. Cut inside and you'll find one of my Guernseys, put it on, put it on and see to it the rest of 'em have Guernseys in future. Ask Mrs Peace,' then turning to his wife, Alicia, who had only ceased being present since his death, he groused, 'Have to think of everythin' around here . . . man's life's not his own . . . worn down with responsibility, that's what I am. Hi Sawby, more madeiry,' and waving his empty glass.

She caught Gyles' eye, read therein a reflection of her own nostalgic memories as Gyles lifted his glass towards her, 'Here's to the old octogeranium,' he toasted. 'Hope the shootin's as good where he is as it has bin for us this mornin'.'

She drank to that and was promptly launched by the men into the equally traditional shot by shot, stand by stand recapitulation on the morning's sport until she became aware of Anne's absence.

'What happened to my daughter?' she enquired.

'Felt a bit under the weather,' said Andrew hastily, having been already primed. 'Nothin' to fuss about, I think she must be teethin'.'

Presently they moved to table and Raikes went round with the footwarmers, tucking one over each pair of female feet. She then followed Sawby who carried the great steaming, napkin-wrapped steak and kidney pudding, handing red cabbage as was also statutory, while George dealt with the other vegetables.

'Cooked en salmi,' quoted Ninian reminiscently, helping himself hugely. 'Remember how the old boy insisted upon reciting the *modus operandi* every blessed time?'

'One presumes Christine,' said Gyles smilingly, 'that there is Mrs Parsons' famous treacle tart to follow?'

'Of course,' she affirmed, 'and the old silver bowl for the Jersey cream.'

A little later the cry went up from Gyles, startling Sawby by its similarity to another voice long since stilled, 'Where the devil is the Stilton! Sawby you haven't forgotten the Stilton damme?'

Almost trotting, Sawby just managed to reach his master's side on the last word, to which he appended, 'May I cut your lordship a wedge of Stilton before your treacle tart?'

Gyles beamed, then began expounding precisely as his father had done upon the correct way of cutting Stilton.

His old friend and guest, from across the table leaned forward and murmured, 'I trust, Gyles, you are limitin' the dinin' tonight after this Brobdingnagian feast?'

It was all the same and it set up a special ripple of security among them in those uneasy times of post-war difficulties.

'Makes one feel that ghastly war never happened, eh Harvey?' remarked another guest of his opposite number.

'Wonder how long it can last though,' came the depressing response.

Christine said softly, 'As long as can possibly be managed,' taking the port decanter, half-filling her glass and passing it on to her neighbour. By this time the servants were seated on packing cases tucking into their own pudding.

Gyles confided to his second son, 'I'll show you the game

book tonight when I fill in today's bag. I have a sneakin' suspicion that if we do as well this afternoon as we've done this mornin' we shall have an all-time record on our hands. It's most excitin'.' He broke off to exclaim, 'Good Lord look! Mama!'

The assembly surged to its collective feet as the dauntless little Dowager veiled, swathed in furs, walked towards them smiling graciously.

'Don't move everybody,' she called, 'I felt I just had to join you for a few moments.'

Sawby rushed up with a chair. When she was seated she explained, 'Plum – our old coachman – brought me in the dog-cart. Most invigoratin'. Gyles the port's with you, pray circulate . . .'

When the decanter reached her and she had poured a little into her glass, Gyles lifted his own to her. 'To you Mama,' he said smilingly, 'may you join us like this for many years to come.'

'I have every intention of so doing,' she retorted tartly, turning up her veil and sipping appreciatively. 'How was the mornin' pray?' So all had to be re-told before the guns moved off again, the beaters already heading round a field of kale.

Then Plum appeared to arm the Dowager to her trap, but she lingered on to have a few words with Sawby first.

'Was it ghostly?' she asked him knowing full well he would understand.

'Painfully so, my lady. Especially when his lordship called for the Stilton. It might have been his late lordship, gave me quite a start. For the rest I think it went off pretty well all things considered.'

She stretched out a tiny gloved hand and patted him on the arm. 'That's the trouble with growin' old Sawby,' she told him, 'and sometimes, later on of course, you will find, as I do, that one wonders which part is real, the rememberin' or the participatin'. It is one of the penalties of old age. Now good day to you and I trust you had an adequate luncheon yourselves.' She turned away. The butler stood looking after her. He watched as Plum gave her his arm and as the unlikely pair moved together towards the waiting vehicle, he thought, as he saw her being handed in, tucked up and cosseted, 'I wonder now how much she remembers of that other dreadful drive all by herself,'[1] before re-entering the marquee and being abruptly and to them unaccountably sharp with his staff.

'Wot's bit 'im?' grumbled George, packing up plates. ''E was alright until a moment ago, now 'ees like a randy bull.'

The truants strolled across Lorme land into Danement land, taking a short cut across the field which Charles' ancestor had won 'in fair combat' from Anne's, and so reaching the stables where Charles' small, red sports car stood waiting on the cobblestones.

Half an hour later Charles braked to his customary screaming halt and complaint of rubber on gravel outside a small lath and plaster hostelry before which dangled a graphic sign declaring itself somewhat ghoulishly to be the Stock and Gallows Inn. Over the lintel ran the statement 'Jeremiah Bowden. Licensed to sell Beer and Spirits.'

Their entrance caused much the same stir as the arrival of two peacocks would do among the St Paul's courtyard pigeons.

The landlord bustled forward to shoo them hastily through the sawdust floored 'public' into the saloon bar beyond.

'Ef only I'd knowed you was coming Mr Charles sir!' he backed up towards a dark oak settle and began polishing it with a corner of his old-fashioned leather apron. 'If you just set down here Miss Anne I'll fetch the missus seein' as how you fancy a bite to eat.'

'Don't fuss there's a good chap,' Charles begged him. 'We're playing truant an' this is Miss Anne's first visit to a pub.'

The landlord straightened up in alarm and so far forgot himself as to demand, 'Does 'er leddyship know you're 'ere Miss?'

'Of course not so don't you say a word will you?' the girl laughed. 'I say don't I know you? Weren't you and your wife at our last Barn Supper?'

'That I was Miss, fancy you rememberin'.' He seemed reassured by this and accustomed as he was to the vagaries

[1] Book 1, *The Lormes of Castle Rising*.

of the gentry decided that so long as he produced his wife the visit would acquire an air of respectability if the affair got out. 'Though I do wish you 'ad warned us so as we could 'ave done summat special.' He told them, obediently drawing a foaming tankard of ale, mixing a shandy gaff and carrying both back to their table.

'Now just you sup at that and I'll fetch Ma.'

'Your home made bread and some cheese will do,' Charles called after him, thus raising an outraged cry of protest.

Mrs Bowden emerged wiping her hands on her apron, bobbing, and saying doubtfully 'I've a piece of fresh-made rook pie in its own jelly Master Charles but I don't suppose that would be to your taste.'

'Why not?' asked Anne, 'I've never tasted rook pie. Do let's have it Charles.'

So Rook Pie it was, flanked by a jar of pickled eggs, a bowl of crisp lettuce hastily picked from the garden, a loaf of Mrs Bowden's home made bread and a rough pat of farm butter. They made a splendid meal.

'Rooks are tricky, aren't they,' Anne said suddenly, and with her mouth somewhat over full.

'You have to wring their necks the moment they are shot, I do know that,' Charles replied. 'Let's ask Mrs Bowden.'

The woman was brought in again and after her pie had been pronounced 'scrumptious' she confided 'There's still one old woman in Upper Aynthorp who makes 'em near as good as mine though I say so as shouldn't. We only takes the breasts and upper thighs, leaving the trotters to make the jelly set from the carcase stock, o'course we adds onions, bayleaves and a good pinch of country spices. There was a time too when she'n I was called upon to roast swan for the gentry's buffets. Nasty fishy flesh I found it but anyway them days is gorn. No one eats hedge'og any more either, which is tender and delicate baked in clay – well no one except them dratted tinkers; but there now you don't want to 'ear such things I'm sure, so I'll leave you in peace.'

'Don't go,' Charles pleaded, 'I've had an idea and I bet you could give me the answer. What about the carp in Lord Aynthorp's lake?'

The woman looked horrified. 'Now Master Charles that don't be a lake, as well you know, that's a stewpond where them fishes was bred in bygone days for the table, same as the white pigeons in your dove cote.'

'What! That old thing that m'y father still lets some of our retired estate workers maintain?' Charles registered disbelief.

'That's right sir, why when I was a girl we 'ad pigeon pie reg'lar and I've sometimes wondered why you don't encourage they fer selling. My nephew what went to America said that over there they call 'em squabs and they're specially fattened up to make mighty fine eating.'

'That's an idea,' Charles grinned. 'We could market a whole range and call 'em mediaeval delicacies, what else did they eat in olden times that we don't eat today?'

Mrs Bowden called across to her husband, 'Pa, did you hear the young gennuman's question? You know more about them days than wot I do.'

Bowden nodded. Charles added, 'Draw yourself a pint too Bowden and bring it over here. This could be very interesting.'

Presently Bowden closed and locked the doors, Mrs Bowden trotted off, returning a few moments later with a bottle of her own cowslip wine and some thimble sized glasses.

'Talking's thirsty work,' she announced setting down the opened bottle. 'But you'd best go cautious with this for it's mighty powerful if you haven't the habit of it.'

By the time the two truants drove home their mind was full of stewponds, stuffed carp, and pigeon breeding, though they drew the line at suggesting to their parents badger netted in the pool which was still in existence, or indeed the shooting of bittern.

When they parted outside the castle Anne put out her hand and said shyly, 'I've had a perfectly splendid day although it was so beastly to begin with. Thank you so much.'

Charles bent over the small, now distinctly grubby paw, kissed it lightly, jumped back into the car and as he drove off Anne was sure what floated back to her over the engine's roar was, 'I'll come and fetch you tomorrow, then we will go and see the penguins.'

She floated upstairs not wholly as a result of Mrs Bowden's cowslip wine.

Christine met her mid-way. 'Ah there you are darling, I hear you had a headache, is it better now?'

It was undoubtedly the cowslip wine which made Anne reckless. 'No Mama,' she said, 'I just ran away from the shoot. I think it's all so beastly. Young Charles found me and took me out for a drive. We've been learning about what our ancestors ate and we've got a perfectly splendid idea we'll tell you about at dinner.'

'Well you certainly look radiant now,' Christine smiled indulgently. 'Tell us all your news at dinner; but please do not hurt your father by letting him know your feelings, it would be a pity to spoil his day.'

As matters turned out it was not Anne but Sue-Ellen who raised the subject that night. They were eating a *tarte aux herbes* which Christine claimed was 'one of the best things I ever found in our old receipt books,' when the little Countess volunteered, 'It was brought from Normandy like so many of the dishes attributed to English cookery. I translated it from the original when I was quite a girl. Then it was adapted to suit our modern palates. I expect you know my dear that our ancestors used a great many more herbs and spices than we care for today simply because these sublimated the rather powerful condition of winter fish and fowl which had, er, somewhat over-ripened in the primitive storage.'

Gyles nodded. 'What always irritates me,' he told Sue-Ellen, 'is the general assumption that English cookery is indigenous.'

'Well isn't it?' Sue-Ellen's eyes widened. 'Surely the roast beef of old England, Yorkshire pudding, things like that are completely English.'

'They most certainly are not,' Gyles refuted her. 'It was the roast beef of Old Burgundy at the onset. Even the baron of beef was French, "*le grand baron*" in fact; while what is called Yorkshire pudding today was originally called *la gougère bourguignonne* and was brought back from France during the hundred years war by English mercenaries who joined in the fray for adventure, money and loot.' He paused, laid his long fingers tip to tip and resumed, 'I maintain there is no *cuisine anglaise*. Everything came from somewhere else in the first place. The Romans planted vines, introduced snails – by the by, Christine, I hear there's a feller at Batheaston today who hunts truffles with dogs and sells 'em to the fishmonger in Bath who still offers them to his regular customers. The marauding Norsemen taught the fisher folk of what is now called Yarmouth the art of salting herring and suchlike. In fact this was really the onset of importations from France of genuine *gros sel*. When Alfred burned his cakes they weren't cakes as we know 'em but cakes of unleavened bread baked on hot slabs of stone before a fire.

'Frankly the Saxon fed abominably. It was left to the Norman invader to introduce fine cookery to England. His cuisine was of course over-elaborate, absurdly garnished, over-spiced and over-sweetened – with honey; but from what those conquerors brought with them, the so-called English cookery evolved. The English adapted and did so very well in many instances; but the Lancashire hot-pot still derived from the Norman *hochepot*; the Scottish haggis began life in Normandy where it was called a *franchemoyle* and was eaten with *pommes vapeur* which the Scots were content to boil – which I frankly regard as a hanging crime; while it was left to the fugitive Huguenots, who fled from the Edict of Nantes and settled in the West Country, to ease their dire poverty by making and then hawking in the streets little cakes shaped like small suns and moons. Their street cry was "*Sol et lune*" which rapidly deteriorated into "Sally Lunn". But perhaps I bore you?' He broke off with the apologetic, 'Sorry, but it's a particular fetish of mine, tracing the origins of dishes.'

'It's fascinating,' exclaimed Sue-Ellen, 'but I do believe Anne and Charles are bursting to talk to you about their discoveries concerning carp.'

'Indeed?' Gyles turned to his daughter, 'why carp if one may ask?'

'Because Daddy' – Anne felt her way delicately, fearful of disclosing how their information had been obtained, 'we have learned that the lake isn't a lake at all but a very old fishpond and the carp in there are actually descendants of those netted and cooked on Fridays in Henry Tudor's time.'

Gyles nodded, 'Beastly scaly fish they were too.'

Henry then exclaimed, 'Well sir, surely we could sell 'em

to Jewish caterers. I've heard that Jewish people eat a tremendous amount of carp.'

Anne added excitedly, 'Charles was also talking of selling fattened pigeons as squabs, like in America. We understand our old dove cote is simply stuffed with them still.'

Gyles nodded. 'That is possible,' he agreed, 'but have you ever taken the trouble to see it?'

'No Daddy.'

'Well I recommend you to do so. The place is built like a round house with deep, tiered niches all around the inside wall which is tremendously thick. At the back of each niche there is a nestin' box, and regular inspection and muckin' out is done from a curious revolving stepladder which goes round and round attached to a primitive conveyor.'

Suddenly they all began talking at once. Out of the babble emerged Henry's, 'Don't you think, sir, that there might be something in the carp lark too?'

'I'm afraid not,' Gyles shook his head regretfully.

Then Richard who had been silent up to now said, 'If it's those tremendous scales which discourage you sir I can assure you they can be bred down nowadays. Frankly I'd be interested in lending a hand. I am sure you know already that carp are prolific breeders. The female throws up to half a million eggs at a time. With protection and proper care the catches could be enormous.'

The rest of the table had been watching and listening amusedly. Now the Dowager elected to speak.

'If as it appears we are to become tradespeople in order to survive in these precarious times,' she began a trifle tartly, 'it seems a viable proposition to me, my dear Gyles. You should announce them as bred and netted exactly as in Henry Tudor's time when he walked beside that stewpond ardently pressing his suit on Nan Bullen who steadfastly refused to be ravished except upon the marriage bed.'

'Now Mama,' Gyles expostulated.

'Now Mama nothing,' she retorted, 'I simply state that the idea appeals to me. What do you say Christine?'

Christine, who had been struggling to collect eyes, with marked lack of success, laughed lightly but refused to be drawn. Instead, as everyone turned towards her, she achieved her objective and in moments the men were left to their port. Richard instantly took the seat vacated by his grandmother on his father's right, while Andrew moved alongside Charles. It was plain that another hare had been started up among the menfolk of the ebullient family. To them Sawby, with a deferential little cough, eventually brought the information that their presence was requested in the drawing room.

'Damme how time flies,' Gyles brought out his half-hunter, flipped it open, and rose from his chair, 'I would never have believed we had spent three-quarters of an hour over our port, I think we had better postpone the rest of this discussion until we achieve the sanctuary of the billiards room.'

As they left the dining room, 'He's fallen hook, line and sinker,' murmured Henry to Richard, 'nice work Minimus, your de-scaling expertise did the trick y'know.'

CHAPTER 10

Such a Waste of Loving

A few weeks before Christmas the dinner table conversation drifted close to the quicksands of drama for Stephen Delahaye's widow Sue-Ellen. Since that day when she and her father had arrived unheralded and at a most unpropitious moment, the family had taken to the pair of them, virtually on sight. When Sawby showed them into the White Drawing Room none of them had the slightest idea that Stephen had ever married let alone got his bride with child before he was killed in France.[1]

Sue-Ellen charmed them. They also warmed instinctively to her bluff American father, Mr Blenkinsop, whom they all thought bore a remarkable resemblance to Mr Pickwick. A short while later, Mr Blenkinsop received an urgent summons to return to his native America. His ship was torpedoed and went down with all hands. Thus it was as a widow and an orphan that Gyles Aynthorp brought Sue-Ellen and her baby son back to Castle Rising. She endeared herself to them all. She grew into the family. The staff both indoor and out pitied and admired her this side of idolatry; but not one of them knew that Mr Blenkinsop's death had left her an immensely rich young woman, even by de Lorme standards. It was a shock to them. Plum predictably called her 'me luverly little hairess', and wooed her into his harness room with lardy cake and family gossip which she absorbed avidly. She also broke down Gyles' reserves quite unknowingly, until she called him Uncle Gyles and made of him a replacement father figure, taking licence with him which even his own children scarcely dared. She even brought happiness to her unfortunate in-laws Henrietta and Sinclair, taking pains to discuss every detail of baby

---

[1] Book 2, *War Comes to Castle Rising*.

Stephen's upbringing with them both, which had a magical effect upon the ravaged pair. It was not long before any one of the household, on being challenged, would have found it hard to remember a time when Sue-Ellen was not part of castle life.

Now sitting with her fair hair piled high, exquisitely gowned as were all the distaff side grouped around the dinner table, Gyles made the seemingly harmless remark to the table at large which had such a shattering effect upon Sue-Ellen.

'You know m'y dears,' he observed, 'I feel we have been most remiss in not offerin' some donation to those fellers in the river police. From what you boys have told me they were singularly obligin' over the affair of young Rupert.'

Ninian affirmed this, saying, 'Frankly sir they were rather splendid.' Henry added reminiscently, 'Besides bein' extremely hospitable. I've often meant to raise the matter m'self, but somehow it's always slipped m'y memory.'

Petula smiled indulgently. 'You know I once remarked to your son,' she told them, 'that he had inherited one thing from the family, the Norman nose, and assiduously cultivated one other for himself – a rotten memory.'

Gyles raised an eyebrow at this. She went on, 'He reminded me of it recently, saying "my wife says I've inherited the Lorme nose but what it was she said I had developed for m'yself I'm blowed if I can remember".'

As the laughter subsided Christine asked, 'What did happen when you two boys drove to the London docks? You never did tell us the details of that episode.'

So the tale was told again which, for Sue-Ellen, brought back again the one recollection she had tried valiantly to obliterate from her mind. When Ninian found Rupert, and in that ghastly moment thought his small brother was dead, when, in fact, his guard was completely down, *he had called her 'darling'*. Now, memory spiralled back to the aftermath of those events and how she had lain in her big bed, unable to sleep. Instead she re-experienced the wave of intoxicating happiness which swept over her when she remembered what Ninian had said. Both then and again now at the dinner table she was forced to accept that her momentary glimpse of heaven could never be more than just that – because she had too much money and Ninian was too proud.

Lying in the big bed she had calculated his income, translated it into dollars and ultimately wept for the immensity of the financial barrier which separated them.

By morning she was calm enough. She rode with him as usual. When they strolled from the stables afterwards they discussed the progress of her Zoo. This led her to confess that there was little more she could do until the new buildings were completed. This evoked a rumble of content from Ninian.

'That means you are free to come over and give me a hand in finishing Farthings at last. I'm totally adrift when it comes to arrangin' things. You will, won't you?'

So back she went with him to prepare his new home for his bachelor occupation. This was during what Henry called, 'The usual hectic family run-up to Christmas with all its spendin', plannin', and arrangin'.' The castle saw little of the pair. No sooner was breakfast over and her men had received their morning briefing, than they were off, spending all the hours of daylight doing what Ninian described as 'heaving furniture about and arguin'.' Each afternoon when twilight came – the electricity supply was as yet incomplete – they returned full of what had been achieved during the day while all the time Sue-Ellen became more deeply enchanted with the old house and its new owner. Gradually Farthings took on elegance once again under their hands until both house and owner came to represent the apogee of all desire for her.

Every night when she closed her bedroom door she tried to make herself accept that this was the end; but she never quite succeeded; so inevitably reached the point where she considered how she could find a logical way of getting rid of her dollars barrier.

All this flashed through her mind as she sat lost in her remembering so completely that when Ninian turned to her asking 'What came next Sue-Ellen?' she did not even hear him. He repeated the question, adding 'Hi, Sue-Ellen, are you day-dreaming?' and only then she returned to the moment with a start. Recovering herself she managed to stammer out an excuse, hoping that the curious scrutiny to which she was being submitted by the eagle-eyed Dowager did not presage some kind of imminent interrogation. The moment passed. It seemed forgotten by the family, but Sue-Ellen continued to think round and round the subject. In a remote corner of her mind there remained a glimmer of hope. She had reached the point of considering how she could find a logical way of getting rid of her dollars barrier.

She was on the point of deciding to consult Mr Mobberly when this exercise of what she always called, 'thinking things through to their logical conclusion' was brought to an abrupt standstill as a bombshell exploded among everyone, driving every other consideration from all their minds.

The little Countess Marguerite, trotting across the hall with a very large flower arrangement in a very precious old Chinese cooking vessel, suddenly cried out and then fell. The sound of that fall was very slight; but the smashing of the priceless pot brought them running. She had suffered a heart attack. She was carried upstairs by Sawby who picked her up in his arms and bore her there himself. He confided in Mrs Parsons afterwards, 'She was no weight at all. I could hardly believe anyone could feel so light, I tell you she's gone to nothing recently.'

Dr Jamieson was summoned instantly. Constance shooed everyone, even the Dowager from the bedroom, so perforce they sat about in the White Drawing Room, waiting helplessly for Dr Jamieson to tell them just how grave was Marguerite's condition.

After what seemed an eternity he joined them, accepted a chair and began, 'I will not attempt to conceal from you that the Countess has suffered a heart attack. In layman's terms her heart is very tired which is to be understood in so active a little lady of her age.'

'Age,' snorted the Dowager already on the edge of temper through anxiety. 'Twaddle!' she snapped, sitting rod-backed as usual and glaring at him. 'And also fudge Jamieson. The Countess is only four months older than I and I shall not even be eighty until next year, any more than she will.'

Dr Jamieson's mouth twitched. 'Quite so Lady Aynthorp,' he agreed, 'but, with respect, eighty is not eighteen.'

'Pshaw,' she exclaimed crossly, 'why my mama lived to be ninety-three and Meg's was even older as I recall.'

He persisted – but very gently – telling them all, 'I am still compelled to give you the facts. If the Countess has a long rest in bed, which is imperative, as I trust you all appreciate, and if in concert we can contrive a pattern of life thereafter for her which is suited to her condition, then I am sanguine we may keep her with us for many years.'

'Are you goin' to turn her into an invalid?' the Dowager swung up her lorgnette violently, 'for if that is your intention I can assure you now you will be whistlin' up back alleys to the moon for all the effect it will have.'

'Not precisely an invalid,' he answered, pulling his beard, 'but the Countess must relinquish any thought of returning to her flower activities with Aynthorp Enterprises. That you must all accept, too, and also that she is no longer strong enough for gardening. These are activities which would almost certainly prove fatal. You can imagine my reluctance to tell you these things; but it has to be clearly understood that any active life, such as she has lived for so very many years, is now over. It can never be resumed. Given that this may be achieved, I can then outline what she may do, after the essential, long rest in bed for one or two months. She can then be moved during the daytime to a *chaise longue* after which, according to what improvements we then see in her condition, we can discuss what further activities she may be allowed.'

This took some time to sink in. Marguerite was always immensely active, trotting here and there on her lawful and sometimes unlawful occasions; travelling whenever it pleased her to do so; even going to night clubs – perennially participating in anything which appealed to her.

At length Gyles took the doctor off to his Library, leaving the rest of them to digest what he called, 'This shatterin' news.'

At Dr Jamieson's request, the most celebrated heart specialist was then brought to see her; but as his pronouncements were identical, his manner unbelievably urbane and his acceptance absolute that the patient's prime stipulation for survival was 'total rest' this did none of them any good. They were left with Dr Jamieson's original rulings and a very stiff fee to pay for what the Dowager dismissed as pompous reiterations; but after the great man had left them she hauled down her colours and became rather grey herself with anxiety so it was left to Henry to display his talent in such moments of crisis. He had done this over the late Stephen Delahaye affair by easing tension with a proposition which in that instance and indeed in many others had proved both startling and highly acceptable. He did it again now.

Petula watched him begin by rumpling his hair into a shambles. She knew well enough how he adored his *Tante* Marguerite, so fully appreciated that he was now in all his states, a malaise familiar to them all in moments of high drama.

Eventually he exploded into speech.

'We don't need Dr Jamieson to tell us *Tante* Marguerite will be a difficult patient. The worst part, in my opinion both for her and for us is the plain fact that if she remains in those rooms upstairs she will be desperately lonely.' He paused, looked directly at Gyles whose expression was now registering a mixture of alarm and curiosity. 'You know what I think, sir?' Henry asked him.

'Tell me. I believe I may have an inkling.'

'Well then, why do we not bring her down here among us all as speedily as things can be arranged?' Gyles watched him, seeing as did the rest of them, how deeply he was troubled. 'Wouldn't it just be on the cards we could find suitable quarters for her down here? Then once she is near enough, we could all slip in and chat with her, share little tit-bits of news and gossip. Surely we could find somewhere suitable? That way we can at least make her feel she is still one of us. If we could move her down lock, stock and that dratted parrot of hers, plus all her Burnham Beeches of pot plants she adores I'm sure she would be better at once.'

He paused to find out whether all this had fallen upon stony ground, saw that a bit of light was beginning to brighten their faces, took heart from it and so continued. 'I've always been given to understand that stairs are criminal for heart cases. When she is well enough to walk again and if we did this she wouldn't have any. Is that not so, sir?' He plucked up courage to fire this last directly at Dr Jamieson who was watching him quizzically.

'Certainly,' the doctor agreed.

'Well then, what about it?'

Christine's mind was already well ahead of the proposition. She backed her son now, saying, 'Surely it is only a matter of deciding upon the most suitable rooms. There are plenty of course, but far removed from our hub ...'

'It must be somewhere within sight of her roses,' Claire warned.

'So therefore,' the Dowager cut in briskly, 'it has to be on this side of the Castle.'

Henry relaxed. He knew that the bait had been taken. Now he was content to sit back and let matters take their course. *Tante* Marguerite would get her ground floor quarters. Then, he reflected, there would always be someone with her. His mind ran on from there: Christmas was coming; he and Pet must make her a very special Christmas tree of her own. He was so deep in this he failed to notice their final acquiescence or that Christine and Gyles had left the drawing room, arm in arm, talking softly as they went.

They were back very quickly too. 'We have found the perfect rooms, Mama,' Christine announced, her face flushed with excitement.

'Where?' everyone chorused.

Christine sat down again. 'It really was obvious,' she told them; then she explained.

There was a small withdrawing room immediately behind the one in which they now sat. It had long been unused, but it did lead to a much larger and more elegant French-windowed room which overlooked both the big herbaceous borders and the twin crescents of rose gardens. It was known to them by three names, so when they spoke of it they either spoke of it as 'our wicked Lady Marguerite's Room', or 'the King's Room' (he being Charles the second who was contemporary with the naughty lady); or if it were Henry, 'the Bawd Room', since they all knew that the beauty had used it whenever the King visited her, which was not infrequently, and not just for parlour dalliance. They now remembered that only one item of particular interest remained in that room as, when the museum was refurbished and reopened not long since, all the best pieces had been taken from it leaving only the King's Gift – a beautiful silver

table which his lovely mistress used as a coiffeuse for which
the King also gave her a silver-framed looking glass shaped
like a heart. Beyond this long ago scene of seductions lay a
small ante-chamber.

'Now,' Christine told them, 'Gyles says we may trans-
form that ante-room into a bathroom for *our* Marguerite,
something very special of course, turn the withdrawing
room into her boudoir and use the King's Room as her
bedroom.'

The atmosphere brightened momentarily. Henry had
given them something to plan! And plans they always found
were irresistible.

Christine concluded, 'I suggest *Belle-mère*, that I go to
London in the morning. Pet will come with me. Between us
we shall bully the people concerned for their sworn undertaking to complete by Christmas Eve. Then, if you agree,
Doctor, we can wheel Marguerite down in one of those full-
length basket affairs we used for our convalescents, taking
her right across to the Home's lift, after which she can be
wheeled straight into her new suite.'

'Includin' that sepulchral old Boney,' Henry reminded.

'Indeed yes,' his mother nodded, 'she could never be
without her parrot, I agree.'

'Meanwhile,' Henry added happily, 'Pet and I will see
that her special Christmas tree is ready and in position,
either in her bedroom or boudoir accordin' to her condition; but either way one or other of us will give her the
presents from them and help open them *very gradually*.'
Typically he added, 'If we time the whole operation carefully enough, all the shiftin' could be done while she was
progressin' from up above which would be much better
because then she would not see either room without it
containin' all her treasures. Then on Christmas Day we
might just be able to arrange for us to be with her for long
enough for her nurses to get a bit of time off and a decent
meal. It's terrible for anyone to have to work all the time on
Christmas Day.'

They were off once more, spending in excess of prudence
and keeping fear at bay through Henry's suggestion.

As it transpired, their beloved invalid was too exhausted
after her attack to make any protests about anything for the

first week. She contented herself with little murmurs of, 'Silly me! I just cannot remember when I ever fainted before' and showed a tendency to nod off in mid-sentence.

This at first terrified everyone until Dr Jamieson ruled, 'Best possible thing. I have always maintained that sleep is the greatest healer. The more she drowses the better it is for her. She's doing very well so far all things considered and I am quite satisfied.'

It heartened them. Sawby was of course sent for and given a very full explanation of what was toward. Thus all the plumbers and decorators were made welcome. Belowstairs united in sympathy and genuine affection for Marguerite's way with staff was compelling – save for a few disapproving sniffs from Palliser, which were only to be expected. When she made a few sour comments these drew fearful wrath upon her and when she remarked, 'All that money wasted when most likely she'll go any minute,' Palliser was sent to Coventry while the rest of them took the greatest possible interest in each stage of the transformation. Nothing was told to the patient, who was becoming brighter by the day until she suddenly demanded the presence of all the 'Flower Arranging gels' when it dawned on her that Christmas was fast approaching.

Another Council of War was held with Constance and Dr Jamieson presiding. They both were unanimous that it was best to let the girls visit the little Countess. They even took it upon themselves to see them all first in order to ensure they fully understood what they must say and do.

At first they had been dismayed by the prospect of handling the Christmas orders without their autocratic little arbiter; but when Victoria and, surprisingly, Claire too took charge, with Claire displaying an unsuspected talent for the work and Victoria demonstrating her gift for organisation, they all settled down very well and in the end they notched up higher figures than had ever been achieved before, thus creating a record and contributing a surprisingly large amount to the company's funds.

Sawby privately considered his wife was the one who should have replaced the Countess, but she had other ideas which she dilated upon as the pair walked to and from their cottage and the Castle.

'Albert dear,' she reasoned with him, 'I have been thinking about it myself, of course; but don't you see we must make sounder plans for the future. Mrs Parsons won't last for ever. Nor will Chef neither. His heart is too set on that dream restaurant of his. If I'm all tied up with flower arranging *they*'ll never think of me to replace him; but if I stay close to him, learning everything I can like I'm doing now, who knows but his lordship and her ladyship might allow me to replace him if not both of 'em, for there's other talent in that kitchen nowadays, which I could bring along nicely.'

Sawby halted in his tracks, looked down upon his small wife and asked, 'Appelby talent?'

'You've guessed it, my girl, your step-daughter and your step-son. If we can train both of 'em, then on goes the Sawby tradition!'

'How my dear, how?' She was the only person who could fuss him and she fussed him now.

'Take my boy out of the kitchen and that butchery which I don't deny is useful for him to know. Start him small and lead him on gradual, pantry boy, under footman, head footman right to you my dear, when you are ready to retire and not before. Meanwhile you just leave my girl to me.'

He looked thoughtful. They walked on until as they rounded the curve and came once more in sight of the huge façade, then a great wave of pride swept over him. He patted her hand, 'You're a marvel my love and just as you say I'll leave the girl to you.'

All this time Sue-Ellen fluctuated between an instinct that she must douse her tiny flicker of an idea, and an overwhelming desire to feed its minuscule flame, working out permutations and computations upon the basic theme *Get rid of my money*. Very gradually she came to accept that like the young man in the New Testament she was unlikely to succeed. Money grew tentacles. She saw hers coiled already around the handful of men she employed on her Zoo, her dependents in a country which was beginning to wilt under its own tentacle squeeze – unemployment. Another Sue-Ellen tentacle reached out towards the many hundreds whose jobs in her American factories spelled peace of mind to their womenfolk and security to them. She reminded herself that those jobs for all those unknown people were secure due to the bulwark of dollars her father had built for their protection in times of recession. There was a whole octopus quota of tentacles in her commitments there!

When she had 'thought through' to this point there remained young Stephen whose tentacles wound strongest of all.

She sat on her heels in her dressing room, encircled with gifts, wrapping papers, ribbons and labels and stared at them blankly. As they came into focus, 'Even these constitute a problem!' she thought, looking at the one she had chosen for Ninian. What could she give to the man she loved when she had almost unlimited means and he was as stiff-necked as Ninian? She compensated, characteristically, by buying lavish gifts for everyone else, including Johnathan for whom she bought a whippet of a Hardy rod complete with every conceivable addition she could persuade the distinguished old salesman to produce for her and including a massive pair of fishing boots which made a difficult parcel. Back she went onto her heels. She must ask Harry's opinion of her 'work out' on the complex problems of gifts. For her no virtue could accrue from giving to someone you loved. It had to be something longed for by someone disliked intensely to whom you gave gladly for any of *that* to happen. 'So,' she concluded, tying a complicated bow almost viciously, 'no virtues for Sue-Ellen tonight!' Frustratedly she extracted a card from the heap, scribbled on it 'Happy Christmas and good fishing Johnathan, this was my late husband's but it seemed a sin to let it remain unused, when you throw such a very pretty fly so please enjoy it. Sue-Ellen.' Sighing deeply she decided ruefully that the feet of Ananias were already sounding in her ears. She turned at last to Ninian's. Picking up a sheet of Castle Rising writing paper she scribbled on it, 'Dear Ninian, these were my father's. It would give me great pleasure to see you wearing them now that Daddy is gone. He was a darling, a fat and kindly man who Hen says looked like Mr Pickwick. I think you would have liked each other very much. Happy Christmas. Sue-Ellen.' Another flagrant untruth!

She laid the paper to one side, picked up the little

rectangular box, pressed the spring and looked at the two rows of black pearl dress studs sunk into their satin padding which she had bought last week at Garrards, clapped the lid back again and decided, 'Lower than a duck's stomach with all these lies, that's me', and thought she had never been so unhappy in all her life.

Someone scratched on the door. She shook her head, to splash off tears which hung on her lashes, called, 'Come in', and looked up to see Henry's face round the door.

'Any admittance? I see you're busy doin' your presents?' He was hesitant, spotting the tearstains, absorbing at once the significance of the festive disorder on the Bokhara rug.

She jumped up, dusting snippets from her skirt. 'No, I've almost finished,' she pushed narrow feet into her shoes, 'do you want me for something special?'

He walked towards her slowly. 'N-no, just Pet and I thought you might like to see *Tante* Marguerite's Christmas Tree.'

As he spoke he reached the rug, knelt down beside her as she turned the parcels over in search of Marguerite's gift . . . then he took a flyer . . . very softly he said, 'I once thought I hadn't a hope in hell with Petula, yet now she's my darling wife.'

She stared. 'Is it so obvious?' She choked, ashamed.

He nodded, 'Both of you though, not just you alone.'

'Forget it, Henry. It's what you would call tilting at windmills I believe.'

'That was how I saw me and Pet,' he agreed, 'what was that awful definition of faith which exactly fits, I've forgotten it?'

'Believing what you know to be untrue?'

'Yes that's it. I know a better one. It comes from a feller *Belle-mère* knew very well. Rum sort of chap, kind of a mystic; anyway he said, "Faith is a crutch on which men lean till knowledge comes to cast the crutch away." I should latch onto that one if I were you. I'll swear yours is still unfinished business . . . I suppose it's your filthy lucre ain't it?'

'I s-suppose so, but Henry it's all pie in the sky, he's never said anything except one "darling"!'

He held out his hands and pulled her to her feet. 'Put yer

faith in old Asquith,' he advised, 'just wait and see, that's my advice. I say what a flamin' cheek, talkin' like this to you. I do apologise.'

'Corn!' she exclaimed. Then leaning forward she kissed him on one cheek. 'It is just darling of you; but now let us go and see your tree and give my parcel to Petula ...'

They had silvered a spruce completely, they had hung it with silver bells and icicles; draping fat swags of silver tinsel between the branches from which the smaller parcels dangled from crimson ribbons. Their wrappings were silver too, as was the fairy who flew from the top with her wand and wings outstretched. They had planted the tree in an old silver bucket excavated from the silver room and all about it larger parcels were massed.

'Do you like it love?' asked Petula.

'Like it?' echoed Sue-Ellen. 'It's magical. Oh won't she be enchanted!'

She was. Sue-Ellen standing back as they brought her in, found no cause for anti-climax but, despite this, she shivered. Marguerite looked so tiny! Her hair had been exquisitely dressed, her eyes were sparkling, but her hands with the rings sparkling too as she clasped them in delight, seemed almost transparent.

Behind the doors to her bedroom children began to sing 'Silent night ...' They were the Nursery folk, Chantal and Justin, Sue-Ellen's Stephen, Rupert, Richard, with behind him the older ones, Christian and Claire's Peter Christian and Priscilla, with Rosemary's Charles-Louis and Dominique just in front of them newly assigned with their mother to spend this Christmas with the Family.

When the voices stopped: 'Oh, darlings, that was beautiful,' Marguerite cried, holding out her arms to them. Then they crowded round her until she was enmeshed in them while from the other doorway Christine and Gyles stood watching.

Then they came in, one by one as the children slipped away, having been carefully briefed. Before they went each one handed a parcel to Petula who added them to the immense pile, enhanced now by flowers in long boxes, flowers in pots and one huge arrangement done for her by the flower girls which Petula had put on a white pedestal nearby. Marguerite's eyes rested upon it thoughtfully. 'Yes,' she decided, sighing contentedly, 'they can do very well without me now. Haven't I taught them cleverly?'

Christine bent over her. 'We felt, my darling,' she told her lovingly, 'that we could not bear you to be so far away from us. So we planned this as a little surprise for just while you are recovering from your silly faint. Selfishly maybe we wanted you as near to us as possible so that we can slip in at all hours with the latest *"on dits"*.'

Marguerite chuckled softly. Sawby folded back the double connecting doors. He too was seen to be holding an arrangement which he and his wife had risen at dawn to complete for her.

Constance slipped back to the head of the long wheeled chair. Sawby cleared his throat, only a tiny muscle under one eye giving him away.

'Wishing you a very happy Christmas and a speedy recovery my lady,' he said. 'And now, if you please, will you enter your temporary bedroom which is a gift to you from the family.'

Constance pushed her in very slowly, pausing inside for her to exclaim at the famous silver table and looking glass, now her coiffeuse, and arranged with all her scent bottles and hair brushes.

'Oh dear,' Marguerite exclaimed, 'I shall never be able to leave it! It is ... so ... delicious ... my favourite turquoise ...!' She gazed at the bed drapes. 'Exquisite my dears. Do you suppose this Marguerite will be haunted by that other one? Will she be witness to naughty past scenes of dalliance with King Charles?'

She exclaimed at everything. She insisted on being wheeled here and there until Dr Jamieson came in to banish everyone, saying, gently, 'Now Countess you must go back to bed in this beautiful room. I do not want all the excitement to tire you.'

'Fiddlesticks!' she retorted, 'I feel splendid. If I do agree to being returned to bed, you old tyrant, I insist upon a small glass of champagne. You have bullied me for too long and I am now rebellious.'

He humoured her. He allowed the champagne, once she was safely between the silk sheets, and it was all pronounced a perfectly splendid surprise. 'Better,' she added naughtily, as the door closed behind him, 'than all that old fuss-pot's specifics'. But within moments the champagne sipped and the glass relinquished, she had fallen asleep and her presents remained unopened.

As soon as their Christmas festivities were ended, Marguerite insisted on Mr Truslove being brought to see her. She claimed she had time on her hands and wished to go over her investments with him. She explained, Gyles thought somewhat speciously, but abstained from comment, 'With all this gossip about and our old Pelican totterin' on the brink of retirement I must be sure my investments are exactly as I require them to be. Don't fuss now Gyles, I will not let him tire me.'

Again Dr Jamieson was asked and again he concurred, so the old family solicitor was duly invited to luncheon and Grantham despatched in the newer Royce to collect him and drive him down in comfort. Sawby showed him into the Library where he took a glass of Madeira with Gyles. He was a trifle shaky on his attenuated legs but as astute as ever and having sipped he dated the wine in his glass correctly as usual, confirmed that he was indeed 'retiring to make way for my son' – the Lesser Pelican – and further informed Gyles that at last his only son was to marry after a ten-year engagement the well-endowed human wren of his choice. He then asked to be conducted to the Countess and was warned that luncheon would be served at one-thirty.

The pair were left alone together for an hour. Then Marguerite shook the little bell at her side and leaned back against her pillows. 'Thank you my friend,' she smiled, 'I feel much better now. Pray do not be shocked Mr Truslove at what I require you to do.' She inspected his disturbed countenance, decided his feathers were 'sorely ruffled' and began chiding him. 'Surely after all these years and all you have experienced with this family throughout those years, such a little thing as this cannot disconcert you now? If you really are uneasy let me tell you *I know what I am about.*'

He nodded vigorously. 'Oh yes, Countess, I feel sure you do . . . nevertheless . . .' he was pecking more violently than ever, darting his head forward and back as he had always

done but with increased vehemence. 'M-most unorthodox
... really ... very, er, disconcerting too for some parties ...'

'Pooh,' she shrugged, 'when has orthodoxy had anythin'
to do with Lorme behaviour pray?'

He raised his old eyebrows at this. 'Well,' he admitted
with the ghost of a smile, 'I have asked myself the same
question once or twice, I am bound to admit.' Then there
came from him a curious, wheezing sound like an old clock
working itself up to strike, making her eyes sparkle with
amusement as she realised that for the first time in all the
years she had known him Mr Truslove was laughing.

'Tee, hee,' he wheezed, 'tee, hee hee, really most extra-
ordinary ... tee hee hee.'

On this he took his leave of her and toddled out still tee
heeing as he worked his way slowly towards the White
Drawing Room.

When the New Year came it brought with it a thaw. Gyles
and his sons began dividing their time between hunting and
the new pedigree cattle. The first of the new in-calf heifers
began to drop their calves and this dominated their conversation until Christine, thoroughly exasperated, complained, 'Really Gyles, these endless *accouchements* are quite
revolting during dinner. They quite put us off André's
delicious dishes, pray reserve them for when we are not
at table.'

The little Marguerite remained in bed. She seemed
content, which was contrary to their expectations. She
barely enquired as to the progress of the flower arranging
activities now, but delighted in her increased proximity to
the family; played chess with Gyles, backgammon with the
Dowager and allowed the younger ones to initiate her into
the complexities of mah-jongg. She also wrote many letters,
sitting propped up in bed wearing one or other of the
exquisite 'half-negligés' as she called the little wrappers
which Lucien half designed for her.

She corresponded regularly with Piers who was able to
reply to her. She seemed deeply interested in his progress;
and was very down for several days after Lucy had been on
one of her flying visits during which she told her that
Spahlinger had said it would be a very long time before Piers

would be allowed to resume normal life. She brightened considerably though when Piers wrote himself.

This is a red-letter day for me. I have been given permission to draw at last and I have walked in the grounds. You and I are both on the mend I know; but we must both be patient. I long to see you all again and to be with my tiny wife. She came to see me last week. As you know we have been kept apart for a long time. When I did see her she looked absurdly young although she is nearly twenty-nine now, while I, with my prematurely white hair and new lines on my face, am beginning to look older than God (here he inserted a drawing of a bearded ancient and then went on) Lucy gets very cross when I call her my child-wife. Of course I wait in vain for a letter from Lucien. He detests writing letters I know, but Lucy is very good. She tells me all about both his work and his fairly hectic-sounding play too.

He signed himself, 'your loving Piers'. All this was duly passed on to various members of the family. Only the Dowager accepted the truth, although she dissembled with great care; but even as she talked to her Justin through the mists of the hereafter, fortifying herself by these ephemeral communications against her longing for an end to their separation, she knew that Marguerite had come to terms with her passing with a courage which was as great as her determination to cast no unnecessary shadows over these remaining days. She was as gay as her waning strength permitted. When this flagged she made flimsy excuses to be alone with her Alicia. Only then would she lie back, close her eyes and perhaps put out her hand, so that she could hold on to her 'Licia's' while she drowsed.

No one, not even Gyles, had any inkling of the strain this imposed on his Mama. She remained straight-backed, tart, autocratic and just as meddlesome as ever. She sparred with her eldest son and provoked an outburst of wrath from him at one of her high-handed mischiefs. The only human being who knew the whole truth was her old coachman Plum. To him she spoke freely, well aware that all the tortures of the inquisition would not cause him to break her confidence.

As January passed into February she began taking daily constitutionals. These always took her to the stables. Plum learned to expect her and like an industrious mole he burrowed out tit bits of gossip and scandal to make her chuckle for a moment or two. All he said to his wife was, 'It's the only thing mother as brings a twinkle to them eyes of hern, wots gettin' lonelier and lonelier as the little Countess wanes.'

'Is she goin' then love?' his comfortable and comforting wife asked softly as they sat by the stove one winter evening.

'Ar,' he nodded sadly. 'She'm on 'er way orright; but she'm come to terms wiv' it. Thought wot will 'appen to 'er liddle leddyship it chills me blood ter think on. They've bin that close Ma since 'is darlin' old lordship was took – you carnt imagine!'

Gyles and Christine talked too and held each other's hands as they sat beside the fire in Christine's boudoir when Pearson had undressed her, tidied their room, turned down the bed.

On one such night Christine said forlornly, 'Gyles I am afraid.'

He gripped her hand, having no need for explanations. She continued, 'All our old darlings are leaving us. Soon there will be none left. Then we shall be the old ones in their stead.'

Later on she added, 'I had always thought there could be no lonelier moment than when one's parents die; but now I realise that even that can be eclipsed when the time comes that there is no one left to call us by our Christian names; besides no one who can bully us any more.'

'Like Mama,' said Gyles quickly, 'we all have to face such thoughts my love. It is part of the pattern of living. It comes to haunt me too but I try to force it from me because it is a thought which becomes unbearable. Imagine what a light will go out when Mama leaves us; when there is no one left to provoke and exasperate me – even on occasions to make me feel like a small boy again.' He drew her close so that her head was on his shoulder. 'It is the ultimate loneliness for two people who love each other as we do because the older generation has always wielded such tremendous authority over us. As to *our* separation . . .' His voice ceased. He felt her answering shudder. 'Mama has been only half a person since our master-bully left us.'

She turned in his arms to face him with brimming eyes. 'Even so we shall be exactly the same,' she told him, putting her hands up to his face protectingly. 'In my better moments I pray that you may go first and I be left; but when my spirit falters I shrink from that and beg that I may go first.'

Gyles reminded her, smiling compassionately, 'We must all take the Swan's Path. Even if you went now I would be able to look back thankfully on all the years you have made golden for me.'

'Oh so would I,' she agreed, 'oh, so would I.'

The shadow cast by the tiny figure in the elegant bed lay heavy over them all. Even Anne and young Charles, growing perceptive in their sudden discovery of each other, found that they were unable to speak of it because of the little Countess for whom they too were afraid.

Life went on of course, but every so often Gyles found himself bayed by premonitions of trouble and yet more trouble while he worked, hunted and even entertained. It was all as sawdust in a mouth which had become grim.

One crisp blustery day in late March they were hunting over King's Ride. Hounds had just surged from Puck's Spinney, a russet flash bespoke their quarry and 'Gone awaaaay . . .' sounded joyously as the russet flash stretched over the rise, hounds in pursuit, the field strung out and galloping. Gyles felt his mare stumble. He reined in, dismounted and found she had gone lame. Feeling very sorry for them both he turned to begin leading her back to stables. Limping mare and walking rider began a slow return towards the valley bowl in which the old, grey castle sat enthroned. Gyles had already worked out the shortest line he could take. It took them both by a field in which a score of the new cattle grazed. He looked them over admiringly as he went by slowly, so slowly that a slight movement from one beast – standing apart – caught his eye. He stopped dead, staring, then hastily tethered the mare to a tree, and was through into the field as fast as his long legs could carry him. He approached the heifer. She moved away limpingly, made uneasy by his approach. Talking to her quietly Gyles followed and after several abortive attempts he reached her, took hold of her head and began forcing her jaws apart. Peering into her mouth he stiffened, stooped to the ground to grab a foreleg, turned the leg so that he could examine the hoof. Then he repeated this with all four hooves. There was no gainsaying it! Hooves and mouth were both heavily blistered. He let her go. He stood up with shoulders which seemed to sag under this sudden shock. Then he untethered the mare and continued on his way, his mind reeling as the full import of those blisters penetrated.

When he reached the stables he shouted for Plum who came running. 'Has she gorne lame then my lord?' he panted. 'Now never you fret, she'll be as right as rain, old Plum'll take care of her. Just bring 'er in 'ere and we'll fix her, she looks like she's only slipped a shoe; but what a mortal pity wen you was in for such a thunderin' good run.'

'Damn the bloody hunt,' Gyles threw him the reins, 'you know what to do so just do it. If it is serious send for Pickering, he's the best horse vet in the county, and then come up to my office as quickly as you can, I can't wait now.' And so saying he turned and began a long, loping trot back towards the Castle steps.

Plum remained, clutching the reins and staring after him incredulously. 'Dang us,' he apostrophised the mare, 'look at 'im trottin'! I ain't never seen 'im do that afore, so wot's got into 'im I dursent even guess.'

He learned soon enough. Gyles flung himself into the hall, shouted 'Sawby', and when the man appeared, he demanded, 'Where's Mr Henry? Don't stand there staring man, this is urgent. Find Mr Henry.'

Sawby stammered, 'Mr Henry, my lord, went over with Mr Trimmings to his farm. Is there anything I can do?'

'Yes,' said Gyles curtly, 'put Mr Knowles on the telephone, I'll take him in my office.'

Moments later, while he drummed on his table top, his telephone bell shrilled. He snatched the receiver. 'Good afternoon Knowles ... could you get over here just as fast as you possibly can ... ? no right away I think I have some big trouble on m'y hands ... What? no, don't waste time now man I'll explain later ... yes.... I'll be waitin' in some car outside.' He rehung the mouthpiece, sat on, still drumming and staring blankly until Henry hurried in. 'What's wrong, sir?' he asked with no preface, 'I thought you were huntin'?'

Gyles ignored this. 'Just tell me something. If cattle spring blisters inside their mouths and on the hooves, *what does it signify?*'

Henry's hand flew to his head. 'Not ours sir?'

'Yes ours, now answer me.'

'Christ,' exclaimed his son, 'it's the first clear sign of foot and mouth, but which of ours and where?'

Gyles told him, adding, 'I have already sent for Knowles, he should be here any minute.'

Henry stood, one hand still on the door, staring at his father. 'Then you had better know sir,' he said slowly, 'that Timms' cattle have got it too. If I'm not mistaken half his herd is down with it already ... oh what devilish bad luck! ... I wonder who else is affected?'

Gyles nodded. 'Thanks for tellin' me,' he said grimly, 'our pedigree beasts! Well anyway we shall know the worst when Knowles has examined 'em. What a bloody awful thing, just when we were comin' along so well.'

'I am so sorry sir,' Henry muttered lamely.

'So shall we all be before this is over,' Gyles retorted. 'We shall all be quarantined. Such beasts as get over it will then be virtually worthless. Once the milk yield drops it never rises again. The rest'll just die; then we shall have no milk to sell, no butter or cream to make. All we shall have on this land or any other that is contaminated will be death carts of beasts for buryin' in quicklime, empty pig styes, stalls, fields, and when it is all over some of us will go to the wall. Others will be forced to sell land in order to carry on. It will take years to recover what we thought we possessed when we all came down to breakfast this morning.'

He ran one hand through his hair, smiled ruefully. 'It seems it's catchin',' he acknowledged, 'now you had best come and sit here. Begin ringin' round, order all our lot to contain their cattle immediately if they are not affected as yet. Tell 'em to make sure none stray onto our land which we now know is perilous. Then find out how many of us have been hit so far and don't forget to get on to Uncle Charles....' He broke off as, 'Save yourself,' said Charles

Danement from the doorway. 'I take it you've got it Gyles, from what I heard you sayin'. Well so have I.' He walked in, continuing, 'That splendid bull of mine, Goliath, is my first victim. I just came to find out how you were off for Jeyes fluid because I've rung my local chap and he's just laid in fresh supplies so I thought I might get your first supplies at the same time as my own.'

Gyles and he looked at each other. 'It's a pretty kettle of fish ain't it?' Gyles growled, 'take a pew Charles, we can do no more until Knowles gets here.'

Charles nodded. 'Just let me tell my feller, he's waitin' outside. He can off load some Jeyes for you on his way home to me. I'll be back in a moment.'

'Poor old Charles,' Gyles mused when he had vanished, 'he can ill afford this packet. It was marginal whether he came in at all and now he must be devilishly hard hit.'

Henry was speaking to Henham Castle. Now he leaned back, put his hand over the receiver. 'It's himself,' he told his father, 'I'm just waitin' till the language subsides! He's got it alright. Christ what a sod it all is.' Then hastily, withdrawing his hand, 'Of course I'm here sir, you were sayin' . . . ?'

Gyles turned on his heel and left his son to it.

By nightfall everyone in the county knew that many were hit, including both Danements and Lormes. The authorities had been informed. Knowles was still out in the fields checking the stock, and buckets were being commandeered for the Jeyes, while the entrances to every contaminated farm and estate were being closed and the notices were going up, 'No admittance for any unauthorised Persons. BY ORDER. Foot and Mouth Disease.'

By next morning carts piled high with sacks of quicklime were beginning to lumber across the land to the pit where Rupert had fallen. Gyles deemed this a fitting place in which to bury their dead. The immensity of the outbreak became known very gradually. It soon got round though that the whole country was stricken with another outbreak similar to the one of the previous year which had not touched them then. A few days later the first of Gyles' new stock died and were carried off to the pit. As the disease took hold, the badly infected milking cows and nanny goats showed the ominous drop in milk yield. Then the in-calf heifers began aborting. Some developed the chronic mastitis which affected their udders and eroded their teats. Then the first of Charles' goat herd died, two of Gyles' sows aborted and they went next. So it went on. The tally mounted daily. Andrew and young Charles mooned about with no deliveries to supervise, no records to keep. The butter women were sent home and the cattlemen stood about in miserable clusters. Cream orders were automatically cancelled, and all that remained for the delivery vans was game, poultry, flowers and eggs.

Hunting had ceased too, so Ninian spent much time with Marguerite, who took great pleasure in telling him exactly what he must do with his gardens. She made him draw plans for her and she taught him how to plot herbaceous borders, filling in the crescents he had drawn on the large scale outlines with the names of the plants to be installed. 'Pay no attention to the dictatorial rulings about all the tall ones going at the back and all the short ones bein' relegated to the front. Break it up, it's always more beautiful. Drop heights down gradually in some places leavin' a big space right across the bed and let it be filled with a spread of low growing colour which will *blaze* out whether it's petunias, those frilly ones which are delicious, or those beastly things I always forget and call bloody love, what do I mean, Ninian?'

'Love lies bleeding,' he told her obediently.

By this time Gyles, sick at heart, began entering his losses preparatory to tackling his claims against insurance. In between he visited his tenant farmers, gave what consolation he could to their tearful wives. 'It's the silence,' one choked, 'that's what hurts most. All those empty stalls and pens and styes, it's horrible!' By now the area was permeated by the smell of Jeyes fluid, the hedges powdered with the dust which the winds lifted from the quicklime. It lay in a fine film over adjacent hedgerows and the bursting buds died beneath it.

When at long last the outbreak had been contained, the final tumbril of carcases had rumbled to the pit and Authority gave them all clearance they were still partially dazed by the suddenness with which their Nemesis had descended upon them.

Gyles determined that for a full year he would have no more stock on his land, and then he had to face the final blow for him. He accepted that he would have to dismiss his redundant labour.

For Sir Charles the outbreak had been nothing short of disastrous. His small dairy herd had been wiped out; he had lost his goats, all his beef cattle were gone too, besides a large and prosperous piggery which had been a most valuable source of revenue. Then Charles became adamant against his using the smoke houses for at least three months. So they too stood idle. No deer were allowed to come from Clangowrie and to add to his troubles the salmon catch proved to be the lowest for many years. When he totted up his bill Charles faced the one thing calculated to make him demented. He would be forced to sell more land and with it one of his two remaining farms. The tenant in any case could no longer carry on. The poor chap was far from young, he had lost two sons in the war and now had no incentive left with which to carry on.

As to a funeral both families turned out for that sale. Lormes and Danements sat about on shooting-sticks in the yard where the byres were emptied. Thus Beedale Farm passed into the alien hands of a builder who had done very well during the war and made many friends in government, thereby obtaining some fat contracts when war was over. These had made him a comparatively rich man. Added to this, another neighbour and old friend of both families found himself in like case so again there was a farm sale. This one too went to the prosperous builder.

Gyles, summing up at his own table, was forced to admit that, 'At least the blighter has absorbed our redundant labour and I must own I am thankful for that if for nothing else.'

Perhaps the aspect nearly as grim for these men was the emptiness of their lands. Then, as an entity, they learned that the country had lost a total of over twenty-four thousand cattle, twenty-one thousand sheep, nearly ten thousand pigs and forty-nine goats, to which Charles appended his *vale* by pointing out that 'twenty-four of those goats were mine.'

All this time Marguerite remained in her turquoise hung

bed, upon which her ancestor and her King had indulged themselves with innumerable tumbles.

By mutual agreement the epidemic was kept from her absolutely, while Petula re-shaped her nursery plans. Now the twins had their baths, tied themselves into their fluffy white dressing gowns and pulled on their matching slippers with the rabbits' ears, both of which Justin flatly refused to relinquish even though he was what Nanny Rose described as 'a great big boy of seven'. He silenced her the day he riposted, 'I don't care if they are "sissy" as Rupert calls them, I'm not so there!' – then instead of taking them into the Nursery and reading to them from Nanny Rose's old rocking chair, Petula took them down each evening to visit 'Madame Meg', Chantal's own special name for her great-great-aunt so that *she* could read to them instead. The ritual was unchanging: Petula would take them to the door, open it, push them in and they would run to Marguerite where Justin would make a formal little bow and Chantal dip a wobbly curtsey. This done they would break into chatter as they scrambled onto her bed, being very careful to do so at the foot as they had been instructed. The trio would exchange news of the day. 'Madame Meg, I cleared a three foot post and rail this morning,' Justin would say.

'What were you ridin', my love?'

'Polly, she's a twelve point two Welsh pony, and we cleared a hedge with a ditch in front of over two feet wide and the hedge was two and half as well, an' even Plum said it wasn't 'arf bad for a liddle feller,' making Marguerite chuckle at his mimicry of Plum language. Chantal, not to be outdone, would then chant her seven times seven and all the time two pairs of round topaz eyes would be fixed expectantly on the silk sheet where it was folded back under those fragile little hands.

'Very good,' Marguerite would say approvingly, allowing one corner of the Charbonnel and Walker chocolate box to show outside the sheet. Then she would withdraw the box and give them their chocolates.

Once their mouths were full she would take the current story book from behind her pillows and the twins would sit like mice while she read to them.

Petula opened the door very softly one evening while the

reading was in progress, to hear, '"Oh my paws and whiskers," he cried scuttling along, "The Duchess will be most annoyed!"' so that ever afterwards when someone spoke of her this was the picture which leaped back into her sight from her storehouse of memories ... of the firelight peacocking in a dance of flames, of the lamplight as it fell on the high-dressed white head and on the two small figures, Justin with one fist doubled up under his chin, his eyelashes throwing a line of shadow across the down of his cheeks and of Chantal with her head tilted to one side, her 'Lorme' hair forming a curly aureole about her little heart-shaped face ...

She would recall too how she always changed for dinner while the reading was in progress, and that on this particular occasion she had stood in the doorway until the reading ended. 'More Madame Meg ... more please ... we're not a bit sleepy and Mummy isn't back yet,' they clamoured.

'Oh yes she is,' Petula said firmly, 'you must not tire Madame Meg, so come along now, just say goodnight and thank you very much.'

They did this, then scrambled off the bed while Marguerite removed her spectacles. 'Unflatterin' things,' she said disaparagingly, looking up at Petula and nodding in approval. 'Children,' she said, 'doesn't Mummy look pretty?' They examined her gravely. 'When I grow up,' Justin announced finally, 'I am goin' to marry someone who looks like you Mummy. Your dress is like wood smoke, so you must be a whaddycallum? Those sprites that live in trees?'

'A hamadryad,' she told him, 'do you know what is the one who lives in water?'

'I do,' cried Chantal, 'it's a naiad Mummy. Alright I'm coming.' Then each in turn put their arms around their Madame Meg who told them, 'God bless you my darlings' and then they backed up and repeated their bow and curtsy.

Always Marguerite's name re-invoked this simple domestic scene. It never failed to make Petula's eyes sting and whenever it happened she found herself regretting, much as she had done at the time, 'It's a shame she had no children ... it's been such a waste of loving!'

The Damned Little Whippersnapper

On Marguerite's 'good days', the after-dinner ritual for the family became divided. While Petula presided in the White or Blue Dining Room, either Henrietta or Primrose deputised for her at a second service of coffee, liqueurs and *petits fours* in what Marguerite called her '*petit salon*'. This equipage would be drawn close to the *chaise longue* where she sat, well propped by pillows, sipping her *tisane*, while the men warmed their brandy ballons in their hands and everyone tried to entertain her.

On one such night in early summer the word went round 'Meg's receivin''. They foregathered, the conversation then turned to Piers' latest letter from Switzerland. Marguerite told them happily, 'He will be returning in early autumn. Isn't that splendid? Lucy is house-hunting seriously at last and will go over to him shortly with a selection of wallpapers, hangin's and all that paraphernalia so that they can choose together.'

Primrose was the first to comment. 'What a mercy,' she said, 'that at last those two young things can have a proper home of their own. I wonder what Lucien will do?'

'Join them,' Marguerite flashed back, 'surely you have learned by now that nothing short of death will separate that pair?'

Constance glanced warningly at Gyles who murmured, 'As I understand it my dear Hetty, Lucien has expressed the wish to have his own private quarters where he can entertain his friends; lead, in fact, an entirely separate life. It's just that the three of them are so involved together over work, and indeed Piers so enjoys Lucien's company, therefore I am confident that it will all work out very well indeed.'

All this gained him was an ironic glance from his aunt and a sub-acid, 'I am not in my dotage yet Gyles, so I will not be

humoured. Don't be a fool! It is a most unnatural arrangement and we all know it.' To their alarm she continued, 'I
have never been able to accept that marriage with your
apparent thankfulness. I have always had a strong suspicion
there is more in it than meets the eye.'

This was so very much in her old vein that they were
nonplussed. Only the Dowager evinced a marked reflection
of Marguerite's views with an animation so long unseen in
either of them.

'Meg and I have often discussed this,' she informed them,
'so perhaps we might well give the subject another airin'
after all this time.'

In went Henrietta up to her slim neck, saying worriedly,
'Oh dear me, should we? I mean ... so bad for Marguerite
don't you think Constance?'

All eyes swung to her. Constance said quietly, 'No I do not
not think so. In fact I am delighted to see my patient so
animated. At this rate we shall have her back on her feet in no
time at all.'

'When you have all quite finished discussin' me as if I
were a child or the village idiot,' Marguerite snapped,
'kindly accept that I am perfectly capable still of makin' my
own decisions. Any subject is as you put it so boringly "good
for me", provided it interests me *and this does*. So shall we go
on?'

It was all so familiar, and therefore so encouraging, to
them that they had nothing to add until at length Gyles
laughed, 'Bully for you darling,' he said approvingly, 'go on
then, tell us your innermost dark thoughts on the tarsome
trio.'

With a complete return to their old manner the two Old
Naughties now looked conspiratorially at one another.
'Shall we?' breathed Marguerite.

The Dowager almost tossed her head. 'Why not?' she
retorted, 'provided you don't think all this excitement is too
much for you.'

Marguerite snapped back, 'Now don't you start 'Licia, oh
and Gyles I fancy a small glass of cointreau if you please.'

'Oh lor!' Gyles rose as he spoke, 'you have got the bit
between your teeth tonight, haven't you?' He managed to
obtain Constance's nod of agreement without his sister

noticing, so he poured the liqueur, set it down beside her and re-seated himself. 'Now pray tell us, what sinister meanin' do you read into the marriage of Lucy and Piers?'

Simultaneously Marguerite and the Dowager chorused, 'We don't know,' then they twinkled at each other. The Dowager continued, 'Consider the facts. Lucy never evinced the slightest flicker of interest *in any young man*. Her season was a triumph of offers, a disaster of refusals. Unbeknown to any of us the deceitful puss plotted and schemed in a manner worthy of that rogue Machiavelli, against the day when first she and later Lucien came into their Grandmama's money. Then what happened? First one and then the other decamped, set up house and business together, into which mischief they then drew Piers Fournes. They made a startlin' success of it. Now let me stop there a moment for I wish to digress. Durin' all this, but at some time or other when Piers was in our Convalescent Home as a patient, you Gyles and I suspect Henry too came to the conclusion the boy was effeminate.'

She broke off to apostrophise her son, 'Don't sit there looking at me as if I were Medusa's head. Do you think we don't know sufficient of the Oscar Wilde affair to draw our own conclusions? Stop bein' prissy with me, I beg you. Right?' She broke off to emit the wraith of a chuckle. 'I believe the Greeks had a word for it as they had for most things; anyway – be that as it may – you suspected Piers, you fussed and fretted for Lucien ... and were later reassured. Am I not correct?'

Gyles was regarding his mother with something akin to awe.

'You harpy,' he exclaimed, 'small wonder Plum insists the pair of you have a finger in every pie.'

'Of course,' she agreed without rancour, 'what else is there left for either of us to do pray?'

This softened him, so he merely nodded. 'Then somethin' happened Gyles, but as I am not adequately clairvoyant and was never a spectator to their goin's on after they left this Castle I cannot say what it was; but somethin' blew up. Nor do I know where Lucy came into it but ... well suddenly that utterly charmin' young painter has a frightful haemorrhage, is declared to have tuberculosis and before any of us can say Jack Robinson Lucy marries him in a hurried, hole-in-corner sort of manner.'

Constance sat rigid in her chair. Her mind was in a turmoil. She was the only one in the room who knew, who had seen and heard what had been mercifully denied to any of the rest of them. She now sent up a prayer that they would stop, knowing that any intervention from her would be misinterpreted dangerously. The Countess would read into it a fear of peril to her health and this could have a dangerous aftermath, as indeed it would with all the rest of them; but what she had listened to with such stricken attention was getting too close ... too dangerously close to the truth.

Christine, in her innocence, came to the rescue, 'Of all the things, mama, I ever imagined you would say; settin' aside the dreadfulnesses you are inferring, this is by far the most distasteful. No, shockin' is a better word. We know, none better, that Lucy and Lucien have been unusually close since babyhood, but then so are many twins and I see no possible justification for speculations of so evil a nature as yours.'

Two bright spots flared in her cheeks and her hands twitched in her lap. 'None of you have asked me what I think; but now I am going to tell you. I think that Lucy loves Lucien more than anyone else in the world. I also think Lucien is quite incapable of loving anyone but himself. He is a brilliant, gifted, egocentric will-of-the-wisp. He is also impulsive, self-centred and of course wholly spoiled by everyone. I think that the mother-instinct is also very strong in Lucy and that for all her schemin' she was touched by an overwhelmin' sense of pity and protectiveness when Piers became so ill. I accept that at that juncture Piers *was* in love with her and that she felt his life might depend upon his having a very strong reason for fighting this dreadful disease. Lucy gave him that reason. We know she liked him immensely – both of them did – but I am certain she married him because of her enormous protectiveness. As matters have turned out he is now recovering splendidly so I see no possible reason to doubt that, in its own curious way their marriage will turn out to be very successful. I do not for one moment entertain the possibility that there is anything more to it than I have explained. And now dear Marguerite do you think it is time you went to bed?'

'No,' Marguerite's eyes were very bright. 'I have not finished my *digestif* and anyway I am not tired. In fact I feel better than I have done for a very long time. Stop fussin', do! And now let us talk of somethin' else.' Her eyes sparkled with their old mischief. 'Anyway Gyles needs some time in which to recover from 'Licia's revelations and that extremely forceful speech of yours.'

'I'm sorry,' Christine was contrite, 'but really!'

'Quite so, quite so,' the Dowager was back-tracking now with a vengeance and again only Constance knew what aftermaths of confabulations between the naughty pair would follow.

Sinclair and John, totally bewildered by it all, were staring at their patent leather pumps, endeavouring to find something to contribute which could oil these very troubled waters.

Suddenly Sinclair found what he considered to be a fortuitous topic. 'In a very short time n-now,' he said with barely any stammer, 'Gilbert will b-be eighteen. What do you suppose he would l-like us to do in celebration?'

'Give him some money I don't doubt,' Gyles grunted. 'That chap's becomin' a walkin' calculator. If he ever contemplates matrimony it will be to the *Financial Times*. What do you suggest Sinclair?'

Sinclair looked doubtful. 'I don't know,' he admitted, 'except that he told that older Brinkman boy he hated parties. I had that from George who overheard Gilbert saying it.'

'Since when,' chuckled Marguerite, 'have you taken to hob-nobbin' with the underfootman?'

'S-since he came to help me dress one night,' Sinclair defended himself.

'I was only teasin',' she said hastily, 'don't be so stuffy dear!'

The topics, as they all agreed later, were disastrous besides being in the worst possible taste; but the return of her sparkle to Marguerite was at least some consolation. Now she said, 'I should think the solution is fairly obvious. Just ask him when you next write. It is not until the end of July, so you have plenty of time in which to do so. In fact, I would write for you if you preferred. Gilbert is, I suspect, more likely to be frank with me, whereas with you dear he might feel nervous of hurting your feelings.'

Sinclair grasped at this straw. 'Oh would you? He is such a difficult young man, half the time I simply do not understand him at all.'

Then Constance did stand up, shake out her skirts and say persuasively, 'Dear Countess do you think we should begin to think about putting you to bed?'

'Why not indeed,' she smiled. 'Tomorrow I will prepare a rough draft for Sinclair. Then he can read it to assure himself I have been sufficiently tactful, eh?'

She leaned forward and tapped him with her fan. 'You have provided me with ample food for reflection – all of you.'

They had never seen her in better form though, as Christine confided, mounting the staircase on Gyles' arm, 'How anyone could find such stimulus from that awful conversation is past imagining. They are a dreadful pair Gyles, but oh whatever should we do without them!'

The letter was drafted during the morning, presented for Sinclair's inspection and Marguerite spent the best part of the afternoon re-writing it. It took so long because she kept pausing to gaze thoughtfully at her rose gardens; but even the Dowager, who spent the entire evening with her, failed to learn anything about those thoughts.

Four days later Gilbert's reply appeared on Marguerite's breakfast tray. It was a curious one, she felt it was slightly guarded; as if the writer had something to conceal, though nothing he wrote gave grounds for thinking so. He wrote:

> Dear Great Aunt Marguerite,
>   Thank you for your very kind letter. If I could choose I would say luncheon with the family on my eighteenth birthday. I am not very good at parties. They make me feel awkward and I never know what to say to people.
>   I believe you mentioned that you had shares in British Consolidated so know you will be pleased that these have just gained five points and are tipped to go even higher. Enclosed is a cutting from the *Financial Times*. It gives

you the picture very clearly as always. Congratulations! There is nothing more gratifying than learning one has made a sound investment.

This is as you know my last term. I cannot pretend I am sorry. It has all become such a waste of time.

I hope that your health has improved (like your shares) and that both will continue to do so. Please remember me to my parents and please convince them for me that I only want what I have said.

Your affectionate great-nephew Gilbert.

'He's not my affectionate anything,' she murmured crossly, adjusting her spectacles and turning to the newspaper cutting.

When this had been absorbed, 'What a shrewd boy!' she exclaimed, for the habit, as with all lonely people, of talking to herself was becoming very much stronger since her heart attack. 'I wonder what he would think of my other investments, I think I will try to find out when he comes home, I really will.'

Her active mind, always acutely honed to what she called 'promisin' developments', found it 'fascinatin'' that Lord Brinkman – she thought of him as 'that successful counter-jumper' – should take so great an interest in Sinclair's unprepossessing son. The matter vexed her. Eventually she asked Sinclair and Henrietta.

Sinclair replied, 'We hope, my dear, that the boy will go on to the 'Varsity. It has been arranged. He is undoubtedly brilliant. His reports are excellent; but we shall just have to wait and see.'

All this without the vestige of a stammer, she noted.

She pressed them. 'Do you not consider Gilbert spends too much of his leisure with those dreary Brinkman boys?' This query made her wrinkle her nose in distaste.

'Well you see dear,' Gilbert explained, 'he likes so few people. I do not think them harmful. Just rather common for which they cannot be blamed surely? They have done very well too. I only wish that I could afford to launch Gilbert properly in the City, he has such a remarkable interest in, er, all that sort of thing, stocks and shares you know. Not,' he appended hurriedly, 'that he ever says much to me ... but one gains that impression ...' His voice petered out, indecisively as usual.

The next time the topic was raised the Dowager chose to denigrate Gilbert. Marguerite exclaimed, 'Oh no my dear love, do not underestimate him. He advised me three years ago to invest in some shares, now I wonder if I can remember the name? Oh yes I have it, an American petroleum company. Of course I thought little of it at first; but when I consulted Sue-Ellen she told me she owned a great many of the same shares and held the very highest opinion of them so I bought some.'

'How many?'

'Oh, quite a lot,' she was determinedly vague, 'and it's been such fun ever since, watching them rise and rise ... even though he is so young Gilbert does seem to have a very definite flair for that kind of thing. Extraordinary really when one considers he is your son Sinclair.'

'How much?' The Dowager pressed her. 'Now come on Meg it is not like you to be secretive.'

Marguerite twinkled. 'Well now,' she excused herself, making a little deprecatory gesture, 'I have so little use for money these days and as you all know my dear husband made over almost everything to me when ... when we separated.'

'Almost everything? I thought he had to give up all his worldly goods before taking his vows,' said Gyles abruptly.

'He did, dear; but there was the matter of his – I do not recall the name, but it is a sort of dowry which men take with them into monasteries.'

'Oh that,' Gyles sounded relieved, 'but he left you very comfortably off did he not, even so?'

Marguerite looked at him sorrowfully. 'He left me a very rich woman indeed, but he still gave generously to the Order.' Her eyes were heavy with unshed tears. 'Oh how different my life would have been if that had never happened.'

All contrition now, they began trying to comfort her; but when Constance drifted in, her arms filled with flowers, to enquire if all was well, she became worried.

'Oh dear Constance ... such exquisite blooms! How very thoughtful,' Marguerite murmured as she took and examined them, then laid them aside. 'And now my dear if I may I think I would prefer to go back to bed.'

Constance and the dowager exchanged glances across her head. Her family departed. The day nurse was sent for and the fiat went forth that no one could join her for coffee after dinner; but later, in the drawing room when Constance asked very softly, 'Was something said which upset the Countess?' Lady Aynthorp nodded. 'All our faults,' she owned, 'we were talkin' about money, nothin' there to worry her of course; but it led to her husband, I take it you know the story?'

Constance shook her head. 'I thought that he was dead?'

'Who was dead?' said Gyles, looking across at them.

'It's alright, Gyles, Constance has never heard the story of Marguerite and Jules.'

'We seldom speak of it,' Gyles told her, 'lest it cause Meg pain; but, briefly, they were the darlings of French society, deeply in love but childless. They were supremely happy for a number of years. Then one day Jules told her that he had felt a call towards the religious life. Shocked as she was, Marguerite of course raised no obstacles. Shortly afterwards Jules wound up his affairs. He left everything to Meg except the money he took to his order and then, well, the little wounded creature fled back here to us where she has remained every since. It was a most tragic affair.'

Sue-Ellen was playing chess with Ninian at the time. She looked up on hearing Constance's initial query and remained clutching a pawn and gazing incredulously at Gyles.

'How truly dreadful,' she exclaimed when he had finished. 'Oh the poor lost little love, Uncle Gyles would you not say that to begin a life dedicated to God on such a cruel act was to build a house upon sand – in the spiritual sense?'

'My dear,' he replied, 'I have asked myself the same question many times; but as I grow older I become singularly reluctant to stand in judgement on such matters. I think the only answer I can give you now is that I am not the Almighty and while I have my reservations concerning the rightness of what Jules did, in the final account it must rest between the two of them . . . and their God, when they eventually meet.'

In her own unhappy state Sue-Ellen was immensely

vulnerable to such a story. This one banished sleep. It
bewildered her too. She laid Jules de Tessedre's irreversible
decision against Ninian's attitude to marrying great wealth
and by morning she had at last decided what she could not
possibly do, if not wholly what she must do. For her, the two
men's attitudes came together under the simple head, 'man
does what he must at the point where he stands.' During the
long night hours she had wondered greatly whether she and
Ninian were so placed because they had once been untrue to
each other in some past, unfathomable circumstance and
were now reaping the bitter harvest of their own acts. She
had always found it impossible to accept the proposition of
one life one death one judgement. Such was altogether un-
acceptable to her because as she had once said to her father,
'It makes God unreasonable'.

'How,' she argued, 'can a helpless deaf and dumb cripple
be judged on one such life, equally with, say, a Genghis
Khan or any other human who lives a life of dedicated
cruelty and power seeking? God to me, Daddy, must be
wholly reasonable, wise, just and compassionate. Surely
that's what He is all about?'

Her father had asked her to explain more fully, making his
comment non-committal. 'Well now, honey, just supposing
you go on and try to tell me how you think He operates.'
Then sat rocking peacefully, only the tip of his cigar glowing
in the darkness.

They were on the wide porch of their Texan home
with the heat of the night all around them, only a
great fan overhead creating a small enclave of cool for
them.

'I think,' Sue-Ellen began hesitantly, 'that, once upon a
time every man and woman was *both*, man and woman in
one, His complete creation. Then somewhere, somehow, we
went so very wrong that we were divided. That to me is the
reality of the story of the Garden of Eden. It's actually said
in that bit about Lillith whom you remember "laboured and
rent herself in twain". After that the two halves of us had to
live as separate entities until we had cleared up whatever
augean stable it was that we created for ourselves. Then and
then only do we come together again as twins. Some people
call it "The Wheel of Re-Birth" to which we are chained

until we complete the cycle. I do not of course believe the proposition that we live all our lives here. I think there are many other planets where we live out many lives as well as on this one. Wherever we are we always have the choice as to whether we struggle to get nearer to completion, or just allow ourselves to slide back.'

She remembered what she had said that night to her father, as she pushed back the bedclothes and went to the window to draw the curtains. She stood watching another miracle, of a new day's birth. As the light came, revealing the gardens, they seemed to be trying to communicate with her; but try as she did she could not read their message; but the certainty grew that even if she and Ninian never came together *this time*, she could never again make her home anywhere other than England.

Someone else was awake in the darkness at Castle Rising. He lay with his hands linked behind his head, wondering what his employer would have to say if he went to him with the idea which had taken so strong a hold on him during recent weeks.

How indeed would Lord Aynthorp receive his proposition? Then he too flung back the bedclothes, dressed and went out into the July morning. He walked to the lake where the old black swans were preening and cleaning, and their half-grown cygnets were putting tentative paddles into the shallows. He watched them for a while, then moved on until he came to the beginnings of the rise which led to the saddle back. Eventually he climbed to the top and stood looking down at all the ageless beauty below. The sun was now touching up the Castle windows. It gilded the trees in the home park, it shone down on the men who plodded from their cottages to begin another day's work. There was only one thing missing. There were still no cattle being driven to pasture, no pigs in the styes, for Gyles had adhered to his decision that no more cloven-footed creatures should enter his land until a full year after the epidemic which had cost them all so much.

Suddenly it seemed to Johnathan Brownrigg that he was making much of a small matter; that most of his unease stemmed from a rather base fear that Gyles would be angered into dismissing him. He too had grown to love it all and the world outside seemed a predatory, unwelcoming place after living at Castle Rising. It angered him that he could be so selfish so, turning abruptly, he began retracing his steps until it dawned on him that now he was enjoying the exercise, the crisp air with its promise of great heat to come until, as he climbed the terrace steps, he found himself whistling.

He went in and asked Gyles if he might see him after breakfast.

When he followed his employer from the breakfast room, with Diana walking between them down the corridor to Gyles' old office, entering the shabby room and when at last in that room the door closed and Gyles invited him to 'take a pew m'boy and tell me what's on yer mind', he found himself marvelling that he could have entertained any doubts as to how this sensitive, perceptive man would react to what he had to say.

'Well sir,' he began, 'it concerns Rupert of course but, as it were, by Rupert out of another couple of charmin' youngsters here, so I have decided to risk your displeasure. I am of course reluctant, after your many kindnesses to do anything which might seem to diminish my great appreciation of all you have done for me, furthermore above and beyond these considerations I have had to contend with a matter of telling tales out of school.'

'You are in a pother aren't you,' Gyles sympathised. 'Well you can be assured I will regard whatever you say as confidential.' He leaned forward. 'Why don't you stop bein' so deuced formal and just tell me what's on your mind?'

Johnathan grinned a little ruefully. 'Alright sir. Part of what I have to say is precious like tittle tattle so we'll start there. My colleague, your tutor for your grandson Justin and for Mrs Delahaye's son, wishes to leave. He will be coming to tell you himself at any time now that he has made up his mind he is not suited to teaching.' He paused and into that pause Gyles murmured, 'Queen Anne's dead y'know Johnathan.'

He looked up, startled. 'You knew sir?'

'Of course I did. The feller's as restless as a cat and not to put too fine a point upon it, bored with it. I shall accept his resignation whenever he offers it, and then send him off immediately.'

'Oh,' said Johnathan, 'well now ... that alters things a bit.'

'Are you inclined to tell me why?' Gyles' voice was dry but to complete Johnathan's bewilderment he saw from his eyes that he was laughing at him. Still he hesitated, marshalling his thoughts. 'Well then,' he began, 'you'll, er, you'll have no one to tutor them.'

Gyles laughed outright. 'My dear chap that is a fairly obvious conclusion ain't it.'

'Yes it is sir, I'm sorry. What I want is to have all three of 'em you see. I think my exclusive attention builds up a complacency in Rupert which is dangerous. He thinks he is special, which is not a good thing. What's more I think I've more or less got his measure now and while I admit he's a holy terror I find him stimulating. Now, I feel sure, although there may be many shoals ahead, we should start preparing him for the rough and tumble of school life. He is the same age as Justin who is a splendid little chap. Rupert is also a year younger than Stephen who is as sound a small boy as ever I may hope to meet. The contact with two such little fellers could be of inestimable value to your holy terror. I've given it a tremendous amount of thought and I am sure even if Rupert does play up, the other two will prove a match for him ... now that he's learned it doesn't pay to go beyond certain bounds.'

All Gyles said was, 'I see.'

'Can I have a shot at all three of them together? Would Mrs Henry consider it? And what do you imagine would be Mrs Delahaye's reactions? Even supposing you agree.'

Gyles replied, 'There is only way to find out,' then he rose and reached for the bell pull. 'We'll ask 'em. As for myself ...' He broke off as George appeared in the doorway.

'You rang my lord?'

'I did,' agreed Gyles cheerfully. 'Kindly ask Mrs Delahaye if she can be so good as to spare me a few minutes in here, then when you have done so ask Mrs Henry if she will be good enough to do likewise in,' again he paused to flip open his father's half-hunter and examine it, 'in about fifteen minutes' time. That will be all thank you George.'

Johnathan looked up uncertainly. 'You were about to say?' he prompted.

'Relax Johnathan, I was merely about to say that speakin' for myself I was hopin' some such idea might come to you. Now that it has I am delighted.'

He went back to his chair behind the refectory table, reached for his pipe and began filling it. 'Care for a pipe?' he asked.

'Thank you sir,' Johnathan dived into his pocket.

Gyles pushed the old pewter jar across. 'Then take a fill and let me say one more thing. I would also like it very much indeed if you could bring yourself to give me progress reports. Justin is my eldest grandson and as such he will one day take my place when his father has done his worst,' again his smile took any sting from his words. 'I shall be profoundly interested in what you made of the boy. Remember he's, er, slightly handicapped.'

'You mean his left foot?'

Gyles nodded. 'Lady Constance has the same handicap, one leg a fraction shorter than the other. Would you ever have known?'

Johnathan shook his head. 'Frankly no sir, it's so very slight, that limp.'

'Oh as to that I am not in the least worried that Justin will retain it. In time it will be as unnoticeable as in Lady Constance, we will just have to be careful while his feet are growin'. I am however deeply anxious as to what the mental effect may be when he gets among his own kind. Little boys are remarkably similar to animals. In any pack the weaker runs the risk of goin' to the wall if he's not personally confident in himself. D'you get my meanin'? A little aggression, carefully implanted, could be all that he needs. For all I know it may be there already. It should be if he runs true to form. Then there's young Stephen. I won't deal with him now, but if you would stay on after we have had their mothers' verdicts on this enterprise I'll do my best to fill you in. We must do whatever is possible to seek out, and if your age theories are right, eradicate absolutely anything of his father in him for not to put too fine a point upon it he was a wrong 'un, through and through.'

When Petula and Sue-Ellen were fully informed of what

was proposed, subject of course to their agreement, the two young mothers reacted much as Gyles had anticipated. Sue-Ellen stood, rather like Richard under duress, her legs straddled, as she prepared to take the hurdle she saw confronting her.

'Has Uncle Gyles told you about my late husband?' she asked, her head flung back slightly to face the challenge.

'Not yet,' Johnathan agreed, 'but he has expressed the wish to do so if you are agreeable to the proposition.'

'Agreeable,' Sue-Ellen exclaimed, 'thankful would be a better word. That young man Abbot is a nice boy but he's totally inadequate. I have been anxious for some time to make a change. Frankly I did not want to seem ungrateful. Now let's get this straight, my late husband was what I have learned to call over here "a thoroughly bad lot". He had so much charm it was indescribable. I fell in love with him knowing what I was in for. In my innocence I thought I could handle him; but I see now that would have been quite impossible. He was the most fluent liar, unbelievably deceitful, ingenious with it and a gay, fascinating, charming companion when everything was going his way. To try and hold him once he was bored – and I suspect on looking back that he had a very low threshhold to boredom – then to exert the slightest control over him was not unlike trying to hold a wet eel in a high wind from a rocking boat.'

She paused, crimson with embarrassment at her own words, to which she added after a short pause, 'Yet he died magnificently. He was decorated posthumously by England's King. That my dear Johnathan is about the only thing you can tell my son about his father, except that he rode well, shot well, was a fine fly fisherman and he danced divinely.'

She swung round to face her 'Uncle' Gyles. 'Don't tell me that that was worse than wicked – because it was vulgar. I know it was. Now,' she faltered, 'I feel lower than a duck's stomach so there. But Johnathan is too nice a person for me to handicap him by withholding the truth.'

Gyles remained completely unruffled. 'I had no such idea in mind, my dear,' he assured her, 'I was about to say, at the risk of bein' fulsome, that you have made just about the most gallant speech it has ever been my privilege to hear.'

His words almost finished her; but she managed to choke out, 'I am so afraid Uncle Gyles, so dreadfully afraid, so please let him to go to Johnathan.'

Then it was Petula's turn. She sat down, smoothed out her shortened skirts and listened as Gyles explained. He was careful to make no reference at this juncture to Sue-Ellen.

'But how perfectly splendid,' she exclaimed. 'Oh, Johnathan I am pleased and so will Henry be. I'm relieved too. If you can spare the time Justin can have two whole years with you before we really need to send him to a prep school and by that time he'll have different shoes, so his specialist says, and he'll hardly limp at all.'

Gyles threw out his hands. 'Well that's that, isn't it? You may care to know Sue-Ellen's opinion is identical with your own.'

'Well of course,' she cried indignantly, 'otherwise she wouldn't be Sue-Ellen. Don't be silly darling.'

She turned to Johnathan. 'We'll talk later, shall we? But now I must go and tell Henry and I want to see Sue-Ellen myself.' Saying which she jumped up and ran across the room.

'To think I worked myself up until I expected to be sent packing,' Johnathan exclaimed ruefully. 'Now sir, is it possible I could bring you my initial breakdown for their curriculum, say after dinner tonight?'

'In the Library,' said Gyles smiling. 'Oh Johnathan, by the way there is one small point, will another hundred a year for each of those extra little beggars meet with your approval?'

That night at dinner the vexed question of suitable gifts for Gilbert on his eighteenth birthday was discussed.

Henrietta complained that her son only liked the very dullest things and her husband Sinclair did little to widen that scope when he said dolorously, 'He seems to prefer figures to fiction, desks to cricket pitches, and I don't know what in the world to buy for him.'

Henry was not much help either when he contributed his mite. 'Give him a pair of binoculars, for keepin' a sharp eye out for a sound investment, Uncle, then you could add some

ledgers for enterin' up endless columns of figures and a
decent suit, he always looks like an unmade bed to me.' Both
Christine and Petula rounded on him.

'You're becoming thoroughly nasty,' said Petula; while
Christine said severely, 'I will not have you children speak
like that of any member of this family. Henry you're a big
boy now and should know by this time that it is . . .'

She was not allowed to finish. In unison Henry, Ninian
and Andrew chanted, 'We know Mother, it's worse than
wicked, it's vulgar!' which at least made Gyles smile, though
he hastily concealed it by dabbing at his mouth with his table
napkin.

Henry forged on. 'Honestly Mum, if we gave Gilbert a
new wardrobe between us now that he's no longer a schoolboy, we could all weigh in with ties and shirts and socks and
things, and get him to spruce himself up a bit before he goes
to Cambridge.'

'Where the rig of the day,' Andrew contributed damp-
ingly, 'is grey flannel bags, a navy blue blazer, five yards of
woollen scarf and one of those whaddycall'em, oh yes, pork
pie hats with the brim steamed down so that it dips like a
respectful butter woman.'

Christine flushed. 'Henry I will put up with a great deal
from you but I flatly refuse to be addressed as Mum, you are
becomin' impossible.'

Predictably Primrose suggested, 'What about a horse?'

'Well what about it, Aunt Prim?' Ninian retorted.
'Gilbert doesn't know more about horses than that one end
wags and the other bites.'

This proved too much for Gilbert's mama who showed
signs of weeping, and this angered Gyles. Eventually what
had begun as a simple discussion developed into yet another
first class family row culminating in everyone except his
seething lordship rejecting their puddings, which caused
another Gallic outburst belowstairs.

'Wot's got inter 'em now?' demanded Mrs Parsons,
profiting by the occasion by helping herself liberally to both
raspberry *mille feuille* and iced *soufflé aux fraises* and
thereafter talking with her mouth full.

'Master Gilbert's birthday presents,' said Sawby grimly.
'The young gentlemen were at their worst. Then Mrs John

made matters worse by suggesting a horse and what Mr
Andrew said after that made Mrs Henrietta cry.'

'She always cries,' mumbled Mrs Parsons with cream
oozing from her mouth, 'there ain't nothing speshul in that.'

'Then,' Sawby ignored the interruption, 'his lordship lost
his temper and fairly trounced 'em. So they all sulked,
refused pudding and 'er ladyship rose very stately and took
all the other ladies with her. George 'ave you drawn covers
and set the port?'

'Yes Mr Sawby,' George sat down abruptly. ''An now 'is
lordship is still carrying on and Mr Henry's just sauced 'im
which ain't done no good neither.'

'Wen I lef' Mr John was suggesting as 'ow Mr Joe
Brinkman might be worth consulting. As I went out of the
room I 'eard 'is lordship say "first intelligent suggestion
anyone has put forward this evening" so mebbe 'ee'll
telephone 'im now.'

'It's a nice pudding too, both of 'em is,' said Mrs Parsons,
reached out to the entrée dishes again.

'I nevvaire make my *créations* for you and you'll get as fat
as a peeg!' André attacked her so sharply that she actually
drew her hand back and stared at him with little beady eyes.
'Wot then?' she demanded, instantly become aggressive,
'it's me or the dustbin. We never does serve them with
the same puddin's twice.' This invoked a stream of French
invective which was truncated by the sound of the dining
room bell.

George looked pointedly at Edward who rose, muttering,
'You're gettin' a sight too lazy my lad,' before vanishing up
the steep stairway.

He was back almost immediately. 'Come on they've all
gorne. We can get cleared away quick and then settle to a
nice little game of pontoon. He wants you Sawby, in the
Library he said.'

Sawby rose. By now he was equally ruffled so as a
departing shot he warned, 'No skipping your work now, and
anyway I do not approve of gambling in the Servants' Hall.'

'Oh Gawd,' muttered George, 'I think I'll go fer a stroll.'
He dropped his voice to whisper to Edward, 'You and me'll
slip off to the Arms eh? We'll be bound to get a game down
there.'

Ultimately, having spoken to Lord Brinkman, Gyles accepted his advice to 'give the boy cheques, he'll be best pleased with those. I am weighing in with a small one, he's a brilliant young feller y'know.' To which opinion Gyles gave lip service; but even so it did provide room for thought.

In the meantime the knife turned for Sue-Ellen when Ninian made it known at the breakfast table that he was planning to move into Farthings now that the electricians and plumbers had completed their work. He told the assembled family he had found a very nice, elderly couple who were prepared to keep house for him. The woman had excellent references and was a good plain cook while her husband had been in service too in a very good household as butler and was able to drive a car when needed. He found them both very pleasant. The woman was a motherly old soul who seemed to have a great liking for his old army servant, who was coming to work for him as groom-cum-valet.

'It will be very comfortable for me to have old Bossy around again,' he said contentedly, 'he knows what I like and will keep an eye on the other two. What's more it's his daughter I've got as parlourmaid. I've left Mrs Potter to lay on a housemaid and someone to help her in the kitchen.'

Sue-Ellen heard all this listlessly. Ninian then turned to her.

'If you'll just come over once more Sue-Ellen to advise me about my pictures; then once they're hung and Mrs Potter has had time to stock up her shelves, I'm all ready to go. Mama please don't look so woebegone I shall be dotting to and fro even before the huntin' starts again. Besides I'm all for havin' a housewarming. Nothin' grand, but, well I want you all to come and inspect my new quarters. Then Sue-Ellen will have to be persuaded to play hostess for me.' To which she made no reply, wishing instead she could give him a resounding box on his ears.

To give him his due, Ninian was doing his best. He too had come through sleepless nights to a determination to make the best of things. Now, had he been challenged, he could have defended himself on the grounds that he was only doing what he thought best by getting himself out of the way of endless temptation.

They hung his pictures together even so. They shared the
picnic hamper André had put up for them. They strolled out
into the garden. That was when he told her that he planned
on leaving the day after on his visit to London.

'And on that day,' Sue-Ellen decided, 'I shall come over
here for the last time to do the flowers for him before he
moves in. With Ninian out of the way I can at least pretend
that I'm doing them for us both.'

That night, when they returned, they found Gilbert had
arrived. A few minutes later Richard rushed in, greeted her
joyously, hugged her without inhibitions and declared, 'If
you knew how I was longing to get back to you and our Zoo.'
He pulled her into a chair.

'Sit down do. Tell me everything that's happened during
term. After dinner we'll go round together, I can't possibly
wait until the morning.'

Just as the soup was being passed, the faint sound of a car
crunching on the drive made Sawby whisper, 'Psst!' to
Raikes. She listened to his whispered instructions, left the
room, later slipped back again, handing over a scribble on a
scrap of paper. . . 'Mr Peter Christian has gone upstairs to
change.'

'Did I hear a car Sawby?' enquired Gyles.

'You did my lord. Mr Peter Christian has just arrived. He
hurried upstairs to change. He will be down again shortly.
Shall I lay another cover or serve him in the breakfast room?'

'In here of course.' Turning to Claire, he smiled. 'We
wouldn't penalise him on his first night home just for bein'
late to dinner, would we?'

This dinner was in marked contrast to the stormy meal
during which Gilbert's presents were debated. He now sat
eating in silence, pausing every now and then to prod back
his spectacles which, as usual, showed a marked tendency
to slide off his nose.

'They always do mama,' he said simply when reproached.
Then he resumed his eating.

'How was your last term?' Gyles asked him.

'Satisfactory, sir, thank you.' Gilbert prodded again.
'Joe's father sent a car for us this morning. He wanted to see
me before I came down here. We went direct to Park Lane.'

'Has the other lad, Lionel isn't it, also left College?'

'Yes sir, he was with us too. Joe came down so that we could have a chat on the way to London.'

'We shall have to have a long talk about your future,' Sinclair then said smilingly, 'after your birthday, though, don't you think?'

'Very well sir,' Gilbert agreed. Then Peter Christian came rushing in, greeted everyone, asked after his great aunt Marguerite and listened sympathetically to the news of her. After which he attacked his soup as if he had not seen food for a week, said, 'Ah, that's better after the grub I've been getting,' and enquired, 'and how's our Henry?'

'As well as can be expected knowin' you were due,' retorted Henry. The pair exchanged grins and the fish went round.

'And how is Sandhurst sir?' Gilbert enquired suddenly.

'Gosh that makes me feel a hundred,' Peter Christian exclaimed, 'it's absolutely top hole but you can drop the "sir" old chap.' He turned to his father and began a long rambling conversation about his seniors, most of whom were contemporary with either Sinclair or Gyles. It was a strictly family evening which, as the Dowager thought, looking back sadly at what happened thereafter, was just as well in the circumstances.

Sue-Ellen was hauled off by the exuberant Richard. As they were walking together towards the Zoo she asked, 'Richard, do you know anything about your ancestress the Lady Mathilde?' He shook his head. 'Not too much,' he admitted. 'She left an heirloom and made some pretty ghoulish predictions about what would happen if the family ever opened it up or lost it, at least so far as I have gathered.'

'And have you opened it?'

Richard shook his head. 'Neither lost nor opened it so far as I know, but why don't you ask Hen, he's the one who's crammed with family history. I say, about those white leopards ...'

Sue-Ellen gave up, resolving to take his advice. In the end she had no need for on going to visit Marguerite after an exhaustive session of peering at sleeping animals and birds by the light of a torch, she found her in bed, with the Dowager doing her *petit point* in a high-backed chair nearby.

They broke off some discussion as she went in, 'Come

along in dear,' cried Marguerite, 'we were just rakin' over the coals of past history.'

'Your history?' the girl queried bending to kiss her tenderly. 'How fascinating, I never tire of hearing about the Lormes.'

'I do not suppose,' said the Dowager indulgently as she drew up a small chair and settled with a sigh of relief, 'there is much you have not heard already. You look tired my child, what have you been doin'?'

'Traipsing around my Zoo in company with Richard; waking up indignant animals and birds. We would be there still if the torch had not expired. I'm exhausted!' Sue-Ellen, nothing if not delighted, secretly agreed with Richard's enthusiasm whole-heartedly. She then prompted, 'There's a tremendous amount of family history I still haven't heard, especially about what I only know of as the Lady Mathilde's bequest.'

'Well now you can relax,' said Marguerite fondly.

'That was the beginning of it all,' said the Dowager resuming her work. 'She was a perfectly healthy creature, livin' in our small original Castle in Normandy when suddenly she summoned her eldest son and told him that she was dying. By then she had not only taken to her bed but had been shriven and was surrounded by her women and children – she had seven sons you know. Well anyway Edouarde, her eldest, came, though somewhat reluctantly. She dismissed the rest and launched herself into a spate of prophecy. According to her, our line would die out in France but would survive through her fourth son Henri who came to England with William the Conqueror in 1066. Well then, as the story runs, she drew from beneath the furs which covered her, a casket. She gave it to Edouarde, who must have been a very acquisitive man, for she was at pains to stress that what it contained was of no value; but she charged him to deliver it to Henri. Meg can you remember the words?'

Marguerite leaned back on her pillows, her eyes fixed upon her sister-in-law. Sue-Ellen thought she looked more fragile than ever before; but still she marvelled at the brightness of her eyes. 'Would you like me to repeat them?' Her eyes glittered in anticipation of this pleasure.

'Oh yes please – if it will not tire you too much,' Sue-Ellen clasped her hands together. 'I am so fascinated.'

'It won't tire me,' said Marguerite very softly. 'The Lady Mathilde, holding out the casket, charged her son that he treat the contents of this casket as an heirloom to his descendants and that he pass the words on thus to his firstborn and so on down the line.' She laid great stress upon what she said next: ' *"for whiles he does so there will be Lormes who put down good roots, bear fruit and seed themselves beyond the limits of my vision"*. She then appeared to weaken ... but after a time she rallied again. She began murmuring as if to herself, "soldiers, courtiers, family men and missish things like Gervaise" – he was her effeminate son or so we are given to understand – "all will weave themselves into the pattern of the English land and hold fast to what they represent, not gaining mighty stature but strong in convictions they hold to staunchly and, above all they will be courtly, gentle knights." She said no more. Later when her family returned and were gathered about her she laughed, "a birdlike sound, intense in pleasurable amusement, like a maid who has played some mischievous jest" ... and so laughing ... she died.'

In the ensuing silence a log cracked below the mantel-shelf, for there was always a fire now. The little Countess complained so frequently that she was cold.

Sue-Ellen sat unmoving, still in the thrall of those words which had first been uttered over eight hundred years ago. At length she spoke, 'Did Henri receive the casket?'

'Oh yes,' the Dowager took up the story again, 'Edouarde journeyed to England and gave it to him as bid. When Henri built his first castle he installed it in a special niche in the Great Hall after his first son's christening at which King William stood sponsor. We have it still my dear.'

'Unopened?' she breathed.

'Er, not exactly my dear,' admitted the Dowager.

Sue-Ellen scarcely dared breathe lest she break the spell. Marguerite than looked at her sister-in-law, 'In the light of certain matters why should we not?'

After this unspoken parley, her old friend nodded and said slowly, 'No my dear Sue-Ellen ... it ... has ... been ... opened.'

'Oh! then what did it contain . . . ?'

'We are not supposed to know. It happened after my father's sudden death.'

'But what was it?' The girl's eyes were shining with excitement.

'Nothing of any consequence, as the Lady Mathilde said. Let me continue for a few moments longer. Superstition can be a most curious factor in men's lives. It is responsible for so many acts which otherwise would never occur. The difficulty is that such a thin line separates superstition from recognition, so very few of us can ever be quite sure which is which.'

She continued, 'The trouble with the opening of the Box lay in the subsequent identification of the act; but whether the fear which followed was engendered by recognition or superstition we truly do not know.'

The *petit point* lay leglected now in her lap. Sue-Ellen experienced a sharp tingling as if she had touched some naked electric current. She was quick to realise too that from this moment neither of them were conscious that she was there and instinct told her that, to them both, this had become a final effort at clarification of some grave problem which had dominated both their lives.

The Dowager began again hesitantly, 'You must never forget, Meg, that we are by nature superstitious. I do not seek to excuse us but merely to remind you that history and events have made us so, even as we are also endowed from time to time with recognition.'

Meg sat forward with a sudden display of energy, 'So we are still no further towards a solution as to whether or not that thing in the Box, which caused the Lady Mathilde to die laughing – remember – could have become invested with supernormal powers. Was Boney right then when he croaked "Pandora's Box"?'

Faintly there came from the *'petit salon'* the parrot's croak . . . 'Pandora's Box, ha, ha, ha, Pandora's Box . . .'. Sue-Ellen shivered.

'But after the Box *was* opened,' the Dowager reminded her with great reluctance, 'everything seemed to go wrong both for us and for England, whose destiny has always been handfasted with our own, country of adoption or no. Death came, and tragedies with the death of the Peacemaker, then the Great War and more deaths; a reckless, wanton decimation of young lives ended before they could fulfil their original destinies. Always the tilt was downwards. Oh, it became a challenge. This as usual developed into a stubborn and defiant struggle to hold on. I admit that caused the graph to rise again; but never to the heights it had attained before. The downward drift has always been maintained. So, is our line doomed? And, if so, is England's too? Wall her greatness diminished until she sinks into some abyss too hideous to contemplate? It is time to come to terms with one salient factor: that we shall never know in this life what set it off; but where it concerns this family it is hard to credit that the opening of that Box could possibly play a major part.'

'And yet,' murmured Marguerite, 'the potency of inanimate objects can never be gainsaid. Otherwise what of the Cross? Oh I agree that we can never be absolutely sure but, from William and the Saint's bones across which he swore that oath, to our Talisman . . . well,' she spread out her hands eloquently, 'save only for our "runts" Castle Rising and the Lormes have had as a fine a run as did your Justin when he rode to hounds that last time. That ended in death did it not?'

The Dowager resumed then. 'Again we can debate endlessly on Justin's last words. Did he say "no" to something Plum did when he held him, and then, quite separately, "open the box", the last words he spoke before death came for him. Or did he say "don't open the box" in that moment of passing from one world into the next and possibly therefore having further sight?'

'It is all conjecture,' Marguerite exclaimed, 'we can never know while we are here. That is the logic of the problem. If we knew, then our knowledge would dominate our every act completely and that would be the end of the limited free will in which we have such absolute confidence. Therefore all we can do under universal law is to live it out exerting maximum effort in tryin' to safeguard that which we cherish so jealously in defiance of any signs or portents.' She lay back on her pillows as if suddenly exhausted.

When she spoke again her words seemed to come with difficulty and then they were no more than a whisper. 'All the same I *do* believe that we would have done better if we had left that Talisman alone.'

They watched her anxiously for a while. She appeared to be sleeping. Then the Dowager leaned over and whispered to Sue-Ellen, 'You had better slip away now my dear. We will speak more about it all some other time.'

Sue-Ellen's eyes went back to the little figure on the bed as she rose and left. 'She *must* be sleeping,' was her last thought as she closed the door for, as she passed the bed, the face on the pillows seemed to have shed its age and was as tranquil as the face of any sleeping child.

To her surprise she too fell asleep immediately she climbed the little velvet steps and slid between the lavender-scented sheets in the great high four-poster bed with its stiff brocade hangings. In the morning she awoke completely refreshed. It seemed as if during her unconsciousness, her own way had been made clear to her in whatever state she had passed those sleeping hours. Now her forward mind was clear too, fortified and resolute. Come what may, and despite even Ninian, she would never again even consider the possibility of leaving what had become her chosen place. Unaccountably maybe, she felt as if she had come home.

When Gilbert asked if he might have his breakfast in bed, explaining that the cold baths and early rising at Winchester had been the most disagreeable part of his school life, they all decided to send up his presents with the tray.

When he came down, *Financial Times* folded and under one arm, as usual, he also carried a sheaf of papers. He thanked everyone with such earnestness that they were surprised.

Phrases such as 'most generous of you' . . . 'thank you so much' . . . 'it really was most kind', came tumbling out. Altogether, when Sawby announced from the doorway of the Library in which they had all foregathered, 'Luncheon is served my lady', they all went into the dining room in great good humour.

This persisted until Christine laid down her table napkin preparatory to rising, when Gilbert said abruptly, 'Do please stay Aunt Christine . . . er, it would be so nice to have you with us over port.'

Surprised glances were exchanged between them. Christine picked up her napkin and replaced it on her lap.

'Very well Gilbert, we shall be happy to stay.' Sawby sent George scurrying in search of extra port glasses. These were distributed. Silence overtook them all. Henrietta sat beaming, Sinclair looked very pleased; but Gyles shot a suspicious glance in his nephew's direction. He received the decanter, poured, circulated and when the tour was completed, raised his glass and wished Gilbert a very happy birthday.

Unknowing Henry raised the curtains upon the ensuing scene by enquiring mildly, 'When do you hope to go to Cambridge?'

Gilbert looked at him thoughtfully, prodded his spectacles back into position and clearing his throat replied, 'I do not intend to go to Cambridge, Cousin Henry.'

'N-not go to C-C-Cambridge!' stuttered Sinclair, 'why on earth n-n-not?'

'It would interfere with the plans which I made four years ago sir.' He sounded extremely composed, even to lifting his glass and taking a sip of port.

'May we enquire what plans?' Gyles asked, leaning back in his great chair and surveying the slight figure through his monocle.

'Oh yes, sir,' Gilbert turned towards him. 'At the risk of boring you I will explain quite fully.' He raised himself a fraction in his chair in order to withdraw from underneath the folder of papers on which he had sat throughout luncheon. The family watched, with varying expressions of curiosity and surprise.

Gilbert then pushed forward his dessert plate in order to make room for the folder, opened it out, cleared his throat once more and began. 'Some of you may remember the year in which you allowed me to invite Joe and Lionel Brinkman to spend their holidays with me.' He looked around questioningly, collected nods and resumed. 'We had already spent many hours together at College during which we discovered that our interests were identical ...'

'What interests, f-f-for heaven's sake?' exclaimed Sinclair.

His son frowned slightly at the interruption, replied with the one word, 'Money,' then resumed. 'We had already formulated certain plans when they first came here. As you may also remember Joe brought them both down here in the car his father gave him for his seventeenth birthday. Well anyway, we decided to use birdwatching as a cover for what we had planned and before term ended I had spotted a certain advertisement in several national newspapers,' he broke off to pull a cutting from his folder then read from it, saying, 'It announced "Sale of Surplus War Materials".' Then he went on to enumerate some of the items listed.

'I spotted the one which gave me the idea. In the end we all three drove to Dover for that sale. Joe did my bidding for me because he looked older. Thus we obtained for five pounds a total of fifty thousand Bibles which had been issued to the troops. They were redundant. I won't bore you with the full details, just that we paid a carter two pounds to bring them to a very large barn which we had rented. We supervised their storage, locked the barn and then went back to College. By that time of course we had all three worked out the details concerning the disposal of my Bibles down to the last farthing.'

Irrepressibly Henry murmured, 'I bet you did!' drew a frown from his father and subsided.

'Lord Brinkman had invited me to spend the next holidays with Lionel and Joe. In the end, and this was the one bit of good luck we had not expected, we learned that both Lord and Lady Brinkman were going to Africa but that the Park Lane house was to be kept open for us, staff, chauffeur, everything.'

By now even John Lorme had ceased turning the stem of his port glass round and round. He like the rest now sat with legs stretched beneath the table watching and listening intently.

'Just before the end of term,' Gilbert went on, 'we put an advertisement in the personal column of the *Morning Post* and *Telegraph*.'

'Are we permitted,' Gyles enquired, 'to ask the contents of your advertisement?'

Gilbert put up one hand. 'Not yet sir, if you please. All in good time. We had already purchased the exact amount of brown paper, adhesive, pens, and ink we had calculated we should need. Then because of Lord and Lady Brinkman's absence we had everything delivered to Park Lane. Joe gave the necessary instructions to the staff to put everything into their ballroom. We also arranged for twenty-four clerks to present themselves for temporary employment on the morning after our return, at eight thirty am.

'The Brinkman chauffeur collected all three of us in Lord Brinkman's car, and on the way to Park Lane we went to the accommodation address which had been engaged to receive all the replies from our advertisements.' He paused to interject, 'I should have explained that we had pre-paid for advertisements to continue twice weekly for three weeks. Lionel wanted to go in to find out what our first crop was like but Joe thought this unwise as, like me, Lionel was so obviously a schoolboy and it might have made the news-agent suspicious. So Joe went in and, as you know, he is a big chap, who looked much older than he was even then. He came out with armfuls of letters. That was when we all knew that my idea had succeeded. You see it had to yield us sufficient working capital to enable us to set up our own business and form a company as soon as Lionel and I had finished at Winchester. In the meantime when Joe left he went into his father's business to get as much experience as he could.'

By now, for the first time that anyone could recall, the assembly was listening with such incredulity that several mouths were agape.

'For the next three and a half weeks we worked all hours; but when we were only one day away from the new term we had finished.'

'Finished what for God's sake?' exclaimed Ninian, staring as if his cousin was a freak.

Gilbert again delved into his folder and withdrew a sheet of typescript – figures, of course.

'With deductions,' he said, reading from the sheet, 'embracing every item of expenditure including even our luncheon in Dover (because the Bibles were not put up for sale until the afternoon) paper, string, blotting paper, adhesive and postage, which was a considerable item, as you will appreciate, we showed a total net profit of forty-five thousand pounds.' Saying which Gilbert closed the folder and leaned back in his chair. 'We had agreed,' he added, 'to divide the profits equally, so we made fifteen thousand apiece.'

'How?' came from a dozen throats.

Gilbert smiled thinly. 'It was so very simple, it seemed there must be a catch somewhere. But there wasn't. Our advertisement read: "What every young couple ought to know. Send a five shilling post order with name and address and this book will be sent to you in a plain brown wrapper." We sold the lot. People are such suckers for anything which sounds as if it might be smut! And that in itself is a useful thing to have learned.'

The Dowager rose, so the men rose with her. 'Thank you for telling us your story Gilbert,' she said with glacial courtesy, 'and now it is time for my afternoon's rest, so pray excuse me.' Henry just made the doors in time for her to sail through with her head in the air.

Christine was the next to leave. She found her mother-in-law standing at the French doors of the Blue Drawing Room. 'Who is that?' the Dowager asked without turning.

'I, *Belle-mère*, Christine.'

She turned round, her hands crumpling and uncrumpling a scrap of embroidered lawn. 'What ... a ... perfectly repellent little boy,' she shrugged her shoulders eloquently.

At the head of the table Gyles sat on grimly with the male members of his family. On one pretext or another the women and girls had all fled. Gyles was exerting maximum self-control in order not to inflict more pain on Sinclair, whom he now saw was squirming with revulsion.

'I ... s-simply d-do not b-believe it,' Sinclair stammered, 'why Gilbert, that is s-s-soiled money, you have s-swindled all t-those p-p-poor y-young people!'

'Really?' Gilbert's eyes gleamed behind his spectacles. 'I prefer to consider it a commendable business venture. How many men of my age do you think would have been shrewd enough to see the potential and then carry it through successfully?'

'That is s-simply n-not the p-point,' Sinclair's face was quite white and his hands were shaking. 'It's sh-shameful.'

Gilbert elected to be patronising. 'People like you always say the same about really big financiers when things go against them. Yet there is seldom more than a hair's breadth which stands between them and either a knighthood or a seat in the dock at the Old Bailey. It's all part of the excitement. Take it another way if you like, business is a matter of being considerably smarter than the rest, the suckers. You ask any millionaire who has made his millions and not merely inherited them, just how he made his first ten thousand pounds. You will never get an answer because, if revealed to a man like you, he would know it would only lead to vehement condemnation. Well I'm no exception. I knew you couldn't, as well as wouldn't, finance me when I grew up so I just kept my eyes open for the right opportunity and when it came I took it. Now I can go on alone. I don't need anyone's help. With Joe and Lionel's money we have an initial capital of forty-five thousand pounds. As a matter of fact we have more because Lord Brinkman told his sons he would willingly double any money they made before they were twenty-one. Lord Brinkman has forked out another thirty thousand to his sons which makes a total of seventy-five thousand, plus the compound interest on the lot for three years at five per cent. He is immensely proud of us. He told me so yesterday when he added still further to the kitty by giving me a birthday cheque.'

Sinclair's face had undergone a change. Where he had paled, so he now flushed until he was an ugly crimson. Gyles, whose control had already reached near-breaking point, saw this, remembered Sinclair's stroke and exerted a superhuman effort not to increase the pressure by an explosion.

'J-Just what do you intend d-doing next?' demanded Sinclair through clenched teeth.

'That is what we discussed yesterday amongst other things.' Gilbert was still unruffled. 'We have already formed a separate company, Joe and his father are on the board with a brilliant young mathematician friend of ours. Unfortunately Lionel and I cannot sit on the board until we are twenty-one; but Lord Brinkman and this other chap only hold a couple of shares apiece while all the rest is divided equally between us.'

'B-but your share was only half the amount!'

'Yes father. We agreed to let Lord Brinkman arbitrate. He ruled that none of the money would have been forthcoming if it had not been for what he calls my brilliant idea; so I have an equal third.'

'And what do you intend doing with this capital?'

Gilbert eyed his father thoughtfully. 'I wondered when you would ask me that. All three of us attended that original sale. All three made a particular note of the range of surplus goods which were unloaded. We remarked afterwards that it had all been government stuff. Government is always making blunders, always over-buying, or finding they have bought foolishly. Being government they merely off-load. This constitutes an enormous perennial super-cargo which they simply chuck overboard for a song if you get my meaning. It represents, handled properly, what we believe will prove an endless supply of merchandise which we can buy up very cheaply and then unload again at considerable profit to ourselves. Our great advantage against some of the little dabblers is that we already have funds to spare, so, when we see something offered which we may have to hang on to for quite some time before it becomes profitable to sell, we can afford to hold on while these smaller men have to go for a much smaller return because they cannot afford to wait.'

Henry was already rumpling his head, another ominous sign. Gyles' eyes were contemptuous. It was a close call as to who should speak first. Henry actually opened his mouth to speak but his father cut in.

'Scrap merchants in fact,' his voice was chilly. And Henry added, 'Glorified rag and bone men you mean, sir.'

Gilbert stiffened.

'If you're going to adopt that attitude there is nothing more to be said,' he snapped, 'the name of our company – again with Lord Brinkman's approval – is Delman's Associates Ltd. Del from Delahaye and the latter half of Brinkman. Our offices are in Lord Brinkman's new mammoth building whose overall name is Brinkman Incorporated, and our address is,' he paused, produced his wallet, withdrew a card, and held it out to his father. 'It's all on there, sir, if ever you want to sell anything – in bulk of course.'

Sinclair looked at it distastefully, took it as if it were a dead mouse and finally laid it down in front of him and brushed his fingers fastidiously.

That was when Gilbert decided to push his luck. 'Aren't you going to congratulate me father and wish me luck?' he asked calmly.

'It takes a bit of adjustment,' Andrew murmured, 'to become accustomed to a scrap merchant in this family.' He pushed back his chair. 'I'm in need of some air, come on Nin and you Hen, let's sort out Peter Christian and play a few sets of doubles before tea. I suppose I must wish you well Gilbert,' he added reluctantly, '*chacun à son goût* and all that. What's troublin' this family is *quel* bloody awful *goût*. However I expect you realised that right from the start.'

Gilbert began putting the cutting and the sheet of figures back into his folder. 'It's reciprocal,' he said evenly, 'I think you are all bogged down in the past, with your *droit de seigneur* attitude to your workers. I think you'll have to pull your socks up pretty soon or you'll find your dream castle tumbling about your ears, and I'll tell you one more thing. No, two things,' he corrected himself, 'I'll be a millionaire before I'm twenty-five; but if you don't watch out, and I recommend that you for a start take a course in business management, you'll get in a hell of a mess with your Aynthorp Enterprises. I could show you how to double your profits and halve your costs; but you wouldn't listen. So you'll have to take the consequences.'

Andrew coloured up at this. 'Why you damned little whippersnapper,' he exploded, 'none of us would touch your methods with a bargepole judgin' from what you've told us today. We'll manage alright; but there will be one enormous difference, we'll come out of it with clean hands, yours are filthy already.'

Gilbert rose. For a split second he stood looking at Andrew with a curious expression on his face. 'Oh, for heaven's sake,' he said exasperatedly, 'why don't you grow up and stop talking like a silly schoolboy.'

He timed his exit, as he was to do on so many future occasions, so exactly that as he ended his hands were on the twin door handles. He just opened them and walked out. The family only saw him once again, understandably briefly, and after a very long time.

CHAPTER 12

The Gordian Knot

Had Gilbert's last words been directed to Henry it was unlikely that he would have given them a second thought. Andrew was younger, more vulnerable and considerably less sure of himself than his eldest brother and so they rankled. He tackled Sue-Ellen. 'I say old girl,' he began, trying hard to sound casual, 'can you tell me anything about courses in business management?'

'Whatever for?' Her eyes widened. 'I've never even thought about them. Is something troubling you over "AE"?'

He came straight out with it. 'Well if you must know it was Gilbert. He said "AE" would go to the wall if we didn't pull our socks up, he also said he could show us how to halve expenditure and double profits.'

She laughed. 'Why not try me?' she suggested. 'It may be nonsense but Daddy trained me and he was no slouch when it came to business. We can do two things without anyone else knowing about it; take me round with you while your people are at work, let me watch them, probably ask a number of tiresome questions and then afterwards, show me your books; between the two I should be able to tell you if there are things which need adjusting. It's probably pie in the sky but it wouldn't do any harm just to have a look.'

Andrew accepted eagerly. The result was that Sue-Ellen found herself so swamped with work that she had little time to spare for anything else. Richard had her up long before breakfast and kept her hard at it in the Zoo until it was time for them to dress for dinner. When this was over she and Andrew vanished into 'In Transit' where she outlined her proposals for Aynthorp Enterprises, pointed out areas of unnecessary wastage and pored with him over the company books. During one such session he broke off to ask, shyly, 'I say, you wouldn't let Vikki sit in with us would you? After we're married we want to work together all the time and she's a corker for organisation. She told me today she wondered if you'd brief her too.'

Naturally Sue-Ellen agreed and thereafter the duo became a trio. As this was very much to her taste she was no longer lonely in the evenings, either being drawn, with some skill, by Christine into various entertainments or else sitting working with them until she was so tired she fell asleep the moment she climbed into her big bed.

Ninian was gone but try as he would he could not restrain himself from telephoning her almost daily to discuss his day to day problems or merely to report on his progress as a man of property. His reactions to Gilbert's disclosures had been wholly predictable. 'One gets 'em in every regiment, y'know, often every company – I call 'em square pegs in round holes. Come to that every family has 'em as far as I can see. The nub of the problem is to find holes into which such fellers fit. It's no use trying to shape 'em into standard ones. They're odd bods and that's all there is to 'em. Why, I remember one who drove us all hairless until I found him totting up mess accounts for the mess secretary who couldn't add two and two together. It turned out the chap was a wizard with figures, he loved 'em as a shepherd loves his sheep. He was deuced good at 'em too. Once I'd settled him in Q stores to assist the quartermaster he merged into the background and gave us no more trouble. The only thing I find devilish puzzlin' with Gilbert is how his parents ever spawned such a rum little beggar.' And that for Ninian dismissed Gilbert. When pressed he admitted, 'No I don't think he's a true-blue runt, not in our assessment of 'em anyway. He may sail a bit close to the wind; but he's so shrewd I think he'll come about alright. I don't anticipate scandals from him – just oodles and oodles of money.'

The unfortunate last words made him gloomy, even drew from him 'Wish some of the rest of us had the same talent.' After which he drew back into his shell and soon made an excuse to 'cut along home', explaining hastily, 'I've simply masses of jobs cryin' out for attention.'

Gyles refused to be drawn. All anyone gained from him was a tight-lipped, 'The less said the better so far as I am

concerned.' But Christine could have told how ever afterwards her husband referred to Gilbert as, 'that damned
young Shylock'.

When Petula asked Henry he said dismissively, 'All the
Delahayes are peculiar, even Stephanie, who's doin' splendidly with her Henry and the boy, but she's not A1 at
Lloyds. Just imagine preferrin' to bring up the kid herself
and flatly refusin' to give him all the advantages of our
nursery! Gilbert's just as peculiar; happily for us he thinks
the same of us so he keeps out of our way. I could never
find anythin' to say to the feller. He's got no standards.'

The Dowager, whose memory was still acute, promptly
recalled the nickname old Nanny had given Gilbert in the
days when she was bullyragging Lucien so consistently that
Lucy was forced to draw attention to the parlous state of the
Nursery. That was when she had learned that old Nanny
called him 'Mr Moneybags'. The Dowager found it the *mot
juste*. She even told Gyles and Christine when they were
alone together, adding, 'Old Nanny may have been wrong in
some things but she was a remarkably shrewd judge of
character. I must have a chat with Nanny Rose one day and
see if she can throw any light on what earned him the
sobriquet. There's more to it than just his obsession with
The Financial Times.' Off she went again with her usual
vigour returning in triumph to Gyles with Nanny Rose's
tale of Gilbert, at the outbreak of war, bewailing that he was
too young to profit by the fortune which lay waiting for
anyone who could corner black materials when everyone
was rushing into mourning.

Rose remembered, 'Pore Nanny cried when Master
Gilbert told her. Then she called him a little monster to
think of trying to profit from all the sorrowing women who
was losing their husbands and sons in France.'

'So you see,' the Dowager concluded, 'Gilbert was at it
even then. Nanny was right, he was and is Mr Moneybags
and if you ask me he always will be.'

Once again Gyles only grunted when this was told to him,
but his face was grim.

It became grimmer still when he studied the figures
Andrew brought him, setting out the half-year's takings by
their company.

He laid these against the returns for the previous half-year and their concomitant expenditures. Finally he made a rough estimation of their long-term losses resulting from the foot and mouth disease. It was depressing reading.

Christine was unwise enough to choose this moment to remind him that Andrew and Victoria hoped to marry soon and that it was obvious to her than young Charles Danement would be presenting himself any day now to ask for Anne's hand in marriage.

'Charmin'', said Gyles. 'The gel will have to have some sort of private income, young Charles ain't got much; and old Charles has taken a sore toss over this same affair.' He rattled the papers he had just shown to her. 'Speakin' comparatively I'd say he was harder hit than we.'

'Oh surely not?'

He nodded sombrely. 'He had less for a start, which gives him less room for manoeuvre. I shouldn't be at all surprised if he didn't have to sell land before very long. At least we haven't come to that my love.'

The wind of change was indeed blowing coldly over both families in that summer of 1922; unlike the weather which was brilliant. The heat was in fact becoming intense.

Marguerite complained of it. Gone were her claims of always feeling cold. Instead she became visibly drained by the rising temperature. It sapped her remaining vitality which made them all uneasy, though none of them would ever admit to this or acknowledge the possibility that anything grave beset her. Meanwhile the Dowager went about fanning herself and the staff paused frequently as they worked, to mop or lean panting against the walls. Below stairs became a smouldering cauldron of discontent.

One August afternoon, when the heat lay particularly heavily upon them all and no wind stirred, the sky began to darken. The swans withdrew from the lake to seek shelter with their young. The hens clucked distressfully and great flashes of lightning began streaking across the skies, while distantly the throaty rumble of thunder disturbed the Zoo's inmates. Yet no rain fell. The monkeys began to chatter excitedly; the big cats paced restlessly up and down; the young deer huddled together for comfort and Hanibelle lifted her trunk and began trumpeting dolorously.

Sue-Ellen came out of the polar bears' enclosure. They spent their time sunk to nose-tips in the sun-warmed water. She met Mick plodding towards her trundling a load of straw for the monkeys. He halted his barrow when he reached her, pushed his cap back and began mopping the streaming sweat from his face. ''Tis sinful weather madam,' he muttered, 'more like India than England! I'm sweatin' like old Farmer Murphy's pig!'

Sue-Ellen smiled. 'The animals don't like it either,' she agreed, 'if only the storm would break!'

'It'll flay us alive when it does,' Mick warned, ''tis the wrath of God that's coming and no mistake.' He sketched a hasty cross. 'I never could abide the thunder.' His words were almost drowned by a tremendous clap which broke seemingly right above them.

'Holy Mother of God,' he cried out, 'send us some rain will ye before we are kilt by a thunder bolt or struck wi' lightning. Lady you'd best hurry along inside 'tis divil's weather as is on its way this night.'

Sue-Ellen hesitated. Richard she knew was still in the enclosure spreading fodder for the white buffaloes.

'Alright Mick,' she agreed, 'but I'll just run back to Master Richard and get him to keep me company.'

She turned and ran. As she did so another blinding flash pierced the sky across and almost immediately afterwards came another tremendous thunder clap which exploded deafeningly. She ran on, spotted the copper head in the enclosure and called out, 'Richard, Mick says it's going to pour with rain, come back to the Castle with me, keep me company.'

Richard turned. 'Alright,' he shouted back. 'Hang on a sec.' As he let himself out of the iron gate and shot the bolts cautiously the lightning flashed once more and the thunder exploded an instant later with daunting violence. He ran to her, caught her hand. 'Come,' he urged, 'any minute now the floodgates will open.'

They ran. They reached the farther side of the peripheral cages and were trotting side by side when, preceded as always by an immense, waiting stillness the rain came down in great fat drops, falling so violently that it stung their bare arms and faces. In seconds they were wet through.

Sue-Ellen's soaked cotton frock clung to her, impeding movement. Richard's cotton shirt clung to him too, while their shoes began squelching as they ran on, laughing. 'We'd better go in by the garden door,' Richard panted, 'there'll be hell to pay if we puddle all over the hall.'

The sheeting rain had by now increased in violence. It was falling so strongly that they found it difficult to see. It poured through their hair, hung on their eyelashes and blurred their vision of the way ahead. When they stumbled to the nearest garden door they leaned against the inside, panting and gasping. 'Gosh,' Richard exclaimed, 'that was rather splendid don't you think? Much nicer than having a bath.'

Sue-Ellen put her hands to her hair and began wringing it out on the cocoa-matting. Then she tugged off her shoes. She too was completely breathless, but after a moment or two she exclaimed, 'Richard what is the time? I think we are dreadfully late for tea.'

'That won't matter,' said Richard, looking comical as he gripped the seat of his white cotton shorts and squeezed.

Sue-Ellen giggled. 'That looks very vulgar,' she gurgled, 'really Richard it looks quite dreadful.'

'Alright then,' Richard agreed cheerfully, 'go and tell mother I've wetted myself.' Then suddenly he sobered. 'I say you can't run the gauntlet with the servants like that, I can see right through your frock ...'

Sue-Ellen shrieked. 'Then turn round, go ahead of me you wicked boy then they'll only see the outline of my ... er behind.'

She seized his shoulders and began frog legging him forward. They were lurching a bit, too, and choking with laughter. Thus they entered the big Servants' Hall to see to their utter consternation that all the servants were gathered round the big table having their tea. Incredulously they turned and stared.

'Crikey,' Richard exclaimed, stopping hand to mouth.

Huddled behind him Sue-Ellen coped. 'Pearson,' she called, 'I am drenched and not quite respectable. Could you please get me a towel or something to wrap around me, just until I get upstairs?'

The staff were gaping, open mouthed. Sawby of course

rose to the occasion. 'All turn to face the stove,' he commanded, 'at once.'

It was too much for the drenched pair. They doubled up, with Sue-Ellen sobbing, 'Oh dear, thank you so very much, but you do all look so very funny.'

Pearson had leaped to her feet. The rest stared obediently ahead of them, those on the farther side of the table swinging round in their chairs to face the stove. As they did so Mrs Parsons toppled over and went down in a welter of red petticoats, white drawers and black-stockinged legs.

Pearson ran to Sue-Ellen, holding out a bobbled red tablecloth. 'Bless you Pearson,' she grabbed it gratefully and dropped her voice to explain, 'this wretched dress is *quite transparent.*' And all this time Pansy and Sawby struggled to re-invert the upturned cook whose legs were flailing as she exhorted and abused them.

Sue-Ellen wrapped the bobbly cloth around her, scuttled across the Servants' Hall and ran up the steep stairs leaving a trail of water behind her. The pair fell through the green baize door, out into the hall just as Gyles was crossing with Diana at her heels.

'What on earth?' he exclaimed, staring at them disbelievingly.

'Got caught in the rain father,' Richard explained. 'Sue-Ellen's frock has become transparent, so we came by the garden door and then we had to wrap her up and even then she trailed up leaving a stream of water behind her . . .'

Gyles put one hand to his mouth. 'She is still leaving a trail of water,' he pointed out. 'You had better get upstairs as quickly as possible and give yourselves a good rub down.' The thunder drowned his words.

'Give yourselves a what?' shouted Richard.

'A good rub down,' Gyles shouted. He so rarely raised his voice that it made Diana bark.

'You're puddling,' Richard shouted to Sue-Ellen, enmeshed again in laughter as he surveyed her comical figure. 'Oh lor!' He broke off, turned and fled as the Dowager appeared from the White Drawing Room, raised her lorgnette. She examined them, 'Bin swimmin'?' she enquired maliciously.

Gyles shook his head. 'No Mama, they got caught in the

rain. You two get up those stairs and dry yourselves. I will ring for fresh tea and order you some hot toast.'

They joined the Family in record time, only their heads bore testimony to their drenching. Claire poured, they ate hungrily and everyone listened as they recounted their shared adventure. When Sue-Ellen came to the moment when Mrs Parsons overturned, Gyles really laughed, his grimness temporarily banished.

'That,' he told Sue-Ellen, 'is something I would have given much to see.'

'We fled,' admitted Richard, 'the last I saw of Mrs Parsons was all red petticoat, frilly drawers and great black legs waving madly.'

Christine choked. 'Stop it Richard, my sides are aching.'

Gyles rose, crossed to the windows and began peering out through the veil of rain. 'This will do the ground good,' he approved. 'Not before it's time though; but it does look like the real thing. If it lasts through the night it will prove a godsend.'

'Not much chance of any tennis today,' Andrew joined him to stand looking out disconsolately.

'You're like children,' Christine chided them. 'Why not settle to a nice game of mah-jongg?'

'Oh mother,' Henry teased, 'you'll be suggestin' tiddley winks next.'

It was all very domestic, very trivial and it had the effect of lifting the general gloom.

That evening in the drawing room after a little preliminary wrangling Andrew, Henry, Anne and Petula settled to their mah-jongg. Richard curled up with another of Frank Buck's books, and the room became almost tranquil. Just then Petula led her chattering twins down the staircase on their way to their great-great Aunt for chocolates and their bed-time story. She tapped on the door. The nurse's face appeared.

'Oh not tonight if you please, Mrs Henry!' she was almost gasping. 'We're not feeling quite the thing.' She closed the door abruptly in her face. The twins began clamouring, 'Mummy why can't we go in? Mummy please . . .'

'Poor *Tante* Marguerite has a headache so you will have to

put up with me instead darlings,' Petula told them, her mind elsewhere.

'You have got chocolates haven't you?'

'Yes,' she rallied, 'I have chocolates for you; but if you would just run up and wait for me, I would like to use the telephone before I read to you.'

Chantal wriggled, a sure sign she was uncertain. 'You will come quickly Mummy?'

'Very quickly,' Petula promised, 'cross my heart.'

'Oh come along Chantal,' urged Justin, 'the sooner we go the sooner Mummy will have finished with her telephone call.' He caught his sister's hand. 'Right. Five minutes.' Petula smiled, 'Be off with you now then ...'

She watched them take the first treads, then she flew to the nearest telephone.

She spoke to Constance and heard her reassuring voice, 'Now don't worry love I will be over in moments. What a good thing Charles left his car outside! She was perfectly alright you know when I left her at four o'clock, on the *chaise longue* too, not in bed. So relax. Are you still there?'

'Still here,' Petula assured, feeling her heart thumping less, her fears abating.

'I should telephone Dr Jamieson if I were you,' Constance advised. 'Just tell him what you've told me and ask him to meet me there.'

After Petula had spoken to Dr Jamieson she went back to her children. She read them their story, gave them one extra chocolate each for being so very good, heard their prayers then tucked them up and said goodnight. Then she changed hastily and ran downstairs again. There was no one in the drawing room. She drew back the curtains and peered out experiencing a great wave of relief as she saw the Jamieson car outside.

She began pacing up and down, fearing to go to Marguerite, realising that probably no one knew there was anything wrong, trying to decide what to do when the call came down again.

The minutes passed. Edward came in with the drinks tray. He gave her a respectful, 'Good evening madam', set down the tray and began plumping up cushions, straightening rugs, slipping some magazines back into their china holder and generally giving the lovely room back its self-respect. Petula watched him unseeingly. When he went out closing the door behind him she was assailed by a sudden feeling of loneliness. She began her pacing again, a slender figure in a chiffon dress whose flame petals floated out as she moved so restlessly.

Gyles and Christine came in. They were laughing and Gyles' arm was around his wife's slender waist.

'Hello darling,' said Christine, 'you are early,' the words fading out on her lips as, 'Pet, is something wrong?'

Petula shook her head. 'Not for sure. It's just that, oh dear I don't want to frighten you, but when I took the twins as usual to *Tante* Marguerite for their bedtime story, nurse stuck her face round the door and said, "Not tonight Mrs Henry if you please, we're not feeling quite the thing." Then she closed the door again. I began to worry. In the end I telephoned Constance, she is in there now I believe. She asked me to ring Dr Jamieson so I did and his car's outside now. Oh and Constance said *Tante* Marguerite was perfectly alright, *and* on the *chaise longue* when she left her at four o'clock, so it's probably just a storm in a teacup, but I just had to ring . . . in case.'

Gyles put a protective arm about her shoulders. 'Why, you're shaking my dear. You did exactly what we should have done I can assure you.' He looked questioningly at Christine who stood with one hand to her throat.

'Oh Gyles,' she said.

'Now please, Christine, sit down and compose yourself. We can do nothing until Jamieson comes out. I'll ring for Raikes. She can stand guard and ask him to come to us the moment he reappears.'

Raikes took up her position at the entrance to the long corridor, by which time the servants knew that something was amiss.

Gyles went to the drinks tray and poured himself a whisky, first giving Christine a thimbleful of brandy and standing over her while she sipped it. Then Henry and Andrew came in so they had to be told too, and on and on it went as the various members of the family came in gradually.

Once they knew that there was even the possibility that

something was amiss with Marguerite all conversation withered. The whole great building seemed suddenly to have assumed a mantle of silence in which the ticking of the clocks was strident and intrusive.

Still no one came to tell them anything. By now, like a forest fire, their fears had spread to belowstairs, creeping to the Steward's Room where Palliser sewed and sniffed; seeping in among Chef André's stoves and out to the scullery maids where they stood washing parsley.

Chef worked on in total silence once he knew. The only sound came from a bubbling sauce, a spit and sizzle as he basted guinea fowls, the clink of a knife and the crack which startled them all as little Boots emptied a hod of coke into a gaping, crimson maw.

From time to time, pairs of eyes lifted to the ceiling as striving to see something of what went on above them.

The click of the *petit salon* door as it opened sounded like another thunder clap. Dr Jamieson came out, bent his head to hear Raikes' subdued message, nodded, and tugging at his heard went towards the White Drawing Room. As he came in they all froze, whether standing or sitting. Henry with hand outstretched for a salted almond remained with it poised as he turned his head.

'She is alright – at present,' the Doctor said. 'I will tell you of course and I will hold nothing back. I am bound to say I think nurse became scared, but who should blame her with such a precious patient in her care.

'This set up a chain reaction.' He went on, 'First to you Petula and then to Lady Constance and myself. According to nurse she was sitting beside the Countess doing her crochet. She says the Countess seemed to catch her breath and then went into a choking fit. She did all the usual things until the Countess nodded and croaked, "Enough nurse, I am quite alright now thank you." She took a sip or two of water, lay back and said, seemingly quite cheerful, "that's better. I must have caught my breath." A little later she flung out one hand rather suddenly, grasped nurse's wrist as she bent over her and gasped "Pain ... probably indigestion."

'That was when you, Petula, knocked on the door. It explains why the woman was so hasty with you. When she went back to the Countess she found her lying quietly with her eyes closed. Nurse spoke to her. She opened her eyes. "Poo", she exclaimed, "that was nasty. Do you think I might have some bicarbonate of soda?" Nurse hesitated, and at that moment Constance came through the French doors.

'She gave her one of the special pills we keep for these occasions, then I arrived and the long and short of it is I think she teetered on the edge of another heart attack; but that it has been averted, for the moment.'

Claire and Christian, who came in just after he had finished speaking, forced yet another recapitulation, after which Dr Jamieson said, 'If I may, I would prefer to remain here for a while. Then either Constance or I can be with her for the rest of this evening. We will see what happens after she is safely in bed. She is being extremely naughty I may say at not having her usual sponge bath. She almost bit my head off.'

This time his words ended on a rumble of thankfulness and small laughter.

'Indomitable eh?' he smiled at them, accepted some sherry and their invitation to sit down and sip it in comfort.

'We will take Constance in to dinner with us if you do not mind,' said Christine, 'then she can come and relieve you, perhaps in the meantime you would like to telephone your wife? Poor soul we have ruined her evening.'

'It was ruined already,' Dr Jamieson told her, 'my wife's mother is staying with us and she has retired to bed with a mild head cold, so poor Kitty is condemned to an evening of trays and complaints. The good Lord deliver me from women who enjoy ill health.'

Thus he rallied them; but when the turn and turn about dinner for both he and Constance had been completed, she insisted on returning to her patient, while Dr Jamieson returned, ostensibly to enjoy some of Gyles' excellent port with the men. But once they were alone together he let the mask slip and Gyles faced a very worried man at his dinner table.

'She's so fragile,' Dr Jamieson shook his head sorrowfully. 'For the past few weeks it has been almost impossible to persuade her to eat *anything*. She has so little in reserve that a recurrence now would almost certainly prove fatal.'

Then the shadows really came down upon the assembled men. Only Gyles, Sinclair and John could remember the Castle during the years she was away in France captivating French society with her Jules. For the rest there had never been a time when Grandfather Justin was not doing battle with his mischievous sister; or when she had not flitted through the Castle rooms filling them with her exquisite flower arrangements, or tending her roses and enslaving the outside staff. Henry, going later with Petula for their regular peek at their sleeping twins, felt an agonising constriction in his throat as he remembered waking and seeing Marguerite's beautiful little face bent over him when he was small. He went from the night nursery muttering, 'Oh bloody hell', for which Petula did not reprove him.

Constance returned to them to report, 'No change. She is awake but neither of us can persuade her to take even a sip of André's *bouillon* . . . she *must* have some nourishment.'

'She will,' said the Dowager abruptly. 'Jamieson, may she take the extract of a smashed, raw fowl cooked *au bain marie* in a bottle of champagne?'

'Certainly she may Lady Aynthorp.'

Out of the room and on across the hall went her ladyship. Through the green baize doors she marched, on down the staff staircase, raising startled heads from below as they saw her and rose to their feet.

'I apologise for disturbing you,' she said huskily. 'I want' – her eyes roamed over them, 'Ah? Chef André, I require your skilled service at this late hour for the Countess who will die if she does not take some nourishment.'

'*A votre service madame.*'

She nodded, and together they marched into his kitchen, but not until she had sent Sawby in the opposite direction jingling the keys of the cellars.

André vanished into his *garde manger* and came back dangling a plucked raw hen. 'Now smash it, please,' said the Dowager, '*il faut que ce soit presque fondu.*'

She pursued André and his dangling hen to the chopping block. She stood watching as he reduced the bird to a juicy pulp. Then when Sawby reappeared with the champagne she instructed him, 'empty the contents into a jug and give the bottle to André.'

This having been done, with several bright, interested glances at his instructress, André paid flesh and bone into the champagne magnum, poured some of the champagne over – just enough to cover and then rammed down the cork once more. Finally he swathed the bottle in cloths and stood it on a block of wood inside his tallest copper saucepan.

A babble of French then flowed between the two.

'Wot's they saying?' Mrs Parsons whined querulously.

'I am saying Mrs Parsons,' the Dowager advanced towards her, 'that that bottle and its contents must simmer throughout the night. In the mornin' Monsieur André will strain the fluid off, put it upon ice and when it is a light jelly we will feed it to the Countess in teaspoonsful. Now good night to you all and thank you.'

Head held high, she mounted the stairs once more, and no one could ever have guessed that there went an old and tired woman whose only surviving confidante was almost certainly very close to death.

At midnight Dr Jamieson came in again. 'She is sleeping,' he told them. 'Lady Constance and I will stay. Rest assured we will summon you instantly if there is any change; so please be good enough to go to bed.' To give point to his request he extended his arm to the Dowager. 'May I take you to your room?' he asked.

She rallied to him. 'Bully,' she chided, and they smiled gently at each other; but she took his arm and a little later on Constance scratched on her door and persuaded her to take a little pill that would ensure she had some sleep.

The night passed quietly enough. Constance sent up messages with all the early morning tea trays that the Countess had passed a quiet night and was sleeping tranquilly. Soon after the trays went upstairs a small, veiled figure slipped through the side door towards the lych gate and vanished into the old chapel. Here the figure knelt for a very long time, rising with a little difficulty and surprising her entire family by being discovered at the breakfast table.

She enquired of Sawby as to the state of her 'Elixir' which was older than she. He told her, bending over her gently, 'Chef André presents his compliments my lady and it is ready and waiting.'

Constance came in a few minutes later. She reported, 'The Countess is awake and asking for you Lady Aynthorp.'

The Dowager rose immediately. 'But has she taken any nourishment my dear?' she asked.

Constance shook her head.

'We will see about that,' the Dowager declared, 'Sawby, pray bring me the elixir at once.'

When it came she took the tray and marched with it across the hall. At the breakfast table Constance met Gyles' questioning eyes.

'There goes my last hope,' she said ruefully, 'but if anyone can persuade her to take nourishment it is that perfectly splendid old person, your mother, my dear Gyles.'

Once inside the bedroom, by now at her most autocratic and intimidating, the Dowager faced the nurse who rose from beside the bed. She waved her away imperiously. 'Run along now nurse, do. Have your breakfast or something but kindly leave the Countess to me.'

Nurse went. The Dowager picked up the tiny napkin from the tray, then bent over her sister-in-law. Marguerite opened her eyes. 'Ah ... there you are ... I've missed you ...'

'Maybe,' said the Dowager, 'let me tell you that you will be glad to see me go again if you refuse to put some of this inside you in double quick time you naughty one.' As she spoke she tucked the napkin under Marguerite's chin, dipped a teaspoon into the little silver bowl and held it out.

'What ... is ... it?'

'Our elixir. Now come along let us have no more nonsense.'

This widened her eyes, she stared a moment, then said, 'Ha! you think I'm dyin', don't you? Well I'm not. Spoon away ... damn you.'

When the bowl was emptied the Dowager wiped her lips, withdrew the napkin and sat down beside her.

'Now admit it Meg, that was delicious wasn't it?'

'Oh yes ... I want some more.'

'Not for an hour my love. You'd be tipsy!'

Marguerite put out a tremulous hand for her to hold.

'Sleepy,' she said – then – ' 'Licia.'

'Yes love.'

'I dreamed ... of ... Justin ...' her eyelids flickered ... 'and Mama. They were having a shockin' squabble ...' she chuckled faintly as her eyelids closed. Then she murmured, 'I feel ... splendid.'

The Dowager sat on beside her. Beyond the windows the sun flooded the garden beyond, sparkling on the rain-drenched leaves. She smiled tenderly at the tranquil little face; but when Constance tip-toed in, raised her eyebrows as she saw the empty bowl and the Dowager nodded back contentedly, Dr Jamieson, who had followed her in then moved around her, picking up Marguerite's free hand from the laces on which it lay, and his fingers closed over the tiny wrist. Then he withdrew it, straightened wearily, met the Dowager's eyes and turned away, his own heavy with regret.

'Gone?' the Dowager's shaking lips just managed to shape the word.

He just nodded, quite unable to speak.

It was Constance whose hands went out with infinite tenderness. It was she who drew the sheet over Marguerite's face which seemed suddenly transfigured by great tranquillity.

Marguerite de Tessedre had slipped away so quietly that even the Dowager had failed to see her go.

Constance bent again, this time to the stiff-backed tearless watcher whose tired old lips were moving now in prayer. She put her arms about her. She made no resistance but just let Constance draw her to her feet and with her protective arms around her lead her from the room without a backward glance.

Once the door closed behind them she stiffened suddenly and drew herself away. 'I ... will ... tell ... them ... my dear ...' she said stiffly, but patting the arm from which she withdrew.

'Are you sure? Why not let me do it for you?'

Back came her voice more strongly, 'Because Marguerite would have wished it so.'

Constance relinquished her. She stood back. She watched as the Dowager's head came up once more, but as she moved towards the dining room her figure became a blur.

The weeping servants closed the Castle's eyes, folding

shutters, drawing curtains across, shutting out the brilliant sunlight which now seemed such a mockery, which is always its way in such circumstances.

During the afternoon Marguerite was carried by her kinsmen to their little chapel as had been done when Justin Aynthorp died.

This time, it was Petula, Anne, Christine, Primrose and Claire who worked there, their heads covered by scraps of lace as they moved about lighting the candles and arranging the flowers.

They filled the chapel with them until the small, still figure of alabaster whiteness lay resting beneath a panoply of flowers. At the last they laid white freesias between her folded hands and turning went to the venerable stalls, where they knelt and prayed.

As they left the chapel they were replaced by the menfolk who took their places at the four corners of the raised catafalque; Gyles Aynthorp, Henry de Lorme, John Newmarket and Sinclair Delahaye, who had stammeringly insisted upon exerting his privilege to accompany them. They would presently relinquish their guard to Ninian, Sir Charles, his son Charles and Andrew who in their turn would at length stand down for Eustace Bartonbury, his eldest son Ralph Lord Steyne, Richard de Lorme and Harry Devening, Stephanie's husband.

At a very early hour Lucien and Lucy arrived. Together they carried the cross of flowers which Lucy confided her brother had spent most of the night making himself. They went straightway to the chapel, laid their flowers at her feet, Lucy withdrew to a stall to pray and Lucien turned towards the organ loft where he settled himself at the organ and played for the little Countess, only relinquishing the instrument when Mr Prewitt appeared atop the familiar steps.

Thus was she guarded until her body was laid to rest, by which time they knew well enough she would have gone beyond their reach.

To their even greater surprise Gilbert walked in very quietly when they were all assembled for the simple service. When it was over he hurried back to the immense chauffeur-driven Daimler which awaited him. He barely spoke to any

of the family and was driven away immediately, the family
crest gleaming on all four doors, much to his father's and
Gyles' astonishment and displeasure.

Harry conducted the service. The choir sang 'None but
the weary heart' for her. Gyles, Eustace, John and Sinclair
carried the small coffin to its last resting place. Then they
returned together through the opened door into the crisp
sunlight and walked back to the castle between the massed
ranks of villagers who flanked the path on either side. Henry
walked with Sue-Ellen's son Stephen on one side and his
Justin on the other, his mind thronged with memories of his
most favourite and beloved of great aunts.

He remembered her bending over his cot when he awoke
yelling from a nightmare. He could almost feel the scented
softness of her as she lifted him reassuringly into her arms,
and the instant comfort which dispelled all fear. Remembering then passed from his babyhood to himself as a schoolboy, standing atop the castle steps with the carriage, Plum
on the box, drawn up in the drive, his portmanteau and
tuck box already stowed in readiness to drive him to the
station and his first term at Harrow. In turn he kissed his
Mama, shook hands with his father, was enfolded once again
in Marguerite's fragrant embrace and again experienced the
feel of the brand new golden sovereigns she slipped into his
hand.

He was like a man drowning as one after the other these
progressive scenes developed on the retina of memory.

Justin suddenly slipped one hand in his as Henry was
recalling his entry into Marguerite's boudoir. Boney, her
parrot, was screeching at him on this, his wedding morning,
and he in all the splendour of his wedding garments was
receiving his special private gift from *Tante* Marguerite
while Boney climbed his cage squawking disapproval.

His small son nearly brought him down when he gave him
a huge nudge and whispered, squeezing his hand, 'Don't be
sad Daddy, *Tante* Marguerite wouldn't want you to be sad.'
In desperation Henry whipped the handkerchief from his
sleeve and blew loudly, tumbling thereafter into the abyss of
recalling how he had stumbled in as Petula fought for her life
and that of the twins in a room above and of how
Marguerite had sustained him.

One by one the men drifted into the drawing room where the women waited behind drawn blinds. Gyles put a drink into Henry's hand. The sound of the siphon of soda water being squirted by Eustace into his whisky was garish in the quiet room. They just stood about now, waiting for Mr Truslove whom Grantham was driving down to them from London. They said things to one another like 'How exquisitely Lucien played did he not?' from Christine, and from Claire 'I think *Tante* Marguerite would have approved the flowers', while the Dowager sat with ramrod back, her hands clasped together in her lap to quell their shaking. The entire castle was mantled by silence in which the ticking of the clocks seemed a most unsuitable intrusion.

Then into that silence came the unmistakable crunch of the Royce's tyres on the gravel sweep below the steps confirming that the 'Pelican' had indeed arrived.

Gyles slipped away and ran down the steps to meet him. The frail old man mounted the steps shakily leaning on his arm. He only spoke once as Gyles steered him into the Library where, as was also their custom on such occasions, he would unfold the last will and testament of Marguerite, Countess de Tessedre while her husband Jules knelt in his stall in the monastery as the Abbot conducted the Mass for her immortal soul.

Mr Truslove just asked, 'Was the end ... peaceful?' Gyles told him and then helped him into the chair at the great round table where the men of the Family had stood to witness the opening of their Talisman.[1]

The old man seemed unaccountably nervous and, to Gyles, inexplicably on edge. His hand shook as he accepted a glass of madeira. 'Thank you ... such a grievous separation,' he stammed shakily, spilling a little of the wine as he lifted the glass, and hastily groping for a handkerchief.

Gyles turned away, deeply regretful for the manifest *coup de foudre* Marguerite's death had been to the old lawyer, but even so he was a little puzzled by the extent of it.

He returned to the drawing room, bent over his mother, who rose with some difficulty, taking his proffered arm without protest. Gradually the drawing room emptied as they all went slowly across the great hall to take their places

[1] Book i, *The Lormes of Castle Rising*.

on the chairs which Sawby's footmen and woman had arranged for them.

The old Pelican seemed to have some difficulty in beginning. Ninian, sitting next to Henry, murmured, 'The poor old boy seems to be in all his states. Did he know *Tante* Marguerite all that well?'

'No of course not,' Henry whispered back. 'Must be somethin' else, I honestly don't know ...'

The 'poor old boy' was still shuffling his papers hesitantly. He seemed so distressed that Henry looked away to where his father now sat between his mother and his wife. Almost facing Ninian on the farther side of the old Library sat Sue-Ellen, feeling considerably *de trop*. She had even protested, on being asked to attend, pointing out that she was not 'family' and therefore had no place among them at such a time. She had been cut down by the Dowager who retorted, quite in her old autocratic manner for the moment, 'Fiddlesticks my dear. Pray do as you are asked. Now please sit down.' This clearly brooked no argument. Sue-Ellen obeyed. She too found her eyes drawn to Mr Truslove. She watched him a trifle curiously as he indulged in a positive orgy of throat clearing ... of humming ... hawing ...

She found his nickname very apposite, imagining she could almost see him endeavouring to compose his sorely ruffled feathers after some fracas with a marauder. Then, as she watched, she saw him make a particularly large peck with his attenuated nose and look around him tremulously. The sound of the crackling parchment between his unsteady fingers was like a series of small pistol shots in the silence where he had read many other wills over the long years in which he had served de Lormes.

At last he began, his voice steadying somewhat as he went on. First came the smaller bequests ... 'To Millicent Palliser the sum of five hundred pounds ... to my friend Thomas Plumstead the sum of one thousand pounds ... to Mr Prewitt in fond remembrance of his many kindnesses one thousand pounds ... to Petula ...'

At the sound of her name Petula's head came up in astonishment. '... I give and bequeath my jewellery in the certain knowledge that my pieces will only serve to enhance her beauty ...'

It brought the startled tears to her eyes so that she barely heard 'To Henry Gyles de Lorme, my beloved nephew, the sum of ten thousand pounds with which to purchase some land I know he desires in France ...'

Then Mr Truslove began to falter once again. He cleared his throat, he looked around him like a cornered stag with so frightened an expression on his withered countenance that Henry, dazed by his own bequest, had the sudden thought that 'if the old boy were not dominated by such a rigid sense of the proprieties I swear he'd try to make a bolt for it.'

Finally with a despairing movement Mr Truslove plunged his beak into the opened parchment as if desiring to bury it therein and then on a rising note almost shouted the remaining words. 'The entire residue of my estate ... I leave to my great nephew Ninian de Lorme ... with the sole proviso that he proposes forthwith to Sue-Ellen Delahaye and marries her thereafter; a condition with which I feel confident he will comply with great alacrity since this bequest demolishes the only barrier which separates these two young people from one another ...' Mr Truslove added despairingly, 'Oh dear, oh deary deary me!' and laid the parchment down.

Over the heads of his stunned audience two transfigured faces turned to one another. The look held as Ninian rose very slowly and deliberately. Then his voice rang out, 'Sue-Ellen my love, will you please do me the honour of becoming my wife?'

She rose too, and then cried out, 'Oh yes my darling, indeed I will, most willingly.' The words came clearly through her quivering lips as the tears rained down her small, white face.

Ninian just nodded, then he swung round to the little crouched figure whose hands rested on the discarded parchment on the library table.

'Mr Truslove sir, I trust that meets with your requirements?' he asked a trifle stiffly.

THE END